AN IMPULSIVE KISS

Captivating Kisses
Book 2

Alexa Aston

ARE YOU SIGNED UP FOR DRAGONBLADE'S BLOG?

You'll get the latest news and information on exclusive giveaways, exclusive excerpts, coming releases, sales, free books, cover reveals and more.

Check out our complete list of authors, too!

No spam, no junk. That's a promise!

Sign Up Here

www.dragonbladepublishing.com

Dearest Reader;

Thank you for your support of a small press. At Dragonblade Publishing, we strive to bring you the highest quality Historical Romance from some of the best authors in the business. Without your support, there is no 'us', so we sincerely hope you adore these stories and find some new favorite authors along the way.

Happy Reading!

CEO, Dragonblade Publishing

Additional Dragonblade books by Author Alexa Aston

Captivating Kisses Series
An Unexpected Kiss (Book 1)
An Impulsive Kiss (Book 2)

The Strongs of Shadowcrest Series
The Duke's Unexpected Love (Book 1)
The Perks of Loving a Viscount (Book 2)
Falling for the Marquess (Book 3)
The Captain and the Duchess (Book 4)
Courtship at Shadowcrest (Book 5)
The Marquess' Quest for Love (Book 6)
The Duke's Guide to Winning a Lady (Book 7)

Suddenly a Duke Series
Portrait of the Duke (Book 1)
Music for the Duke (Book 2)
Polishing the Duke (Book 3)
Designs on the Duke (Book 4)
Fashioning the Duke (Book 5)
Love Blooms with the Duke (Book 6)
Training the Duke (Book 7)
Investigating the Duke (Book 8)

Second Sons of London Series
Educated By The Earl (Book 1)
Debating With The Duke (Book 2)
Empowered By The Earl (Book 3)
Made for the Marquess (Book 4)
Dubious about the Duke (Book 5)
Valued by the Viscount (Book 6)
Meant for the Marquess (Book 7)

Dukes Done Wrong Series
Discouraging the Duke (Book 1)
Deflecting the Duke (Book 2)
Disrupting the Duke (Book 3)
Delighting the Duke (Book 4)
Destiny with a Duke (Book 5)

Dukes of Distinction Series
Duke of Renown (Book 1)
Duke of Charm (Book 2)
Duke of Disrepute (Book 3)
Duke of Arrogance (Book 4)
Duke of Honor (Book 5)
The Duke That I Want (Book 6)

The St. Clairs Series
Devoted to the Duke (Book 1)
Midnight with the Marquess (Book 2)
Embracing the Earl (Book 3)
Defending the Duke (Book 4)
Suddenly a St. Clair (Book 5)
Starlight Night (Novella)
The Twelve Days of Love (Novella)

Soldiers & Soulmates Series
To Heal an Earl (Book 1)
To Tame a Rogue (Book 2)
To Trust a Duke (Book 3)
To Save a Love (Book 4)
To Win a Widow (Book 5)
Yuletide at Gillingham (Novella)

King's Cousins Series
The Pawn (Book 1)
The Heir (Book 2)
The Bastard (Book 3)

Medieval Runaway Wives
Song of the Heart (Book 1)

A Promise of Tomorrow (Book 2)
Destined for Love (Book 3)

Knights of Honor Series
Word of Honor (Book 1)
Marked by Honor (Book 2)
Code of Honor (Book 3)
Journey to Honor (Book 4)
Heart of Honor (Book 5)
Bold in Honor (Book 6)
Love and Honor (Book 7)
Gift of Honor (Book 8)
Path to Honor (Book 9)
Return to Honor (Book 10)

The Lyon's Den Series
The Lyon's Lady Love

Pirates of Britannia Series
God of the Seas

De Wolfe Pack: The Series
Rise of de Wolfe

The de Wolfes of Esterley Castle
Diana
Derek
Thea

Also from Alexa Aston
The Bridge to Love (Novella)
One Magic Night

PROLOGUE

Huntsworth, Surrey—1789

JUDSON JARVIS CLIMBED from the carriage that had brought him home from his latest term at school. All the other boys had departed in the company of one or both their parents. An ache filled him each time he witnessed his fellow students greeting their parents, who enfolded their sons in happy embraces before leading them to the vehicle that would take them home.

Not Judson. His mother had died giving birth to him, while his father was continually in poor health and never left home. Because of that, Judson's uncle lived at Huntsberry and was in charge of the marquess' country estate, making all decisions regarding the land and its tenants.

Uncle Jeremiah never bothered to come for his nephew. Instead, he would send the carriage and merely have a footman and the coachman see that the heir apparent was delivered safely back to Huntsworth.

He thanked Tim, his favorite footman, who said, "I'll see your trunk is brought to your room, my lord."

"Thank you for bringing me home, Tim. You are a loyal and faithful servant. When I am the marquess someday, I will not forget your kindness to me."

Tim beamed at him. "All in a day's work, my lord. Happy to be of service to you."

Judson entered the house, being greeted by Mrs. Clippman. He saw pity in the housekeeper's eyes, something he saw repeatedly when other people looked at him. He was old enough to understand that sympathy showed compassion, whereas pity only showed how others felt sorry for him.

"Good evening, Mrs. Clippman. May I see my father, or is he already asleep?"

The last time he had been home from school, Papa had been more ill than usual. He had not received a single letter from his father this term and had tried to keep his growing panic at bay, fearful he would return home only to find Papa gone for good.

The housekeeper shook her head. "Mr. Jarvis told me to give you some milk and bread and see you to bed, my lord," she said apologetically. "I'm certain you will be allowed to see his lordship tomorrow sometime. Your uncle, too."

Anxiously, Judson asked, "How is Papa?"

"I am not a physician, my lord," the housekeeper said crisply. "Mr. Jarvis will be able to tell you all about Lord Huntsberry's condition when you see him in the morning."

He knew the woman could tell him exactly the state of his father's health, but she—like every servant in this household—was terrified of his uncle.

"Then I will bid you goodnight, Mrs. Clippman," Judson said, trudging up the stairs to his bedchamber.

His trunk awaited him, and he opened and unpacked the little he had brought home for the summer. Many of his clothes and other possessions had vanished, as always. He was ten years of age but small in size and stature, leading the bullies at school to pick on him unmercifully. They also stole his belongings. Judson had long ago learned not to bring anything of value to school with him because it would be taken. No one in authority would help him recover it. The school's tutors and its headmaster all turned a blind eye to any bullying amongst the students. If they were asked, they would deny the practice even took place.

A maid arrived with a tray for him. He thanked her and then ate the bread and cheese, washing it down with the accompanying cup of milk. He was determined to see Papa tomorrow morning, even before he breakfasted with his uncle.

Judson changed into a nightshirt, folding his clothes neatly and placing them on the chair next to his bed. He was too young to have his own valet, but Papa had said once he reached twelve years of age, he would be allowed to have one. Even though Tim was a footman, Judson had already decided to see him promoted into the position.

One good thing was that sleep would come easily to him tonight, thanks to there being no one here to roust him from bed and torment him. At school, he was afraid to close his eyes, living in terror of when the other boys would come for him in the middle of the night. Sometimes, only a day passed between attacks. Other times, a week, two weeks, or even a month would go by. He was never lulled into thinking the bullying had come to an end, however. Larger boys always came for him. They treated him cruelly, sometimes beating him until he was so battered and bruised, he could barely move. They never touched his face, though, not wanting to leave a trace of their abuse toward him.

On some occasions, he had been doused in cold water and made to stand for hours, shivering, his teeth chattering loudly. Once, a group had even left him locked outside in the snow, barefoot, wearing only his sodden nightshirt. It had surprised him that he had not died in the bitter cold. At times, he had actually prayed for death to come, not thinking he could endure another minute of the cruelty.

Yet he loved learning. Despite the fact no adult intervened in the horrible attacks on him, Judson soaked up every bit of knowledge imparted to him. He was excellent at maths and gifted when it came to languages, especially Latin, Greek, and French. He knew one day he would be the Marquess of Huntsberry, and he wanted to be prepared intellectually when he came into his title.

He awoke early, washing and dressing quietly before slipping from his room, and heading across the hall to Papa's bedchamber. His uncle had long ago taken over the rooms meant for the marquess, saying they went to waste since his brother only occupied the bedchamber. Resentment toward Uncle Jeremiah roiled through him again, and Judson wished his father would banish his younger brother from the estate. Yet even at his tender age, Judson understood how his father could not handle the duties of his rank, and that Uncle Jeremiah did serve a purpose in the household.

Not bothering to knock, he merely slipped into the room. Usually, a servant sat with Papa overnight, but he saw no one in the room doing so. He went and opened the curtains before going to his father's bedside, taking in his gaunt frame and labored breathing. Papa was incredibly pale, looking worse than he ever had. Part of him believed this would be his last summer with Papa, and he worried about what life would be like with his parent gone.

Judson wrapped his hands around one of his father's, wishing for a moment that he had a different father. One who was healthy. One like other boys had. His schoolmates talked about how their fathers had taught them how to hunt. Ride. Fish. Swim. Papa had never been strong enough to do any of those things, and Judson had never learned any of those skills. He was too afraid to ask his uncle to teach him any of them, and if he asked a servant to do so, they would likely be in trouble and even lose their position if they did so.

"I am thirsty," his father whispered hoarsely, his eyes opening. In them, Judson saw recognition, and his father smiled weakly at him. "My boy."

"I am here, Father. Home for the summer. Let me get you something to drink."

He released his father's hand and looked to the table by the bed. A bowl half-full of broth stood there. Turning back to Papa, he helped him to sit up a bit, plumping the pillows behind his back. Then he reached for the bowl and held it to his father's lips. Papa took a couple of sips and closed his eyes.

"Do you want more?" he asked eagerly.

"No." The word came out defeated.

Judson put the bowl down again and perched upon the bed. He took Papa's hand in his again and sat, content to merely be in his presence. His love of learning had been instilled in him by his father, who was a voracious reader.

Papa's eyes slowly opened again. "Tell me . . . about school."

He had never shared how he had no friends, much less revealed the extent of the bullying. Instead, he only told Papa of the good things, not wanting him to worry.

"I took the spelling prize again this spring," he said enthusiastically. "I also had two poems published in the school newspaper."

For the next few minutes, he entertained Papa with amusing stories of things that had happened at school, as well as his other accomplishments. Judson paid dearly for each academic success, though. Many of the bullies struggled in their coursework, and they punished him for how well he did in every subject.

"It seems you have had . . . a lovely time, Judson."

"I have learned so much, Papa," he said, knowing that was a truth, even as he glossed over how awful the entire year had been. His suffering was nothing compared to Papa's.

"I need to go down to breakfast, Papa," he said. "Get some rest now. I will be back to see you later. I will read to you if you like."

The marquess gazed at him intently, as if he could see into Judson's soul. "Be a good man, my son. I am already so very proud of you." Exhausted, his father closed his eyes and fell asleep.

He leaned over and kissed Papa's cheek before he left the room, making his way downstairs. Entering the breakfast room, he saw his uncle already there. Another man was present, as well, and Judson recognized Lord Blackwell. The earl was a frequent visitor to Huntsworth. Judson thought the nobleman to be a braggart and a drunk.

"Good morning, Uncle Jeremiah, my lord," he said, taking a place at the table.

Immediately, a cup of milk and plate of food were set in front of him by different footmen. He had to force himself not to gobble it down.

"How were your marks this term?" his uncle asked.

"I earned top marks, Uncle," Judson replied. "I scored the highest in each subject of any boy in my class."

His uncle did not congratulate him, but Lord Blackwell said, "You might be smart, but you are still a scrawny little thing, aren't you? When are you going to get some meat on your bones?"

He wished he could reveal that often much of his food was stolen from him by other boys, and that was the reason why he was so thin. Instead, he kept his mouth closed, knowing the earl didn't expect a response from him.

Lord Blackwell, whom Judson suspected had been a bully during his own school days, pushed harder, saying, "It is too bad you are not like your uncle here. Why, Jarvis was the most fit, athletic student during our schooldays. He could shoot with great accuracy and was by far the best rider, both then and now."

"My nephew takes after his parents, Blackwell. You know that. His mother was so fragile, she died giving birth to her brat. And my brother has never been strong. He emerged from the womb a weakling and has been so all his life. Huntsberry always had a tutor at home and never spent a single term away at school."

Judson hadn't known that about Papa and wished he, too, could be educated at home.

Boldly, he asked, "Would that be possible for me to do, Uncle Jeremiah? I am far ahead of my peers in my work. If I were able to remain at Huntsworth and continue my studies with a tutor, I could progress much further and faster."

"No," his uncle said bluntly, squashing Judson's hopes. "School is where you will stay. I do not have time to look after you, since your father has thrust all the responsibilities of the Marquess of Huntsberry upon me, while I can never hold the title."

His gaze pierced Judson. "I should have been the one who inherited everything. I was the one who was always stronger and cleverer. You are a little weakling—just as your father is."

The harsh words washed over him, bringing hurt. He had never had much attention from his uncle, but he had also never been spoken to in such a sour manner. It was obvious his uncle's hatred and resentment ran deeply, for both his brother and nephew.

Judson glanced about the room and saw the pity in one of the footman's eyes. The servant averted his gaze.

Knowing he would be severely punished, he still looked directly at Uncle Jeremiah and said, "But you are a second son, aren't you, Uncle? I am the heir apparent. One day, I will be the Marquess of Huntsberry. And you will not."

His uncle frowned deeply. "Insolence does not suit you, Boy." He signaled a footman. "Remove his food."

The footman did so, and Judson wondered when he would have his next meal.

"Go to your bedchamber. I will deal with you later," his uncle ground out. As Judson rose, he warned, "I better not find you anywhere else. You are not to visit your father without my permission."

"Yes, Uncle," he said meekly, leaving the breakfast room.

Returning to his bedchamber, he was thankful he had already visited with Papa earlier. He could live without the food, but he wondered how long Uncle Jeremiah would keep him from Papa's side.

Thankfully, in times such as these, he was not bored. Reading was his favorite pastime, and Judson enjoyed escaping into other worlds, pretending he was someone brave and strong, such as Odysseus. Underneath his bed, he kept the complete works of William Shakespeare. He pulled the massive tome from its hiding place now. He remained on the floor, opening the book, and placing it in his lap. In case his uncle did come to see him, it would be easy to close the book and slide it under the bed and pretend he was merely sitting on the floor, staring into space.

Several hours passed, and he ignored the hunger pangs in his belly as he read Part 1 of *Henry IV*, chuckling to himself about Falstaff's antics. Then he sensed the door opening, and he quickly placed his volume of Shakespeare under the bed. As he shot to his feet, he saw Tim closing the door. The footman hurried toward him, handing him a wrapped cloth. Judson opened it, finding a slice of bread and a hunk of cheese.

"Eat quickly, my lord," Tim urged. "I heard your uncle is coming to see you soon."

Gratitude filled him. "Thank you, Tim."

The footman winked at him. "Can't have you going hungry now, can we, my lord?"

He hurried from the room, and Judson quickly ate half of what had been brought. The rest, he wrapped back in the cloth Tim had brought it in and placed it on the floor behind the window's curtains. His uncle would never think to look there. If Uncle Jeremiah cared to search the room, he would likely go for the wardrobe first and then the trunk. He might possibly look under the mattress or bed, only finding the volume of the bard. The food should be safe in its hiding place.

Another hour passed, and he wondered if Uncle Jeremiah would make an appearance or not. Suddenly, the door flew open, startling him. He was glad he had moved to the window seat.

"Come," his uncle ordered.

Not knowing where they were going, trepidation set in. He crossed the room, moving toward his uncle, who stepped into the corridor and then moved into Papa's bedchamber. Relief swept through him, but it quickly dissipated when he spied his father. His breathing was harsh and sporadic, and his face was bright red, as if from fever.

Judson ran to the bed and touched Papa's forehead. "He is burning up," he cried. "Send for the doctor."

"I have," Uncle Jeremiah said. "It will not do any good. This is the end. Say your goodbyes."

A lump formed in his throat, making it almost impossible to speak. He forced it down as tears swam in his eyes. Judson cradled Papa's cheeks.

"I love you, Papa. Please, don't leave me."

It was as if his father could no longer hear him, though. His breathing now rattled loudly and was so erratic, Judson worried that each breath Papa took would be his last. He found himself climbing onto the bed, curling up at his father's side, one arm possessively over him.

In his head, he silently repeated over and over, *Please, don't go. Please, don't go.*

His father shuddered violently, and Judson held tightly onto him, knowing this was the end and wanting to convey his love for this gentle, kind man.

Then Papa wheezed a final time—and was still.

Judson continued to lie still, not ever wanting to let go, but his uncle harshly commanded, "Get up."

Reluctantly, he did so, taking a seat in the chair next to the bed.

"I will stay with him until the doctor arrives."

Uncle Jeremiah came to stand next to him. He clasped Judson's shoulder so firmly that a small yelp emerged.

"You will go to your bedchamber and remain in it. You are no longer needed here."

Stubbornly, he said, "I will stay with Papa. I do not want him left alone."

His uncle's fingers squeezed tightly, but this time, Judson refused to make a sound.

Seeing his defiance, Uncle Jeremiah then lifted Judson by his shirtfront, dragging him across the room and to his bedchamber.

Tossing him onto the floor, he said, "You will stay here. Until I return."

Contempt for his only living relative filled him. "I am now the Marquess of Huntsberry. I will do as I wish."

Uncle Jeremiah gaped at him—and then broke out in laughter. Anger burned through Judson.

"You are but a mere boy," his uncle pointed out. "I am your guardian. Until you reach your majority at one and twenty, you will dance to the tune I play."

Judson spent the next three days locked in his room. Servants came at regular intervals with a tray, but not one would speak to him. He spent much of his time at the window, watching the comings and goings since it faced the front lawn. The local doctor arrived soon after Judson's confinement. Then neighbors came, including the Marquess and Marchioness of Aldridge, whose estate bordered Huntsworth. He assumed they came to pay their respects.

Finally, he saw the wooden coffin bearing his father's body leave the house. It was placed in a cart and driven away. Shortly afterward, his uncle and Lord Blackwell left in the marquess' carriage. Judson supposed they were going to Alderton, the nearby village. A section in the church's graveyard was given over to the Jarvis family. He only hoped Papa was being laid to rest next to Mama.

It was late when the carriage returned. Only Uncle Jeremiah climbed from it, and Judson wondered where Lord Blackwell was. Shortly afterward, a knock sounded on his door, and Clippman entered. The butler had deep circles under his eyes, and Judson thought the servant must have sat vigil each night at his former employer's side.

"My lord, Mr. Jarvis wishes to speak to you in the study."

"I am allowed to leave to go and see him?" he asked, not wanting to anger his uncle.

"Yes, my lord." The butler paused. "May I express my deepest regrets to you on the loss of Lord Huntsberry?"

"Yes, thank you, Clippman. I appreciate your words."

The butler led him to the study. It was a room Judson had always enjoyed being in. He and Papa had spent many hours there, reading together, talking over history and religion and even a bit of politics.

When he entered, his uncle sat at Papa's desk. Fury filled him, but Judson knew if he lashed out, it would do no good. His uncle was just as much a bully as those boys at school. He decided he would bide his time. It would take years.

But he would have revenge on Jeremiah Jarvis—and anyone else who had ever hurt him.

Clippman closed the door, and Judson stepped forward. "You wished to see me, Uncle?"

"Yes." His uncle rose and came from behind the desk. "Have a seat."

He took one next to the window, while his uncle sat opposite him.

"The solicitor has come and gone. Everything is official. I am your guardian and the executor of my brother's estate until you reach your majority." Bitterness crossed his face. "Even in death, I do the work of the Marquess of Huntsberry, yet I am denied the title."

Fear filled him. The only thing standing between Uncle Jeremiah and the title was Judson himself. He would not put it past his uncle to do something dastardly and put an end to him. But he could never allow Uncle Jeremiah to see any sign of weakness. He must behave as if nothing had changed. Still, from this moment going forward, Judson would be on guard. He would never drink or eat anything his uncle offered him. He would do his best to never be alone with him. He wanted to live.

And be the best man he could in order to honor his father.

Uncle Jeremiah studied him. "You are too delicate. So very weak. You took the worst qualities from both your parents." He paused. "It will be my job to toughen you up. Make you a man."

Judson did not like the sound of that, but he did not react.

"Remove your clothes," Uncle Jeremiah ordered.

"What?" he cried, leaping to his feet.

"You heard me. As I am your guardian and in charge of this estate, I am not to be questioned. No servant will ever stand against me. Do as I say."

Bile rose in his throat. Even if he attacked, trying to claw his uncle's eyes, he would prove no match for the older man. Jeremiah Jarvis was thirty years of age and in the prime of his life.

Having no choice, Judson stripped off his clothes and stood, jaw locked, glaring at his uncle, whose eyes roamed his nephew's thin, bruised, scarred body.

"I see you have a few bruises," Uncle Jeremiah noted. "It seems your school chums have also tried to make you a man."

"Beating me will not make me a man," he responded, causing his uncle to slap him.

Judson saw stars, but he did not cry out. Did not whimper. He merely stood his ground. He had already had plenty of practice doing so.

His uncle retrieved a cane. "It pains me to do this, but someone has to make a man out of you."

He took each blow without a word. The cane cut into him, and Judson knew he would have scars from it. But he would never give his uncle the satisfaction of hearing a single squeak come from him. He would take anything doled out by this horrible man.

And return it sevenfold when he became an adult.

"You may dress again," Uncle Jeremiah said, removing his handkerchief and wiping the cane. Judson stared at the blood. From that moment, his heart became encased in ice.

He decided he would never feel any emotion again, other than hate. He would allow his hate to grow, feeding it steadily over the years, until he exacted his revenge. On his uncle. On every boy who had struck and mocked him. His father had wanted his son to be a good man, but Judson knew as the years progressed, any good inside him would be beaten away, leaving him thirsting for revenge.

When the time came, he would punish everyone who had wronged him. Injured him. Wounded and harmed and terrorized him. Judson knew it would cost him his soul.

And he didn't care.

CHAPTER ONE

London—March 1807

EXCITEMENT BUZZED THROUGH Lady Lucilla Alington. This afternoon, she would be seeing her cousins for the first time in more than a decade. The three related families lived in various corners of England, and the ten cousins had only been brought together for one magical week in London many years ago.

Lucy was making her come-out next month, along with her cousins Lia and Tia, daughters of the Duke and Duchess of Millbrooke. She had been drawn to the twins when they had met because they were the same age, and she couldn't wait to spend the entire upcoming Season with them as they attended the many social events, looking to find their husbands.

It would be Uncle Charles and Aunt Alice coming to tea today, along with the twins and Lord Claibourne, who was the duke's only son and heir apparent. She remembered Val as a fun-loving, mischievous sort, and he had been her brother Con's closest friend for years. The boys had attended school and university together, even sharing rooms during their Oxford years.

She sat at her dressing table, checking her appearance, wanting to make a good impression on these cousins. They had played well together when they were girls, but she wondered what Lia and Tia would be like now they were grown up. More than anything, Lucy valued family, and she hoped her cousins would become her good friends during these months in town. She also hoped to make other friends during her debut.

A soft knock sounded on the door, and her maid Annie entered the bedchamber. Annie had been promoted to be her lady's maid recently and would go with Lucy to her new household once she wed. She liked Annie's no-nonsense approach, and the maid had a wonderful touch in dressing hair.

"My lady, Lord Dyer wishes for you to come to the drawing room now."

Tea would not be served for another half-hour, so she wondered why Con wished to speak to her.

Rising, she said, "Thank you for letting me know, Annie."

Lucy went to the drawing room, finding Con and another handsome gentleman with him. She came toward them and said, "You must be my cousin Val. Con constantly sings your praises."

He smiled and took her hands in his. "Cousin Lucy. Ah, it has been too long since we have seen one another. That will be remedied this Season, however. You are all grown up and looking ever so lovely."

"Come have a seat," her brother urged. "Val thought he would stop by early and get to know you a little better before the rest of his family arrived."

Her cousin said, "Five of us Worthingtons descending all at once is a little overwhelming. And that does not count Ariadne and Julian, who will not be in town for a while."

Her cousin Ariadne had made her come-out last Season and wed the Marquess of Aldridge in the first wedding of the Season. Ariadne had given birth to their child only two weeks ago, a girl named Penelope.

"Will Ariadne even attend the Season this year?" she asked Val.

"She plans to do so," Val revealed. "Sis wants to help in launching the twins—and you—into Polite Society. Ariadne has said that she and Julian will only attend a handful of events, but she wants to do all she can to help introduce you and our sisters to the right people."

"Julian and Ariadne are also very busy with their orphanage,"

Con said.

"I do not know anything about that," Lucy said. "What orphanage?"

"They have bought and are managing Oakbrooke Orphanage," Con told her. "They both feel very strongly about helping the poor as much as possible. Ariadne and Julian hired a headmistress, and the two women were responsible for hiring the rest of the teachers and staff."

"They try to spend a few days in town each week," Val added. "They volunteer their time at the school, teaching the orphans. Of course, the month leading up to the birth, they remained at Aldridge Manor. It was too difficult for my sister to travel even the short distance to town in her delicate condition."

"Have you seen your new niece?" Lucy asked, longing for babes of her own. She hoped to find a husband and began a family soon, unlike her younger sister Dru, who had remained in the country at Marleyfield and showed no interest in marriage or babes.

"I most certainly have," Val said, pride evident in his voice. "Penelope is the perfect babe. A heavenly creation." He laughed. "It almost tempts me to find a wife of my own so I could have a child to lavish attention upon."

"Wait a minute," Con said. "I thought neither of us was perusing the Marriage Mart at this point."

Val chuckled. "I said tempted, Con. I have no desire to wed at this point in my life. I would rather wait until I come into my father's title, which hopefully will not occur for many years to come."

Lucy looked to Con. "Do you feel the same way? Waiting until Papa is gone before you wed?"

"I do," her brother confirmed. "Until then, Val and I are simply enjoying the bachelor life and each Season as it comes along. We also will be helping you and the twins in finding husbands. Val was charged to do so last year by his father on Ariadne's behalf, and we intend to do the same for the three of you girls this year."

Her cousin added, "There are some wonderful gentlemen who would make worthy husbands. On the other hand, there are a good number of rogues whom we wish to keep far away from the three of you."

"Have no fears, little sister," Con said. "The two of us will review each of your suitors. We want to keep away fortune hunters and men of less desirable character."

"This is wonderful to hear," Lucy declared. "I had no idea the two of you would be aiding me and my cousins."

"Ariadne wound up with one of our very good friends," Val said. "You will meet Julian when they come to town. They plan to do so a couple of days before the Season begins."

"Oh, she must be so disappointed to leave her babe so soon after giving birth," Lucy said.

"That is where you are wrong," her cousin said. "My sister and brother-in-law have no plans to ever leave any of their children behind in the country as all of us were by our parents. Ariadne assured me that each Season, she will bring her entire family to town. She hopes all her cousins will do the same. Frankly, the Season is a time for family and friends to come together, and I do not understand why children are always left behind."

"If Ariadne is going to bring her children to town, then so will I," Lucy said, not certain if Val had things right or not and thinking it was only because Penelope was so young that she had accompanied her parents to town. Wistfully, she added, "I always felt as if Mama and Papa abandoned us each year to head to town for so many months."

"We are a new generation," Con remarked. "Perhaps we can set the stage for change within the *ton*, helping families to stay united. I know I want my own children to get to know yours. Val's and Ariadne's, as well."

Lucy was even more eager to meet her cousins again now, and she knew that would happen soon because her parents entered the drawing room.

"Ah, Valentinian," Mama said fondly. "You came separately from your family?"

He greeted her parents, saying, "Con and I were at White's and decided to come together."

They seated themselves and Mama said, "I am so looking forward to seeing my brother. We were extremely close growing up and have remained so all these years. It is the highlight of each Season getting to spend time with him and his duchess. Are your sisters eager to make their come-outs?"

"They are, Aunt Charlotte. They have seen how happy Ariadne is in her marriage, and they look upon Julian as another brother to them. In fact, the twins even went to Aldridge Manor for Christmas this past year, and they also visited Oakbrooke Orphanage and spent time with the orphans."

Mama sniffed dismissively. "I am not quite certain that I understand why they devote so much of themselves to that orphanage. Yes, it is important for members of Polite Society to help support the poor, but Aldridge and Ariadne have gone a bit to the extreme. I believe they should focus on their own family."

"It makes them happy, Mama," Con said. "And they are remaining in the country now since Penelope's birth."

Their butler entered the drawing room, announcing their guests. Lucy rose, along with the others, wondering what her cousins looked like now.

The duke and duchess swept into the room first, and she thought the pair had not changed much at all. Her uncle's hair was threaded with more gray than the last time she had seen him, while her aunt had a few more wrinkles. Still, she would have recognized them anywhere.

Following them came their twins, and Lucy couldn't help but smile as her cousins' gazes turned to her first. While they both still resembled one another in the face, there were marked differences between the pair. Lia was the shorter of the two, with auburn hair and deep blue eyes. Her curves were obvious, and Lucy thought she and Lia could probably wear one another's clothes with ease. Tia had strawberry blond hair and clear, sky-blue eyes, and possessed a willowy frame.

Greetings and kisses were exchanged, and she saw Aunt Alice sizing her up. While Lucy had never given a thought to thinking herself in competition for a husband with her cousins, her aunt's gaze betrayed that was at the forefront of her mind.

"You have turned into a lovely young lady, Lucilla," her aunt remarked. "I do believe you and my girls will be the most beautiful in this year's come-out class."

"I am so happy to be making my come-out with my cousins," Lucy replied.

Aunt Alice smiled. "Ariadne made a brilliant match last Season. I expect nothing less for Thermantia and Cornelia. And you, of course."

Hearing her cousins' given names surprised her, for she always thought of them as Tia and Lia. Her mother and Uncle Charles had been fascinated by Roman and Byzantine history, along with their cousin George. The three had named all their children after emperors and empresses, though most of the children had rebelled against their unusual names, taking on more diminutive forms of them.

Two teacarts were rolled in, and Mama said, "We adults have much to discuss amongst ourselves, and you young people would be bored by our conversation. Lucilla, you are to pour out for your brother and cousins."

Lucy knew this was a great honor, being asked to do so even before she had made her debut. She had practiced the etiquette of tea many times with her governess and hoped she would not make a mistake today.

"I am happy to do so, Mama."

The cousins all went to the far side of the drawing room, where the second teacart was being placed. They took seats, and she began the process of preparing and pouring out for the group.

As she did so, Lucy said, "Why don't you each make up a plate for yourselves? That way, things will go more quickly."

Val reached and handed a plate to each of his sisters before taking one of his own, while Con picked up one for himself. Her brother distributed the cups and saucers she handed to him. Lucy then poured out for herself and took a piece of strawberry cake and a ham sandwich for herself.

Tia, whom Lucy remembered was the more outgoing of the two sisters, said, "We are thrilled to be making our come-outs with you, Lucy. Have you been to see Madame Laurent yet? Mama told us Madame is the only modiste she trusts in all of London. She made up Ariadne's complete wardrobe last Season."

"No, we have only been in town since yesterday afternoon. Mama has scheduled time at Madame Laurent's shop for us, however. Have you visited her yet?"

"No," Lia said. "Mama needs to write for an appointment. It would be wonderful if we could all go together on the same day and choose materials and styles of the various gowns to be made up."

"Let us ask them after tea if that is possible," she suggested.

The next hour passed pleasantly, with Con and Val describing the various social affairs to them. She could not wait to attend garden and card parties, musicales, and Venetian breakfasts. Most of all, Lucy was excited about the many balls to be held throughout the Season.

"Do you enjoy dancing?" she asked the twins.

"We have had a dance master for three years now," Tia explained. "Lia is naturally graceful and took to everything with ease. I am a bit more exuberant, but I have learned to dance quite well, if I do say so myself. We have attended various assemblies in Willowshire, a village nearby Millvale. What about you, Lucy?"

"I, too, have had a dance master. Mama has retained another one for the next few weeks to refresh me on various steps and dances. Con has escorted me to assemblies in our local village, as well. I think balls will be the most fun of all this Season."

She glanced to the other side of the room and saw it looked as if her aunt and uncle were ready to leave.

"We should rejoin our parents," Lucy said. "I want to ask our mamas about a joint appointment at Madame Laurent's."

The five cousins returned to the adults, who rose. Quickly, Lucy asked about seeing the modiste together.

"That is an excellent idea," Mama proclaimed. "That way, you will have both my expertise and that of your aunt in recommending what should be included in your wardrobe."

She could barely contain her excitement, ready to form a strong bond with these cousins of hers.

"I shall send Madame Laurent a message and make arrangements for all three of our girls to be seen together," Mama promised.

"It was so good to see all of you," Papa told their guests.

Uncle Charles said, "You must come for tea tomorrow afternoon. I insist, Charlotte. Agnes will be there, as well."

Lucy's aunt Agnes had been married to her uncle George, and she was now a widow. Lucy hoped Mama would say yes. She would love to spend more time with her cousins and also see Aunt Agnes.

"We would be delighted to do so," Mama declared.

"Until tomorrow," Aunt Alice said.

They accompanied their guests downstairs, where they claimed their things. As Uncle Charles set his hat on his head, Lucy saw the expression on his face turn odd. Something came out of his mouth, not exactly words, but gibberish. All eyes turned to the duke as he spoke again, this time his words slurring, the right corner of his mouth drooping in an odd fashion.

Then her uncle collapsed upon the marble floor of the foyer.

Aunt Alice shrieked. Lia and Tia stood frozen. Val sprang to his father, stripping off his coat and folding it, placing it under his father's head.

"Send for the doctor," Papa commanded crisply.

"I will go," Con volunteered, dashing out the door.

Suddenly, footmen appeared, along with the butler, and Mama said, "Take His Grace upstairs to the Blue Room," her voice cracking.

Quickly, the servants, directed by Val, lifted Uncle Charles and hurried up the stairs with him. Mama and Papa followed, both of them supporting Aunt Alice.

Her heart went out to her mother, knowing how much her mother loved her brother. More importantly, Lucy needed to help take care of her cousins now.

Going to them, she embraced them together. "Come. We should go back to the drawing room and wait for the doctor."

Lia was the first to speak. "It is apoplexy," she said solemnly. "I visited one of our tenants who was struck by it. He was bedridden until he passed." She began weeping softly.

Tia wrapped her arm about her twin. "We do not know that, Lia," she said fiercely. "The doctor will come. He will fix Papa."

Gently, she took her cousins in hand and guided them upstairs to the drawing room, where they waited in silence.

Con, his hair looking windblown, joined them, saying, "The doctor is with Uncle Charles now."

After half an hour, Mrs. Adams appeared. The housekeeper asked, "Shall I bring tea, my lady?"

She looked to her cousins, who shook their heads.

"No, not now, Mrs. Adams, but thank you."

Another hour passed, and then Papa and Mama entered the room. Her mother, usually so cool and reserved, looked as if she had aged a decade in the last few hours. Papa guided her toward them.

Mama's lips trembled as she said, "There is no easy way to say this. Your papa is gone," she told the twins. "You may come say your goodbyes to him."

Lucy, who had continued to hold her cousins' hands, squeezed them now. She rose, pulling Lia and Tia with her. Both her cousins began to sob.

"Where is Mama?" Lia asked.

"She became hysterical," Papa explained to his nieces. "The doctor has given her something to quiet her. She will sleep for now. He will give you something, as well, if you wish."

"No," Tia said firmly. "Lia and I have one another. And Val. We must be strong for Mama." She looked to Lucy. "Will you come with us?"

She nodded. "Of course."

Accompanying her cousins to the Blue Room, Lucy spied Val standing next to the bed. He came and embraced his sisters, saying, "He went peacefully. One minute, he was here. The next, he was gone."

The twins went to their father. Both looked at him a long moment before kissing his cheek.

Val said, "We will take him home to Millvale. He will be buried in the churchyard at Willowshire. I will have Con escort the two of you home now. Aunt Charlotte and I will handle the details. I will also send a messenger to Aldridge Manor to let Ariadne and Julian know."

"When will we see Mama?" Lia asked softly.

"The doctor said she will sleep until tomorrow morning," Val told her. "See that the servants pack everything. We will return to Kent immediately." He hesitated. "This means that there will be no Season for the two of you this year. We will be in mourning."

The twins nodded, and Val said, "Your time will come next year. What is important is to be with Mama. I will stay with you, as well. As the new duke, I have many responsibilities to see to and much to learn."

Disappointment flooded Lucy. While she understood that her cousins would need to mourn for their father, she had looked forward to their company in the coming months.

Then it struck her. If the Worthingtons were in mourning, would Mama also be in mourning—and by extension—her own family? She hated thinking such selfish thoughts.

Con spoke up. "Let me take you home now."

Tia came and threw her arms about Lucy. "I am sorry we will not be here this Season with you."

Lia joined them, hugging Lucy tightly. "Take care. Write to

us about everything if you would."

"I promise to do so," she replied, still unsure of her own status regarding her come-out.

Her brother escorted the twins from the room. Lucy went to Val, hugging him and expressing her condolences.

Mama said, "I must speak to Lucilla briefly, Valentinian, then we shall sit and discuss what needs to be done regarding His Grace."

Her mother took Lucy's wrist and led her into the corridor.

"I am so sorry for your loss, Mama. I know how much you loved Uncle Charles. I wish I could have known him better."

"I wanted to tell you this changes nothing," Mama said. "You will make your come-out as planned."

"We will not be in mourning?" she asked quietly.

"I will always mourn the loss of Charles," Mama said brusquely. "But it is important to secure your future. You are a very pretty girl, Lucilla, and you will attract a good number of suitors. Cornelia and Thermantia are also striking. They would have been competition for you. I see no reason for you to wait until next year and have to fight for a husband with that pair challenging you every step of the way."

Lucy thought her mother's words harsh. Even unfeeling. She also knew when Mama made up her mind about something, there was no changing it.

"All right, Mama," she agreed. "I will continue with making my come-out."

Mama smiled, patting her daughter's cheek. "You will shine, Lucilla. Madame Laurent will see to that. She is incredibly creative and will know just how to flatter your figure. We will keep our current appointment with the modiste so that she may start your wardrobe."

She frowned. "But that is two days from now. Surely, we are going to Surrey for the funeral and burial."

Mama snorted. "Women are usually kept from funerals. I see no reason to go. Launching you into Polite Society is my priority."

The reply shocked her. Lucy had not known the Season was so combative.

Mama smoothed Lucy's hair. "I see a great match for you, my dear. Especially with two fewer girls to distract the current crop of eligible bachelors."

"Lia and Tia are your nieces, Mama," she chided.

Her mother gazed coldly at her. "And you are my daughter. My allegiance is to you—and seeing you make the best match of the Season. Ariadne did so last year. It is up to you to make a brilliant one of your own this year."

Mama sighed. "I must go help Valentinian make the arrangements. A coffin must be built in order to transport Charles back to Millvale. We will talk again tomorrow."

Lucy was left in the corridor, feeling numb. She returned to her bedchamber and lay on the bed. Sadness filled her. The loss of her uncle was part of it, but losing out on the closeness she would have experienced with Tia, Lia, and Val was the greater part.

Now, she would go into the Season alone, not knowing a soul beyond Con.

CHAPTER TWO

London—April

JUDSON JARVIS, MARQUESS of Huntsberry, sat patiently as Tim shaved him.

"Almost finished, my lord," the valet said.

"I am not in any hurry."

He only wish he had something to hurry to. His life was one of ease. Great wealth had come to him once he had reached his majority. Of course, he had held the title from the time he was a boy, but his uncle had held the purse strings for almost a dozen years. Fortunately, Judson's father, knowing he was in extremely poor health, had hired Mr. Baker, the leading solicitor in London, to make out his will. He didn't know all the particulars. All Judson did know was that Uncle Jeremiah was at the mercy of Mr. Baker. He could barely spend a farthing without having to clear the expense with the solicitor, something which Judson had not known at the time.

Baker had waited until Judson was ready to go away to Cambridge before he had requested an appointment with the marquess. At their meeting, he had explained that all Judson's school fees and living expenses would be paid for, as well as a quarterly allowance provided for miscellaneous items. Baker then explained how he had, in effect, hamstrung Uncle Jeremiah as far as expenditures went. While Judson had wrongly believed his uncle poured through the estate's money and worried if anything would be left by the time he could claim control, he learned his uncle had lied. Baker—and Judson's father—had protected him well. Huntsworth thrived. Other investments in shipping, land, and banking also were doing quite well.

He had kept Baker on since he managed all the holdings. Now, the solicitor worked only for the Marquess of Huntsberry.

Judson had given Uncle Jeremiah his choice of a cottage, free and clear, on Huntsworth lands, or a small quarterly allowance. He had chosen the latter, taking rooms in town, but the amount was so little that Uncle Jeremiah could not live in style. All transactions went through Baker, and Judson had not seen his uncle in several years now.

He had an excellent steward who sent regular reports, ones Judson didn't bother to read. He never went to Huntsworth, instead choosing to stay in town year-round. Judson knew nothing about running a large estate and chose not to do so. In fact, he had closed the country house and hired a caretaker. The man and his wife checked it regularly to make certain no one had broken into the house. The furniture had been covered and all the servants had been let go with glowing references.

Since he had nothing to do every single day, Judson had grown increasingly bored. He couldn't imagine continuing in this pattern for the next several decades. Because of this boredom, he took risks. Often. He raced his phaeton regularly and had never lost a contest. He rode his horse like a demon straight from Hell. He gambled frequently and couldn't seem to lose. Oh, he did experience the occasional loss, but his luck always rebounded, and by the end of the evening, any loss in a gaming hell had been erased many times over.

He supposed he should wed in order to secure an heir, but the thought of having a wife who would no doubt nag him and children he couldn't care less about simply did not appeal to him. Perhaps in another ten years, he might consider marriage. After all, he was only eight and twenty. In the meantime, he had his needs meet by his mistress. Antonia Amato had served in that role for the past five years. He only kept a mistress because of his fear of disease in the brothels frequented by men of the *ton*.

Judson only saw Antonia once or twice a month. Even then, he was starting to be bored by her, too.

Was he destined to go through life so jaded?

Tim finished shaving him, cleaning Judson's face and dabbing cologne on his neck. It was a blend of Tim's own making. The former footman was clever. Once Judson took control of the marquessate, he elevated Tim from footman to valet, since his uncle had never allowed him to have one, and began giving the servant books to read. Tim proved as voracious a reader as Judson himself, and they spent many hours discussing what they had read, be it novels, plays, or items in the London newspapers.

In truth, Tim was his only friend.

Minutes later, Judson was dressed for the day. He went down to the breakfast room, a small, cheery room that got plenty of sunlight. There, he drank a cup of tea and ate his usual breakfast of two eggs, ham, and toast points slathered with marmalade. After, he took the morning post into his study and went through it. Invitations for the upcoming Season, which began in a week, were flooding in, as usual. Some years, he took in a few of the events. Other times, he skipped weeks' worth of them. Even when he did respond to an invitation, indicating he would show at some social affair, a hostess never quite knew whether or not that would be the case.

Still, the invitations continued to come, simply because he was a marquess. An unwed marquess. That meant he was always highly sought after at any affair he attended. Eager mamas fawned over him, thrusting their daughters into his path. Girls making their come-outs set their caps for him. Or so he'd read in the gossip columns.

The whole Season was a bloody bore.

But at least it gave him something different to do for a few months when he did decide to attend an event. The card room was always full at balls. He would dance a few times, giving hope to many females, and then disappear for hours into the card room. He actually enjoyed dancing, which was why he chose to show up at a ball every now and then. Garden parties were a bore. Musicales were even worse. He cared nothing for music. Antonia had been an opera singer and was always wanting to sing for him, but he had no interest in hearing her.

He did enjoy going to the theater, though. Judson always had a box at several of the theaters in town. He sat in them alone because he had no one whom he wished to invite to accompany him to a production.

Taking in today's round of invitations, he decided not to reply to any of them. So far, he had yet to promise a single hostess he would attend her event. Instead, he would place them in chronological order and decide the morning of whether or not he would go. No hostess in London would deny him entrance into their affair. It would save him time writing replies, and he would simply pick and choose when and where to go as he always had.

A knock sounded on his door, and he said, "Come," knowing it would be Clippman, informing him his carriage was ready. Judson went to White's each morning and drank coffee as he perused the newspapers. It was something he enjoyed.

And there weren't many things he did.

Forcing himself to meet his butler's eyes with confidence, he asked, "Is my carriage ready?"

"Yes, my lord," the butler replied.

Part of him wanted to let Clippman and his wife go, simply because they were a part of his past. They had witnessed the aftermath of what his uncle put him through. Time and again, Jeremiah Jarvis beat his nephew. His uncle had not only been physically abusive, but he had pushed his nephew to physical limits no one should have to face, all in the name of making him a man. Judson had been made to run, no matter what the weather, until he was ready to drop. He also lifted weights. Jeremiah finally taught him to swim, only to have Judson swim daily when he was home from school. As much as he hated the torment he faced from his classmates, it was even more difficult to return to Huntsworth, knowing he would be swimming across the lake on the property even in December.

That was a large reason why he never went to Huntsworth now. His memories of the country estate were ones he wished to forget.

He knew he would never terminate the Clippmans' employment. The couple excelled at their positions, and his London household ran without any problems. Or if there were any, he never heard about them. Still, there were times he wished neither of them knew what he had suffered through. Only they and Tim were left from the old days. The rest of his staff in town had not known him as a boy.

Shoving aside those thoughts, Judson went out to his carriage. His driver knew without instructions to take him to White's since it was part of the daily routine. Because London was on the brink of beginning a new Season, though, the place would be filled. He preferred White's being a calm environment the rest of the year, a refuge which he sought.

He left the carriage once they arrived and entered, Pollard greeting him.

"It is good to see you this morning, Lord Huntsberry. Tommy will bring your coffee to you as soon as you are seated." Pollard looked apologetic, adding, "The place is quite full this morning, my lord."

Judson began walking through the rooms, seeing it was worse than he'd feared. He rarely spoke to others and never sat with anyone at the club. This morning, though, seats were filled in every room, and he realized he would have to sit not only near but with others.

Entering another morning room, he glanced about, spying someone he vaguely knew. Lord Dyer was usually in the company of Lord Claibourne, but today, Claibourne was nowhere in sight. Instead, in his place, Viscount Dyer sat with someone Judson had seen upon occasion, starting last spring. Seeing the only available spot was with these two gentlemen, he approached them.

"Good morning, my lords," he greeted. "Is this chair taken?"

Surprise filled Dyer's face. "No, my lord. Please, join us."

He did so and almost immediately, Tommy appeared with coffee and Judson's favorite newspaper.

After Tommy left, Judson fully intended to avoid any further conversation and simply read his newspaper, but Lord Dyer said, "If I may, my lord, I would like to introduce you to the Marquess of Aldridge. This is Lord Huntsberry."

Not wishing to appear churlish, Judson accepted the offered hand and shook it.

"It seems we are neighbors," Lord Aldridge said. "In Surrey."

He thought for a moment. "Aldridge Manor? You are from there?"

"I am, my lord."

"I am never in the country," he said flatly. "You will only see me here in town."

Aldridge nodded. "That is what my steward told me. Ross has become friendly with your Mr. Wayling."

"Wayling is most efficient. Because of that, I have no need to visit Huntsworth."

He took up his paper, not wishing for further conversation, but he couldn't help but listen to his companions' conversation. From it, he gleaned that Lady Aldridge's father, the Duke of Millbrooke, had recently passed and the two men had attended His Grace's funeral. Judson never read the obituaries in any of the newspapers. He had no interest in who was born, wed, or buried in Polite Society.

"Lucy is incredibly disappointed that she will not be able to make her come-out with Lia and Tia," Lord Dyer said. "She is grateful, though, that you and Ariadne will help smooth the way and help introduce her into Polite Society."

Aldridge chuckled. "It seems a bit ironic that I am helping your sister meet others of the *ton* when this time last year, I knew none of them myself. Thanks to you and Val, though, it led me to wedded bliss with Ariadne."

Judson thought it unusual this new marquess had not known a soul from Polite Society. He recalled the previous Lord Aldridge had no children, despite wedding thrice. This man must be a distant cousin of the deceased Aldridge. He was dressed in a refined manner, but he had the look of someone rough and tumble.

Impulsively, he set his newspaper aside and asked, "Do you ever box, Aldridge?"

"No, my lord, though I have done my fair share of brawling in the past. I do not see the point in studying an art form which has rules. If I ever do take up my fists again, it will be to defend myself or protect my family."

He thought the marquess' answer interesting—and cryptic.

"If you do not pursue boxing, my lord, what are you interested in to pass the time? Racehorses? Gambling?"

Aldridge looked at him dismissively, a look Judson no one had dared give him in years, piquing his interest even more.

"I have a lovely wife and a newborn daughter, my lord," Aldridge continued. "My marchioness and I also devote a good deal of time to our orphanage."

"Orphanage?" he asked, confused.

When the marquess merely glared at him, Lord Dyer jumped into the conversation. "Lord and Lady Aldridge purchased Oakbrooke Orphanage last year. They have staffed it and volunteer their time a couple of days a week, helping to teach the children who reside there. Why, they know the name of every child," the viscount declared.

Hearing that, his opinion of Lord Aldridge improved significantly.

"So, you do not waste your time in pursuit of pleasure."

"I only pleasure my wife," Aldridge said, a wicked gleam in his eye.

Judson burst out laughing, something he could not remember doing for years.

"Why such dedication to an orphanage?" he pressed, wanting

to understand this unusual man better.

With defiance in his eyes now, Aldridge said, "I came from a background unlike those in Polite Society. My wife is the one whose tender heart led to encouraging me to aid those in need. Last year, we took on Oakbrooke Orphanage. This year, we are starting a program which will help clothe the poor and those in need in London. I am fortunate to be in a position now of great wealth and power. Ariadne is the one who has insisted because of our wealth, we must do what we can to assist others who need our help."

He nodded. "Your marchioness sounds most interesting, Aldridge. I cannot think of a single lady in the *ton* who would want to give money to the poor directly, much less be so involved with her time."

An unfamiliar look appeared in the marquess' eyes. "There is no one like my Ariadne," he said softly, causing Judson to realize the pair was a love match.

With a spontaneity he didn't know existed within him, Judson said, "I wish to donate to your cause, my lord. Both Oakbrooke Orphanage and this plan to clothe the needy of London."

Both men looked stunned by his words. Lord Aldridge recovered first and said, "That is most gracious of you, Huntsberry. Perhaps we could have you come to tea this afternoon and discuss the matter. You could meet my wife."

Judson hadn't been invited to tea. Ever. Since he had no friends, invitations to such personal times as tea never occurred.

The marquess added, "There will be other family members at tea this afternoon. Lord Dyer's parents and sister. You are still most welcome, however."

Intrigued by this man and his marchioness, he heard himself say, "I am happy to come to tea, my lord. I will be there this afternoon."

Lord Aldridge provided his address to Judson, and he said, "If you will now excuse me, I am off to Gentleman Jackson's gymnasium."

It surprised him when Lord Dyer said, "I, too, was going to the boxing academy next. Perhaps we might go together, my lord."

This was turning into a most unusual morning.

"If you wish," he said off-handedly but then added, "It was good meeting you, Aldridge. I look forward to meeting Lady Aldridge, as well."

The marquess inclined his head, and Judson left White's in Lord Dyer's company.

"My carriage is this way," he said, leading the viscount to the vehicle.

The two men climbed into the carriage. He had not had to make conversation in so long that he did not know how to even begin as the vehicle started up. Small talk had never been his strong suit.

"I want to thank you," his companion said. "For what you did at school. I know it is many years later, but I do not know if anyone ever acknowledged your efforts, much less thanked you for them."

Feeling uncomfortable, Judson asked, "And what are you speaking of, Dyer?"

"My cousin Val and I were a few years behind you. We saw how you handled bullies. You were quite the champion for boys who were smaller than their peers. Defenseless. Fortunately, Val and I were always a decent size and had one another's backs, but we witnessed you putting a bully in his place. School proved to be a much more pleasant place for so many, thanks to you, Huntsberry."

The viscount's words took Judson back to a time he wished to forget. He had hit a growth spurt and, thanks to the rigorous, physical tasks his uncle forced upon him, Judson had not only grown tall, but he had also grown incredibly strong.

First, he had taken care of boys his own age who had bullied him. When he was done with them, they were simpering cowards who promised never to hurt another boy again. Then he had taken on boys older than he was. Thanks to his size and strength—and endurance for pain—he had made mincemeat of them, as well. Word had spread quickly throughout the population that no one was to bully any boy—else he would face the wrath of Judson Jarvis, the Marquess of Huntsberry.

Only twice after that had he needed to put his fists to good use, catching on separate occasions two bullies who thought to defy his edict. One was left with a broken nose and arm. He claimed he had a terrible nightmare and fell out of bed, injuring himself. The boy always turned and moved in the opposite direction when he spied Judson. Eaton, the other boy, had more serious injuries and had withdrawn from school.

Judson had faced no consequences. Not one boy had stepped forward, willing to speak against him, especially since he was protecting so many of the vulnerable. He had never had friends because other boys had always been afraid to befriend him when he was being bullied, fearing they would be caught up in the web of torment. After he increased rapidly in size and strength, every student was too afraid to even approach him. Being friendless had continued throughout his schooldays and university years.

And even until now.

He looked at the man who sat across from him. Would things change? Might he form a friendship with Lords Dyer and Aldridge?

The thought intrigued him.

Realizing that he had not answered the viscount, Judson said, "There is no need to thank me, Dyer. That was many, many years ago."

"Half the boys were too afraid to speak their gratitude to you, while the other half were merely in awe of you. That was Val and myself. This is years late in coming, Huntsberry, but on my behalf and that of my cousin, now the Duke of Millbrooke, I give a heartfelt thanks to you."

Judson realized he felt a strange glow inside. After so many years of being on his own, aloof and withdrawn from others, hope sprang within him. He might actually make a friend.

And find some purpose in his existence.

CHAPTER THREE

"How do I look, Annie?" Lucy faced her maid, smoothing her skirts.

"Very nice, my lady. That new gown from your modiste fits you to perfection."

She was pleased with the gown. Because of her large bosom and small waist, she had to take care with the way a gown was cut. Not only had Madame Laurent helped in steering Mama and her toward not only gowns in which Lucy felt comfortable and fashionable, the modiste had also convinced Mama on colors which best flattered Lucy's hair and complexion. Though she only had a small part of her new wardrobe, already Lucy felt confident entering the Season because of it.

"We should leave now for my cousin's," she told the maid.

On the way there, Lucy told Annie, "Feel free to stay and have a cup of tea or make your way home and do the same. I will be at Cousin Ariadne's two hours before tea even begins, and then tea will certainly be a good hour or more. You will not need to serve as a chaperone home because I will go with Mama and Papa. Con, too, if he is also there. I think he is coming, as well."

They turned onto the square. Three houses sat on it, two facing each other, with one at the end. The one on the left she recalled as the residence of her aunt and uncle. It saddened her that Uncle Charles was now gone, but Lucy thought Val would make for a marvelous Duke of Millbrooke. Though Val would remain in the country this Season with his mother and sisters, at least she would see some of Ariadne and Lord Aldridge. Her cousin was the first of the ten cousins to have wed, and Lucy couldn't help but wonder what the marquess was like. She was also counting on Ariadne's guidance as much as Mama's as far as the Season went. With Ariadne having only made her come-out last year, she was more familiar with the younger set. Lucy hoped to become friends with her cousin.

She knocked on the door and was admitted by the butler.

"Lady Aldridge is awaiting you in her parlor," he said. "Follow me, my lady."

As they went down a hallway, she couldn't help but admire the beautiful furnishings and paintings. The butler announced her and indicated for her to enter the room. She did, seeing Ariadne smiling widely.

"Cousin Lucy!" she cried.

Going to her, Lucy embraced Ariadne, thinking how beautiful she was. Her cousin's hair was a distinct copper color, while her eyes were a sky blue. Even as children, Ariadne had had a maturity about her, and Lucy saw that was still evident.

"I love your scent," she said.

"It is a vanilla which I mix myself. If you like it, I can give you a bottle to use. Only a dab is needed, and the fragrance lasts for hours. Or if you wish for something else, I would be happy to create that for you."

"Thank you. I would appreciate that. I do love lavender."

"Then lavender it is. Come and sit. We have so much to catch up on."

Lucy expressed her condolences. "I am so sorry about the loss of His Grace. At least he and Her Grace called upon you before coming to town and got to meet little Penelope."

Ariadne nodded sadly. "They were only moderately interested in her. After all, she is a female. Most men care little for females, Lucy. Thankfully, Julian is not one of them. He is enthralled with our daughter. She may only be six weeks old, but he loves to hold her and tell her stories. He tells me he will start reading to her soon."

"My, that is most unusual," she commented, not able to imagine any man doing so.

"Julian is most unique. I cannot wait for you to meet him."

"May I see the babe?" she asked.

"She just went down for a nap, but we can sneak up to the nursery so you can get a glimpse of her."

Eagerly, Lucy followed Ariadne up to the top floor. A nursemaid sat in a rocker, watching over the child. She smiled indulgently at her mistress, and Lucy gathered these trips to the nursery were commonplace.

They stepped to the cradle, and Lucy found herself agreeing with Val's opinion of the babe. Penelope was absolute perfection. The infant had tufts of hair which was a soft red. Her mouth was a little rosebud. She frowned in her sleep, stretching, and then settling down again.

"Isn't she lovely?" Ariadne asked, smiling fondly at her daughter.

"She is beautiful," Lucy agreed. "I cannot wait to have children of my own."

"Come. We need to talk about the Season. That is why I asked you to come early so we could have time alone together."

They returned downstairs, and her cousin spent an hour telling Lucy about the various events. How to dress. What to expect. The strict etiquette to follow. She learned so much that her head swam from all the information.

"I am grateful for you taking the time to share this with me," she told her cousin. "Mama has been more interested in what I look like than how I should behave." She smiled ruefully. "I have always been the good child of the family. Con, being a boy, was always free and a little wild. Mama and Papa always forgive him everything."

Nodding in agreement, Ariadne said, "It is the same with Val. As the only boy, he is the obvious favorite. Thankfully, Val never let that go to his head. He and I are quite close. What of Dru, though? I recall she did not want to play dolls with us."

Lucy chuckled. "Dru is a tomboy, through and through. When Mama and Papa leave for town and the Season, out come her breeches. She marches about Marleyfield in them—and even rides astride. Dru has always done as she pleased, which often gets her into trouble."

"She is what, a year or two behind you?"

"A year. She is supposed to make her come-out next spring, but she tells me she has no interest in marriage or babes. That she will never wed. I, on the other hand, have always looked forward to making my come-out and starting my own family. I suppose that is why Mama has not lectured me on particular etiquette."

Ariadne continued sharing her own knowledge with Lucy, explaining how conversation at balls could be limiting because the dancing was so strenuous. She also told her if a gentleman asks her to dance twice in an evening, that showed his particular interest in her.

"But never, ever dance thrice with a man at the same ball," her cousin declared. "It simply is not done."

"What else?" she asked, interested in all that was being revealed.

Her cousin spoke about suitors calling and the arrangements of flowers they would send. How they only stayed a quarter-hour or so.

Mystified, she asked, "Then when do you get to have a decent conversation and learn anything about a gentleman?"

"Alas, many couples only see one another a handful of times before a betrothal is announced." Ariadne paused. "Are you looking for a love match, Lucy?"

"No," she revealed. "Although I know they must occur, I do not wish that for myself. I only need a husband who will be kind to me and give me the children I want. I do not even expect him to be like Lord Aldridge and see our children very often. It will not matter. I will devote myself to raising them."

Ariadne studied her. "What of when the Season begins? Will you leave those babes in the country?"

Lucy recalled what Val had said earlier. "I do not want to, but I realize that is what is expected," she said, wondering if Ariadne would truly bring her children to town each year.

Determination filled her cousin's eyes. "Let me tell you this. *You* will run your household. You must use your authority and insist that your children be brought to town with you. I have done so with Penelope, and I plan to always bring all our children to town."

Shock filled her, realizing that what Val had said was true. She. "I . . . I only thought Penelope came with you because she was so young."

"No. She will come next year. And the next and the next. So will her brothers and sisters. I have spoken of this to Val and Con. To Tia and Lia. We all have expressed how we felt deserted by our parents for months at a time when the Season rolled around. We have vowed to do things differently. I hate that I only saw you and our other cousins for that one week."

"It was because we live so far from one another. We Alingtons are in Somerset in the west. The Fultons are far north in the Lake District. And you Worthingtons reside in Kent."

Ariadne sniffed. "I can understand that travel between our families' country estates would have proven difficult, but what if all ten of us had been brought to London each year? We could have grown up together. Enjoyed our extended family. That is my plan. I want my children to know their uncle and aunts. As I said, Val and the twins have agreed that is a solid plan. Con has said he would join us in this when he weds and has children. I believe the Season is not merely for social events. It is time well spent with family."

This was something Lucy had never considered. She rarely had seen her parents when they resided at Marleyfield. Mama was always going and visiting her friends during the autumn months. Papa often would go to town when she did so. When her parents were in residence, she barely saw them, and that did not even count the months they were gone for the Season. Ariadne's idea of all the cousins bringing their children to town every year was unique.

And she liked it. Quite a bit.

"Count me in," she said, breaking out in a smile. "As I said, I doubt my husband will be much involved in the rearing of our children, but I would love to see them year-round. It would be a real treat for them to grow up in the company of their cousins."

Ariadne nodded approvingly. "I am glad you think so. I also hope you do have a husband who will be involved in their upbringing. And who knows, Lucy? You might even make a love match. I did—and it has been the best thing that has ever happened to me."

The door opened, and in strode a tall man, lean yet muscled, with an air of danger about him. His pale blue eyes were a contrast to his dark brows and hair. If Lucy had seen him on the pavement, she would have crossed to the other side to avoid passing him. Yet as he came toward them, a gentleness filled his face. He bent, brushing his lips against Ariadne's cheeks.

This was the Marquess of Aldridge.

He gazed at his wife with such great tenderness, Lucy almost burst into tears. She had never witnessed such a look before.

Then he turned his attention to her as Ariadne said, "Julian, this is my cousin Lucy."

The marquess took her hand and kissed it. "My wife has been so happy to hear you were making your come-out this year, my lady. We are both quite fond of your brother. Please know that our house is your house."

Lord Aldridge was such a contrast. Her first impression of him, with his fierce looks which frightened her a bit, now altered considerably.

"I am delighted to meet you, my lord."

"Oh, please. Call him Julian," Ariadne instructed. "Tia and Lia do. We will be in one another's company frequently. Only when we are amongst others not in our family should you behave more formally toward him."

"If you insist," Lucy said, thinking this quite different from expectations her mother might have. Then again, Ariadne's unusual idea of bringing her children to town during the Season would no doubt shake Mama to her very core.

They enjoyed a wonderful conversation, with Julian and Ariadne telling her about Aldridge Manor, his country estate in Surrey, as well as their work at Oakbrooke Orphanage.

"Oh, that reminds me," Julian said. "I have asked someone to tea this afternoon."

"We are already hosting Lucy, Con, and my aunt and uncle," Ariadne protested. "Who is it?"

"Con introduced us this morning at White's. A Lord Huntsberry."

"Huntsberry?" Ariadne asked. "You actually met Lord Huntsberry?" Turning to Lucy, she said, "Huntsworth is the estate adjacent to ours in Surrey, but we have never laid eyes upon the marquess. We have learned, thanks to our steward and his, who have grown close, that Lord Huntsberry gained his title when he was but ten years of age. The Huntsworth steward said the marquess never goes to the country. That the house is shut up, and he remains in town."

"From what we have learned, as a boy, Huntsberry came home to Surrey during school terms. His uncle was his guardian. But after he went to university, he never graced the property again." Julian thought a moment. "I believe Ross, the marquess' steward, said it is going on ten years or more since his employer visited his country estate."

"That is most unusual," Lucy said.

"So, you have met the elusive Huntsberry and invited him to tea?" Ariadne said.

Julian shrugged. "He told me he wished to make a contribution to our orphanage. He was also interested in hearing more about your latest project regarding the poor. I told him to come to tea, and we could speak about his donation and more."

"Well, one more for tea will not upset Cook," her cousin said.

A knock sounded, and the butler entered. "It is drawing close to four, my lady."

"Oh, thank you, Grigsby," Ariadne said. "Shall we go freshen up and continue to the drawing room, Lucy?"

"If you will be there to greet our guests, I will come shortly," Julian said, leaving them.

Lucy wondered why he was vanishing as Ariadne chuckled.

"You must think Julian a terrible host. He isn't. He merely is going to the nursery to see Penelope. In all likelihood, he will bring her to tea to meet you and your family if she is awake. If not, he will join us, but he will have asked the nursemaid to bring Penelope to him the moment she finishes her nap."

She marveled at a titled gentleman who took such interest in his child. And wife. Julian had been most attentive to Ariadne. He had even held her hand. Lucy was unused to seeing any kind of physical affection, certainly not from her parents. It made her think on her cousin's words.

Was a love match a possibility this Season?

CHAPTER FOUR

JUDSON HAD DECIDED to walk to the Aldridge townhouse, which wasn't far from his own residence. He had finally learned to enjoy physical activity after it was not forced upon him by his uncle. Nowadays, he took long walks, rode almost daily through Hyde Park, and boxed. He was comfortable in his body. It surprised him that he felt slightly anxious about this afternoon's tea, though. He was no heathen, but it had been so very long since he had been in the company of others beyond Tim, expected to carry on a conversation.

What would it be like to sit in a drawing room at tea with an actual lady pouring out for him? He must stay on his toes and exercise caution with all he said. Of course, he had had years of walking on eggshells around his uncle and knew how to keep silent and watch what words he did utter. The thought of Jeremiah Jarvis disgusted him, and he pushed the image of his uncle from his mind as he approached his destination.

Checking his pocket watch, he saw he was actually a few minutes early. He had no carriage to sit in and wait until the appointed time. He supposed instead of pacing the pavement that he should knock, where a butler could seat him in a parlor until it was time to bring him upstairs to the drawing room.

Approaching the marquess' door, he rapped on it. The butler opened the door and actually smiled at him. He didn't know servants—besides Tim—smiled, especially at guests. Then again, perhaps it was simply that his uncle had frightened the Huntsworth servants until they feared to do so.

He had no card to present because he never engaged in social interaction with others, so Judson merely said, "Lord Huntsberry to see Lord and Lady Aldridge."

"You are expected, my lord. Please, come in. Lord and Lady Aldridge are upstairs. I will take you to them. If you will follow me."

They went up the staircase and down a hallway toward the drawing room. The butler had Judson wait while he was announced, something he supposed was a social practice, and then he entered. He observed that the furnishings were both tasteful and elegant as he went the length of the room, seeing Aldridge and two ladies standing to greet him.

"It is good of you to come, my lord," the marquess said. Turning to the copper-haired beauty next to him, Aldridge said, "My love, I would like to introduce you to the Marquess of Huntsberry."

He did know enough to bow to the marchioness, and she offered him her hand. Judson took it briefly, saying, "It is an honor to meet you, Lady Aldridge."

"We are neighbors in the country, Lord Huntsberry. I hear you are not fond of country living, however. It is good then that we have met here in town."

She looked to the tawny-haired woman on her right, and Judson turned his attention. She was close to the marchioness in age, and he suspected she was in town to make her come-out this Season.

"My lord," Lady Aldridge said. "I would like to introduce you to my cousin, Lady Lucy Alington."

He bowed again, and the young woman curtseyed before offering her hand to him. When he took it, he gazed into remarkable amethyst eyes, the shade the same color as her brother's, but which seemed more arresting in a woman. Lady Lucy was very pretty, but then again, he had seen more beautiful women in Polite Society. However, something tugged on him as he focused his attention on her.

"It is delightful to meet you, Lady Lucy."

"I am pleased to meet you, as well, my lord."

Judson realized he still held her hand and quickly released it. The abruptness of his gesture caused her cheeks to flush, making her quite appealing.

"Have a seat if you would, Lord Huntsberry," Lady Aldridge said, indicating one next to her cousin. "I am so glad you are able to join us for tea today. My aunt and uncle and their son will also be joining us, as well."

At that moment, the butler returned, announcing the Earl and Countess of Marley, along with Viscount Dyer. The trio joined them, and Lady Aldridge introduced her relatives to him before they were seated again.

As maids rolled in two teacarts under the butler's supervision, Lady Marley asked him, "Are you in town to attend the Season, Lord Huntsberry?"

"I remain in town throughout the year," he replied. "I have a fine steward who manages Huntsworth for me and I see no reason to travel back and forth from the country to town."

His reply caused Lady Marley's brows to arch in surprise.

"Where is your country seat?" Lord Marley asked.

"It is in Surrey."

"We have discovered that we are neighbors with the marquess," Aldridge said. "Our estates are adjacent to one another."

"My, isn't that interesting," Lady Marley said, seeming to evaluate him.

Judson realized that the countess would be on the prowl for her daughter's husband. Amusement filled him, since marriage was the last thing on his mind.

"Lucy, would you help me to pour out since there are so many of us here?" Lady Aldridge asked of her cousin.

"I am happy to do so, Ariadne."

He surreptitiously watched the young woman, seeing her

hands shaking slightly, figuring it was her first time to do so in a social setting. Still, she did a fine job, and he even helped distribute cups and saucers which she handed to him. His participation in the ritual seemed to calm her nerves, and she finished pouring out without a single spill.

Wanting to reassure her, he turned and quietly told her, "You poured out with grace, my lady."

She blushed again, and he thought she must be quite a shy, naïve sort. He hoped her brother, along with her parents and the Aldridges, would keep a steadfast eye upon her and not allow a hungry rogue to sweep in and compromise her.

"My son tells me that he went to school with you, Lord Huntsberry," Lady Marley said.

"Lord Dyer and his cousin were a few years behind me, my lady. We see one another occasionally at White's." He did not mention that this morning was the first time they had ever spoken with one another.

Turning to his host and hostess, Judson said, "Tell me about this orphanage you sponsor," wanting to get down to the crux of why he was here and avoid further interrogation from Lady Marley.

The marquess smiled tenderly at his wife, slipping his hand around hers. It shocked Judson to see such a blatant display of affection.

"I will let Lady Aldridge tell you. She has been more involved in the orphanage than I have."

For the next few minutes, the marchioness animatedly spoke about the orphanage and the classes offered. She sang the praises of a Miss Darnell, the headmistress, and also complimented the teachers and staff.

"When I came to town last year in order to make my come-out, I was moved by the great number of poor I saw teeming in the streets, especially the children. I determined then that it would always be an important part of my life to assist those in poverty in whatever way I could."

Lady Aldridge looked at her husband, her love for him apparent as she smiled. "Fortunately, I wed a man with a kind, generous heart. Julian has been a perfect partner to me, not only in marriage and parenting, but in this endeavor. Thanks to his financial support and volunteering hours with the children, Oakbrooke Orphanage thrives."

The marchioness went on to speak about how she even taught classes there a couple of days a week, and how they balanced country life with time spent in town.

Then Lady Lucy spoke up for the first time. "I would love to go with you sometime and visit the orphanage, Ariadne. It would be a privilege to meet these children."

Lady Marley cleared her throat, a disapproving look in her eyes. "You will have no time to do such a thing, Lucilla," she said sternly. "All of your time will be taken by the Season."

"But surely there is some free time away from social obligations," Lady Lucy insisted. "This is such a large part of Ariadne's and Julian's lives. I am eager to see Oakbrooke."

Before Lady Marley could speak again, Aldridge said, "You are welcome to go with us anytime, Lucy. In fact, we will visit tomorrow morning. Perhaps you would like to come with us if you have nothing on your calendar."

The marquess turned his attention to Judson. "You, as well, Lord Huntsberry. You have told me you wish to donate to our cause. I believe it wise you see the school itself and what we do with the orphans before you make such a commitment."

He thought Lady Marley would protest her daughter touring the school. Then he saw the gleam in her eyes. This woman would think it prudent to throw her daughter into the company of an eligible marquess. He wished he could be blunt and tell the countess that he had no interest in wedding her daughter, but his host and hostess had already been so kind to him. It would be wrong of him to upset Lady Aldridge's aunt.

Still, Judson felt a bit sorry for Lady Lucy. Her father had only spoken once during tea. The countess had dominated the conversation and spoken for both herself and her husband. He supposed the countess controlled every aspect of her daughter's existence and would be instrumental in choosing a husband for Lady Lucy.

"I would be happy to accompany you and Lady Lucy in seeing the orphanage tomorrow morning, my lord," he said breezily. Looking to the viscount, he asked, "Would you wish to accompany us, Dyer?"

Lord Dyer had watched him throughout tea, and Judson had heard talk of how the viscount and his cousin Claibourne had scrutinized candidates for Claibourne's sister during her come-out. It was obvious to him Lord and Lady Aldridge were a love match, so he assumed they had had the approval of both Lady Aldridge's brother and her cousin.

"Yes," Dyer said. "I would be happy to. I will be chaperoning Lucy to events throughout the Season. It seems as if my duties will begin tomorrow morning."

The door to the drawing room opened, and a servant brought in an infant. Judson assumed this was Lord and Lady Aldridge's babe. What surprised him, though, was the nursemaid brought the child straight to the marquess, who eagerly took the babe in his arms. It was obvious Aldridge was comfortable handling the infant, as he cooed to it softly and bent to kiss the babe's brow.

Lady Aldridge chuckled. "You see how it is, Aunt Charlotte. Julian insists upon always being the first to hold Penelope."

"I have two favorite women in the world, my love. Rest assured, you are one of them. And Penelope, naturally, is the other," the marquess said.

Aldridge looked to Lady Lucy. "Would you like to hold your new cousin?"

Judson focused his attention on Lady Lucy, seeing the yearning in her eyes. This was definitely a young woman eager to wed and have babes of her own.

The marquess rose and brought the infant to Lady Lucy. She took Penelope and smiled down at the child.

"Oh, I am so happy to meet you, my sweet cousin. Hopefully, I will have children of my own for you to play with."

Something moved within Judson as he watched Lady Lucy with this babe. A deep yearning tugged upon his heart, something so foreign to him that he couldn't make sense of it. He did not want a wife. He certainly didn't want children. Eventually, he would have to have both, but he didn't plan to have much to do with either of them. Children were the domain of a wife. He had loved his father but had seen very little of him. Wasn't that how it was supposed to be?

And yet the Marquess of Aldridge's behavior had Judson trying to comprehend how a man could feel deep love for his offspring.

Looking at Lady Lucy again, who seemed as if she would take to mothering with ease, Judson wondered if he might want more from life.

Then he put a stop to such foolish notions. He was a loner and would stay one. He would do his duty and get an heir off his wife, and preferably a spare, as well. He would live his life, and he would let his wife live hers.

Suddenly, Lady Lucy was looking at him, smiling. "Would you like to hold Penelope, my lord?"

Judson wanted to flatly refuse, but curiosity filled him. Having no siblings, he had never been around a babe before. Surprising himself, he accepted.

"Yes, my lady. If her parents trust me with her."

He turned his body toward Lady Lucy and accepted the small bundle, cradling the infant in his arms as he had witnessed Aldridge do. Staring down into the tiny face, he was in awe of how perfect her features were.

At that moment, Lady Penelope opened her eyes, studying him solemnly. For a long moment, he and the babe took in one another. He felt the power of the moment, almost as if he and the child formed some type of bond. Then she yawned, making a mewling noise.

Lord Aldridge leaped to his feet, coming toward Judson, easing the babe from Judson's arms, saying, "It is time Penelope be fed." He pressed a kiss upon his daughter's head and handed her off to the nursemaid, who left the drawing room.

Judson found himself shaken by the experience. He fought the waves of emotion rushing through him.

Lady Aldridge smiled gently at him. "You seem to be a natural with children, my lord. Perhaps you will have one of your own soon."

He needed to shut down this kind of talk. Let everyone in this room—especially Lady Marley and her daughter—know that he was not going to be perusing the Marriage Mart this Season. Or anytime soon.

Instead, it shocked him as he heard himself replying, "I will need an heir, my lady. Who knows what this Season will bring?"

CHAPTER FIVE

LUCY APPEARED AT breakfast, finding her brother and father present. Mama always took the meal in her room, rarely seeing anyone in the family before noon. She had told Lucy that she, too, would breakfast in her own bedchamber once the Season began, mentioning the late nights and how it was simply easier to take tea and toast in private before dressing. As it was, Mama had told Lucy she would change gowns numerous times a day, due to needing to wear different gowns to receive guests, as well as for various social events.

She wondered if she would have suitors call upon her. Con had explained anyone interested in her would call the next afternoon and stay for a quarter-hour, and Ariadne had confirmed that brief visit. If the gentleman truly had an interest in her, then he would send flowers, as well. When she had asked Con if he ever sent flowers to anyone, he only gave her a mysterious smile. She suspected he had a mistress, but it wasn't something she cared to broach with him.

As she accepted her tea from a footman and another brought her a breakfast plate with a poached egg and toast points, she wished she could ask her brother what he had thought of Lord Huntsberry. Lucy had been quite taken with him. The man stood a couple of inches over six feet, and his muscular frame was revealed by the fit of his finely tailored clothes. His hair was a rich brown, but it was his emerald eyes that had drawn her in.

She had thought Mama far too obvious in looking over the marquess as a potential suitor for Lucy and asking him questions. Would all mothers behave so boldly when it came to their daughters? Lucy would need to ask Ariadne about it. Mama had been almost gleeful after her own brother's death since it meant Lia and Tia returned to the country. She couldn't understand a competition so fierce that even families would turn upon one another, trying to find suitable husbands for their daughters.

Lucy wished it could be her choice, but Mama had already told her that she was young and inexperienced, and that while Con might advise the two of them on the suitability of a gentleman, Mama would make the decision in the end.

That was why Lucy did not even consider a love match. Her mother would have thought that to be the height of foolishness. What Mama was most interested in included a lofty title and an immense amount of wealth. It was what she had gained for herself when she had wed many Seasons ago, and it was what she expected for her older daughter. Lucy knew she would prove to be as meek as usual and let Mama have her way. It was simply easier than arguing with her.

Dru was different. Her sister continually stood up to Mama, expressing her opinions, which Mama never looked favorably upon. Dru constantly challenged Mama. She had even told Lucy she was not even slightly interested in a Season for herself, because she did not want to wed. When Lucy expressed shock at the idea, Dru had informed her that she would never allow any man to tell her what to do. As much as she loved her sister, Lucy hoped she would be wed before next Season, for she did not want to be anywhere near the clashes which would result between Dru and Mama.

Once she finished her breakfast, Con told her they would be leaving soon. Julian and Ariadne would stop and pick them up on the way to the orphanage. She didn't know if Lord Huntsberry would be present or if he would make his way separately to Oakbrooke Orphanage. She hoped he would be in the carriage and that they might sit next to one another as they had at tea. The spice of his cologne had teased her unmercifully.

"Stop," she murmured under her breath as she went upstairs to fetch her spencer and bonnet. Lord Huntsberry was a sophisticated man and one far too handsome to be interested in someone such as herself.

When she came down to the foyer, Con awaited her. A fresh wave of love washed over her. She had always been close to both her siblings, and she was happy Con would look out for her this Season.

He looked far too serious, though, as he said, "We must talk, Lucy."

Dread knotted in her belly. "Have I done something wrong, Con? Did I pour out wrong yesterday? Or—"

"No, nothing such as that," he assured her. "It is about Lord Huntsberry."

"Oh."

"You are unworldly, Lucy. Unsophisticated. I do not say that disparagingly. I adore your gentle spirit and nurturing ways. Because of your lack of experience, that is why I wish to evaluate your suitors."

He paused, and she asked, trying to mask her disappointment, "And you believe the marquess is unsuitable for me."

Frowning, Con said, "It isn't that. I find it hard to explain. Yes, he is a marquess, so naturally, his title alone allows him entrance into the finest residences and social affairs held in London." He hesitated. "Lord Huntsberry has a reputation as a loner. I never see him with friends. Frankly, I do not think he has a single one."

"But I thought you were friends with him," she protested. "At least, it sounded that way to me at tea yesterday."

"We have never been friends. Or even acquaintances. He is older than I am, so I never had any classes with him. We went to different universities. And since my time in town, I do not see him with anyone at social affairs. True, he dances upon occasion and spends time in the card room, where he wins with alarming regularity, but I never see him talking with anyone else. He did sit with Julian and me at White's, but that is the very first time I have ever witnessed him sit with another gentleman and engage in conversation at the club. Frankly, I was astonished when he accepted Julian's invitation to tea."

Con raked a hand through his hair. "You are a wonderful girl, Lucy. You have a brightness about you that I am afraid someone such as Huntsberry would dim. He's a brooding sort. What I am saying is that I think you can do much better than him."

She snorted. "Tell Mama that. Did you see how intently she watched him yesterday? I thought she might gobble him up and spit him out, chewed into pieces to her liking."

Her brother laughed. "I did notice she inspected him with care. I know she thinks to choose your husband for you. I have already spoken to Papa, though, about it. He and I agree that it should be *your* choice. With our input, of course."

"Truly?" she said, excitement pouring through her. "I have lived in fear of Mama rejecting every gentleman under thirty and marrying me off to some elderly duke."

Con's lips pursed. "If left up to her, she would do exactly that. Mama is all about a man's title."

"And his money," she added, giggling.

Her brother pretended to slap himself. "Egad, how could I forget that? But seriously, I know most of the eligible bachelors, especially after looking so closely at them last Season for Ariadne. I will keep away the rakes and fortune hunters and do my best to steer men with good reputations your way, Lucy."

"But not Huntsberry," she pointed out.

Con shrugged. "I would not necessarily keep him from you. I just do not see him being the man for you." He slipped her arm through his. "If he asks you to dance, you may do so. Unless I find out some dark, deep secret he is hiding from Polite Society. In truth, he never dances more than once with any girl. He has never seemed to be serious about marriage. I do not recall anyone mentioning him even calling upon a young lady as a suitor. Huntsberry may be one of those men who wait until they are forty, enjoying his bachelorhood, and then wedding because he requires an heir."

"Thank you for the warning," Lucy told her brother. "If he approaches me, I will be polite, but at least I know he is not to be given serious consideration."

Adams informed them that the Aldridge carriage had arrived, and they stepped out into a cool, overcast day. A footman laid the stairs for them, and Con handed her up. Immediately, Lucy saw Ariadne and Julian sitting together, with Lord Huntsberry opposite them. Her dilemma was whether she should sit next to the marquess or her cousin.

Lord Huntsberry made the decision for her. He moved toward the window, making room for her, so Lucy took a seat next to him. Con climbed into the vehicle and sat next to her. She found her shoulder pressing against the marquess'. Once more, she caught a whiff of his cologne. At least she wasn't sitting opposite him. She had discovered her tendency to blush around him, and if she had to look at him the entire way to the orphanage, she feared her face would be flaming by the time they arrived.

They talked briefly about the weather, and then Ariadne mentioned the first ball of the Season, which would take place tomorrow evening.

"Have you decided which ballgown you will wear to the opening night?" her cousin asked.

"Mama has said she will choose for me," Lucy said, hating how that sounded even to her own ears. It wasn't as if she were four years of age and needed to be told what to wear.

"I would think pale yellow would suit you well, Lady Lucy," Lord Huntsberry said. "It would be a nice contrast to your eyes, and your tawny hair might pick up shades of the gown, which would be most flattering."

"You think so?" she asked, amazed that a man would know

anything about fashion and suitable colors.

"I agree," Ariadne said. "I will mention something to Aunt Charlotte. I know she can have rather strong opinions about things."

"No," Lucy said firmly. "I will decide which gown to wear. After all, it is my come-out and not Mama's. If I am old enough to wed, then certainly I should be able to choose a gown without her advice."

"Bravo, my lady," Lord Huntsberry said, causing Lucy's cheeks to warm considerably.

"And I will do my best to deflect Mama's wrath," Con said lightly.

Her mother did have quite a temper, especially when someone went against her. Dru had suffered the most of the three siblings because she was so bent on being stubborn herself. Lucy hoped Ariadne would speak to Mama, despite the fact she had protested against it. Her cousin's word would carry more weight than Lucy's, especially since Ariadne had only recently made her own come-out, and she was now a marchioness, outranking Mama.

They arrived at the school, and as Con handed her down, she saw a wagon bearing the name of Gunter's on it.

"Is that the same Gunter's where we ate our ices?" she asked.

"The very one," Ariadne said. "They have a catering business beyond their tearoom. Since Julian and I have not been to the orphanage these past six weeks, we wanted to surprise the children with not only our presence but also with some treats."

A woman stepped from the building and headed toward them. "Ah, Lord and Lady Aldridge. It is so good to see you once more. I see you have brought visitors with you."

"Miss Darnell, this is my cousin, Lady Lucy Alington, and her brother, Viscount Dyer. And Lord Huntsberry, our neighbor in Surrey. They are most interested in seeing the facilities and meeting the children." Turning to the others, Ariadne added, "Miss Darnell serves as headmistress for Oakbrooke Orphanage and also teaches a few classes."

They exchanged greetings and then Miss Darnell smiled. "I see Gunter's is here again."

"Yes," Julian said. "They have brought biscuits and cakes for the children. To celebrate our return to town."

"They will be most appreciative, my lord," the headmistress said. "Won't you all come in?"

Miss Darnell led them on a tour of the school. Lucy was touched when a few of the children in the halls hugged Ariadne and Julian, telling them how much they had been missed.

One boy, whose name was Joseph, said, "I have been working on my geography, my lord, as well as long division. You said both would be helpful to me."

"Yes, Joseph," Julian replied. "I hope your marks have been good since we last spoke."

"They have been excellent," Miss Darnell declared. "Joseph is the top student here at Oakbrooke."

As they moved on, Julian told the group, "I plan for Joseph to come and work for us. He is a bright lad. At first, I had thought to have him start as a footman, but I think he would be happier working with Mr. Ross, our steward." He glanced about the group. "My goal is to eventually help every child here find gainful employment. That may include calling upon my friends to see if they have any positions open in their households."

"I would have to have my own household before I could take anyone on," Con joked. "But Lucy will soon wed. Perhaps you could convince your new husband he needs additional staff."

Julian looked at Lord Huntsberry. "Do not think you will get off easily, my lord. When the time comes, I may come knocking at your door. I can guarantee you that these children are learning to master reading, writing, and maths. They also are being trained to go into service or work for shopkeepers. A few have expressed interest in farming and animals, so I may be bringing some of them to Aldridge Manor so that they might become tenants or work with my livestock."

"I would have to speak with my steward, my lord," the marquess said. "As for town, I only have a skeleton staff of servants. Since I am the only one in the house, my needs are simple. In fact, I do no entertaining, so my drawing room furniture is covered in sheets, as is most of the furniture in the house. I take all my meals in the breakfast room since it is cozy. The rest of the time, I am in my study or bedchamber."

Ariadne laughed. "That will change when you take on a wife, Lord Huntsberry. You will need to open up the entire house. Lady Huntsberry might also prefer country living, and you must open it, too. We would be happy to see you in Surrey."

He shrugged. "When I wed, my marchioness is welcome to live in the country. I prefer town and will always remain here. My future wife will be allowed to live wherever she chooses. If she wishes me to open up my country house, I will do so for her and our children."

Ariadne looked at him oddly. "I see."

Con was right. Lord Huntsberry was not for her. While Lucy knew many couples of the *ton* led separate lives, she would want her husband to at least reside with her and their children some of the year. She wondered why the marquess was so solitary.

"Do you have brothers or sisters, my lord?" she asked as they continued on their tour.

"Neither, my lady. I am not much for family since I have none."

"No one?" she inquired. "No aunts and uncles? No cousins?"

His jaw tightened. "An uncle. We are estranged, however."

She did not question him further, realizing the topic was sensitive to him. Mama had drilled into her that Lucy was not to ask personal questions, and now she could see why.

They watched some of the lessons going on, and Ariadne encouraged them to walk about and help the children. She found herself enjoying herself immensely.

Miss Darnell appeared. "It is time for assembly," she said, and the children in the room scrambled to put away their books and slates and form a line, which moved from the classroom once every child was in place. The others began to follow. She and Lord Huntsberry were the last in the classroom.

"You seemed to become a different person around these orphans," he said. "At tea yesterday, you were very quiet. But you opened up and were laughing often."

"I have always been drawn to children," Lucy admitted. "It is the reason I am eager to make my come-out. Once I find a husband, starting our family will be next. It is all I have ever wanted. I cannot wait to manage my own household."

"Out from your mother's thumb."

She nodded. "Mama is very domineering. She is a lot like my late Uncle Charles, who recently passed. Extremely opinionated."

"And always right?" he asked lightly.

Lucy giggled. "They think so. Oh, Mama is not so bad. She just has firm ideas of how things should be."

"I think she was considering me as a future son-in-law yesterday at tea," he said bluntly.

Heat rose in her cheeks. "I am sorry for that, my lord. I fear Mama will be assessing every unwed man, seeing if he might serve as a potential husband for me. Have no fear, though. I understand you are not interested in marriage at this time."

He cocked his head, studying her. "Why do you say that, Lady Lucy?"

She felt her face go hot. "Con told me you are not often in the company of others. That you have never called upon a young lady."

The marquess nodded his head slowly. "Lord Dyer is correct. I have never chosen to woo another." He paused. "I do worry about you, though, my lady."

"Worry? About me?" she squeaked.

"You are a breath of fresh air," he declared. "And very, very innocent. There are horrible gossips in the *ton* who would tear a lovely creature like you into shreds. And rakehells who might take advantage of your extreme innocence."

She bit her lip. "Might you be one of those rakehells, Lord Huntsberry?"

"No," he quickly assured her. "But you never want to be alone with one. That is a hard and fast rule."

Lucy looked around. "But we are alone together now," she pointed out.

"And we shouldn't be. Because something like this might happen."

Before she could ask what, Lord Huntsberry's arms came about her.

And his mouth pressed softly against hers.

CHAPTER SIX

JUDSON HAD NEVER been reckless his entire life. He was methodical. Prudent. He never behaved in an uncivilized fashion.

But this was madness.

Yet even as his lips brushed against Lucy Alington's, deep inside he knew it was something he had wanted. He didn't understand why he was attracted to the chit. Yes, she was pretty. Even more than pretty. But that didn't explain why he did what he did now.

He supposed part of the attraction could be chalked up to hearing her determination in the carriage. When she had said that her mother would select the gown to be worn on the opening night of the Season, pity for this young woman had filled him. She had turned it around, though, her resolve breaking through. Judson supposed he admired that bit of bravery coming from her. That tiny slice of rebellion.

Because he, too, had felt it his entire life.

Of course, anytime he had acted upon it, Uncle Jeremiah had slapped him down like he was an annoying gnat. The older man's sheer physical size had overwhelmed his ten-year-old self. But as Judson grew in size, his rare remarks of independence became more frequent. Finally, a time had come when Uncle Jeremiah had slapped him—and Judson punched him back.

Never again had the older man laid a hand upon him.

He focused on the kiss now. He didn't want to frighten her. It was obvious that Lady Lucy had never been kissed. Because of that, he wanted it to be a pleasant memory for her. A sweet, inoffensive kiss. Not one of passion or possession. More to expose her to the beginnings of what a kiss could be.

His hand slid up her back, capturing her nape. Her skin was like fine silk, and his thumb stroked her neck, causing her to shiver. He continued giving her soft, easy kisses, ending one and beginning another. Her lips were pillowy soft, and Judson longed to lick them. To taste her. But that would be going too far.

Finally, he ended with a final kiss, breaking it, his mouth hovering just above hers. She let out a small sigh. He released his hold on her. For a minute, her eyes remained closed, a dreamy expression on her face. Then she opened them.

"Thank you," she said simply. "That was my first kiss."

"A kiss can be many things, Lady Lucy. This was an introduction to kissing. I will not be kissing you again."

Her face fell, but she threw back her shoulders, her gaze meeting his. "Why not?"

He smiled ruefully. "Because you need a good man to claim you. One who can be the husband you long for." He paused a moment. "My soul is too dark to corrupt that of an innocent."

Frowning, she asked, "Then why kiss me?"

"I think going into your debut, you will need to be thoughtful as you seek your husband. If you liked our kiss, look for a man who will treat you kindly. Who will make you the center of his world. Do not allow a rogue to turn your head. They are worthless—and dangerous. And I warn you again, so please take heed.

"Never be alone with another man—else you may be forced to wed that man."

She sniffed. "I would not force him into marriage, my lord, nor would I be forced into it myself."

Her response told her just how innocent she was. "You say that now, but would you be willing to enter a ballroom and have all conversation cease as everyone present looked at you as if you were no better than dirt? Or worse, you might even suffer the cut direct. Any friends you made would desert you. You would never find a good man who would be willing to court you, much less wed you."

Her lips began to tremble, and her body followed suit. Judson wanted to hold her so badly his teeth ached, but she must understand the gravity of the situation.

"You would be a pariah, Lady Lucy. Worse, your family would also suffer. Lord Dyer would not be able to find a decent woman to wed because no family would allow their daughter to marry into yours. And I believe I heard mention of a younger sister. Her hopes, too, would be dashed."

"Dru says she does not wish to wed," she said stubbornly.

"But would you risk your reputation? Your brother's and Dru's? Even your parents?" He shook his head sadly. "I am giving you good advice, Lady Lucy. Never be caught alone with a man, or you will be ruined. Especially if he chooses not to have his hand forced and wed you."

"What about that gentleman's reputation? What would he suffer?"

Judson sighed. "The world of Polite Society is not a fair place. I am afraid he would be forgiven—but you never would."

Tears welled in her eyes. He took her hands and brought them to his lips, kissing her fingers tenderly.

"I am trying to help you. You seem remarkably sweet and innocent. I would not see you hurt. Now, come along. We should join the others."

Offering his arm to her, she slipped her hand through the crook of it. He led them along the corridor and down the stairs to the assembly room which Miss Darnell had shown them earlier in their tour. Sweets were being distributed, and the two of them joined in, helping hand these out, along with cups of milk.

Judson made certain he stayed on the other side of the room from Lady Lucy. He felt as if he were Eve and had tossed God's warning aside, eating the apple because of the snake's tempting words. Lady Lucy had been a most tempting morsel, but she deserved far better than a damaged soul such as himself. She needed a husband who would always be there for her and their children.

His gut told him he could never be that man.

Perhaps it was time to wed. Get it over with. Have a few children and guarantee the title would be passed on to another Jarvis. He decided he would find a marchioness this Season.

Because if he had a wife, he wouldn't be tempted to try and make Lucy Alington his.

Lord Aldridge came up to him. "What do you think of our orphanage, Huntsberry?"

"It is nothing like what I expected. I have heard orphanages are places of no hope, but the children here seem joyful. They adore you and Lady Aldridge."

"My marchioness inspires that in everyone she meets," the marquess replied, glancing across the room and smiling softly as he spied his wife.

Judson tamped down the desire to have what this man had. A woman and child he loved. It was simply not in the cards for someone with his past.

"Lady Aldridge neglected to tell me of her next project," he said, drawing Aldridge's attention back to him again.

"Shall we go to Gunter's when we leave here?" Aldridge asked. "Ariadne has wanted to take Lucy. They went to the teashop when they were girls. The ten cousins from three families all met one another in London for a week when the children were young. Gunter's was a favorite memory for them. We could stop for ices, and my wife could share about her ambitious project."

He wanted to say yes, but that meant being around Lady Lucy, and that didn't seem like a very good idea. Still, if he didn't discuss the matter with the Aldridges today, the Season would begin. The couple would most likely have little time to meet with him. From what he gathered, they usually spent two days a week at the orphanage and would be busy with social activities.

"Yes, I will come for a little while. I have another engagement I cannot miss, however."

"Then we will make it a quick visit," the marquess said. "Let me round up everyone."

Miss Darnell came toward Judson. "Thank you for visiting Oakbrooke Orphanage, Lord Huntsberry. Might I answer any questions you have?"

"No, Miss Darnell. I will be sending you a very large donation, though."

"That is generous of you, my lord."

"You and your staff are accomplishing good things here. Lord and Lady Aldridge are right. Those of us who have been blessed with wealth should give back to those in need."

"Well said, my lord," the headmistress said. "Please feel free to drop by anytime. Perhaps you might even read to the children when you visit us."

He doubted he would ever set foot in this building again, but he smiled. "It is always a possibility, Miss Darnell."

Lord Dyer approached him. "I hear we are going to Gunter's."

"Yes. I wish to hear more about Lady Aldridge's next undertaking," he replied.

Their party left the school, making their way to the carriage. This time, Lady Lucy sat next to her cousin. Though they sat across from one another, she never looked at him once. Instead, she glanced out the window at the passing traffic. Judson knew he had hurt her, but he had wanted to make her aware of the possibilities that could happen to young, unsuspecting ladies.

And selfishly, he also had wanted to kiss her.

He *still* wanted to kiss her. Not a light, friendly kiss as they had shared, but a true kiss. It would never come to pass, however. Judson understood he was a moth to her flame, and he was determined to stay away from her and not burn.

Inside Gunter's, they were greeted by name and seated at a

prime table. He couldn't help but wonder what it would be like to patronize places such as this and engage in friendly conversation with others. That would defeat the purpose of why he was in town, however.

Instead, he decided to focus all his attention on the Season. Attend a few events. Find a woman whom he could accept enough to share his name and bed for as long as it took to get her with child. He would hope for a son and heir that first time, but he would also need a spare. His thoughts turned to little Penelope. How delicate and beautiful a babe she was. Perhaps even having a girl or two to spoil might not be too terrible. And it would most likely please his wife to have a daughter.

They ordered their ices, and he noticed Lady Lucy ate hers thoughtfully. He watched her put the spoon in her mouth, savoring each bite, and wished his tongue was what she tasted.

Get a grip, Judson, he silently ordered, turning his attention to Lady Aldridge.

"Tell me about how you would clothe the poor of London, my lady."

As he listened, he decided Lady Aldridge was not only beautiful, but she was also highly intelligent—and very organized.

When she had finished providing him with the details, he said, "I also will be donating to this effort, my lady. You have convinced me that assisting the poor is something important to do for those of us who are more fortunate."

"It is wonderful that you are so accommodating, Lord Huntsberry," Lady Lucy said, placing her spoon into the empty dish.

Her tone was neutral, but somehow, he read disappointment in it. Judson determined not to let her affect him.

"Regretfully, I must leave you now," he said. "I have an appointment with my solicitor. Please, stay," he said, rising. "I will take a hansom cab."

"Will we see you at the opening ball?" Lady Aldridge asked.

"Yes. I plan to attend," he confirmed.

But he would not be asking Lady Lucy to dance. It had been foolish to kiss her. He refused to lead her on further, having their names coupled together because of a single dance. Also, he did not want to give Lady Marley any ideas that he was interested in her daughter.

"Perhaps we might take supper together then," Lord Aldridge suggested.

Ignoring the marquess' comment, Judson merely told his companions, "Good day."

He left Gunter's and began walking, not caring where he went, only knowing he needed to get far away from the group.

And Lady Lucy.

CHAPTER SEVEN

L UCY WATCHED AS Annie put the finishing touches on her hair and then stepped back, admiring Lucy's image reflected in the mirror.

"You will be the most beautiful girl at tonight's ball, my lady," Annie declared proudly.

"While I know I am a bit pretty, we both know there will be girls more beautiful than me at this ball, Annie."

Her maid shook her head stubbornly. "But you are beautiful inside, as well as outside, my lady. The right gentleman will figure that out for himself, and he will make you his wife. Is there anything else you might need?"

"No, Annie. Thank you. If I am a success tonight, it is because of you and Madame Laurent."

The maid left the bedchamber, and Lucy stared into the mirror. She was pleased to be wearing the ballgown she had wanted to, thanks to Ariadne.

Yesterday, after they had visited the orphanage and Gunter's, her cousin had insisted upon coming inside, saying that she wished to see the gowns Madame Laurent had already made up for Lucy. They had gone upstairs to her bedchamber, along with Mama, and Annie had brought out each finished gown.

Ariadne had Lucy step behind each one so she could have an idea of what Lucy would look like in each gown, and she had raved over two of the ballgowns, in particular. Thanks to her cousin's suggestion of which gown to wear this evening, Mama had agreed.

And the gown was the color Lord Huntsberry had suggested she wear, as well.

Why had the marquess kissed her? He had warned her not to be alone with a man because a kiss was a possibility. Lord Huntsberry had sternly told her she would be ruined if she were caught kissing a man, especially if that man did not immediately offer for her.

He had made a good point when she had told him not only would she not be forced into a marriage she did not want, she would not force any gentleman to wed her, either. He had explained to her the effect that would have not only on her reputation—but also her family's. Lucy would take his words to heart. She would always stay in view of others.

But oh, how she longed to kiss Lord Huntsberry again.

She brought her fingertips to her lips, thinking of how his had brushed ever so softly against hers. He had kissed her several times, his mouth pressing against her lips, then separating, only to return again for more. His kisses had caused her scalp to tingle and made butterflies flutter within her belly.

Lucy stood. The marquess had made it clear he would not be one of her suitors, so she needed to cleanse all thoughts of him from her mind. Tonight was the beginning of a wonderful time in her life, possibly the best, a Season where she would attend glittering balls and fabulous parties. Hopefully, it would end in a betrothal, and she would wed and have her first child quickly, just as Ariadne had done. Her cousin and Julian would be at tonight's ball to help introduce her to members of Polite Society. Mama and Papa would also help ease her into the *ton*, and Con would be ever watchful, making certain she was wooed by the right type of gentlemen.

Mama entered Lucy's bedchamber without knocking, something she was used to occurring. Her eyes swept over Lucy, and the corners of her mouth turned up in a smile of approval.

"Ariadne was right," Mama said. "This color suits you. You will gain quite a bit of attention tonight, Lucilla. Remember, you are looking for a gentleman who will be able to take excellent care of you, one who will allow you to live in the manner you have become accustomed to. An earl would be nice, but a marquess or duke would be even more desirable."

"I am hoping to wed a gentleman who will respect me, Mama. One who is kind and will be devoted to me and our children."

Mama waved her hand in the air dismissively. "Those are not the things to look for, Lucilla," she chided. "You need to wed for a title and wealth. Social standing is most important in Polite Society. Do not worry, though. With my guidance, I will make certain that the right husband is selected for you."

Lucy knew better than to protest. She had faith that Con and Papa—along with Ariadne and Julian—would see that she had a good, kind man, hopefully one who would also please Mama.

She went downstairs with her mother, finding her father waiting for them in the foyer. His eyes lit up as he saw her.

"Ah, Lucilla. You resemble an angel. Who knows? You may be betrothed by the end of this first week."

"Is that even possible?" she blurted out.

"Of course, it is," Mama said brusquely. "Some of the best matches made occur early in the Season. A gentleman finds exactly what he is looking for and takes a lady off the Marriage Mart. Look no further than your own cousin as an example. Ariadne and Aldridge were the first couple to wed last Season. Why, Ariadne was the envy of every girl in her come-out class! She has great standing in Polite Society now."

Lucy kept quiet, not bothering to mention that Ariadne and Julian were an obvious love match. Yes, Julian had snapped up her cousin quickly, but she could tell it was because he and Ariadne were so much in love and eager to start their lives together as husband and wife, not because they met the requirements of some arbitrary list.

They went outside to the carriage, where Con awaited them, and traveled at a snail's pace because of the roads being clogged with other members of Polite Society eager to attend the first event of the Season. Con had told her that the opening ball was attended by practically everyone in the *ton*, eager to catch up with old friends and see the new class of girls making their come-outs.

The receiving line was lengthy. Mama spend the entire time they were in it whispering into Lucy's ear, pointing out gowns she admired and identifying important members of the *ton* to Lucy. Her head spun with all this information, and she doubted she would recall a single name.

Reaching the front of the receiving line, they greeted their host and hostess. The countess was someone Lucy had heard her mother disparage before, but Mama was all smiles now as she introduced her daughter.

As they left the receiving line, a footman handed Lucy her dance programme, which gentlemen would sign in order to reserve a dance with her. They entered the ballroom, which looked as if a garden had been brought indoors. The sweet smells of fragrant flowers filled the air.

Things became a blur as friends of her parents came to greet them and wish Lucy a good Season. Ariadne and Julian joined them, as well. Con stood by her side the entire time as various gentlemen were introduced to her. Her brother had told her he would nod if he found the gentleman acceptable, so she constantly looked to him for his approval before handing over her dance card to a man. It filled quickly, and Mama smiled smugly.

"I see you have no other dances left, Lucilla. You still must continue to meet others and act interested and eager as potential suitors make their way toward you. The fact that you no longer have any dances available will be a sign to them, letting them know how popular you are. Why, you may even have some gentlemen call upon you tomorrow, despite the fact they did not have a chance to dance with you."

All Lucy knew was that Lord Huntsberry would not be one of

those callers.

She had seen him enter the ballroom a few minutes ago, and he turned in the opposite direction of where she and her family stood. Without meaning to, her gaze had followed him around the ballroom as he spoke to a few people and signed a few girls' programmes.

Her heart began beating rapidly as Lucy saw he had circled the room and now made his way toward their circle.

The musicians began to tune their instruments when Lord Huntsberry approached them.

"Lord and Lady Marley," he said, bowing. "It is a pleasure to see you again this evening." He also greeted Ariadne and Julian.

Then the marquess turned to her brother, inclining his head. "Dyer."

Suddenly, his attention focused on her, and Lucy felt her heart slamming against her ribs. He looked so very handsome in his evening black, and she longed to spend time in his company.

Bowing, he took her hand and kissed her gloved fingers. "You look like a dream come to life, my lady." Pausing a moment, he added, "And this color is so very flattering on you."

She saw the twinkle in his eyes and told him, "Ariadne helped me choose tonight's ballgown."

"Then I would say your cousin has impeccable taste, Lady Lucy. I suggest you listen to Lady Aldridge's advice throughout the Season and wear what she recommends for each affair."

Smiling gratefully at him, Lucy knew he had said so in order to influence Mama's thinking.

Her mother spoke up, saying, "If you wished for a dance with my daughter, Lord Huntsberry, I am afraid you have arrived too late for that to occur. Her entire programme filled completely within minutes."

She winced, hating that Mama pushed her in the marquess' direction.

He smiled graciously, though. "It is good to know that your daughter will have so many eligible bachelors to dance with this evening, Lady Marley." Glancing around, he added, "I must seek out my first partner now. If you will excuse me."

After the marquess left, Mama clucked her tongue. "I thought he would ask you to dance this evening."

"I would not worry about it, Mama," Con said easily. "Lucy has already proven to be quite popular. I do not believe Huntsberry is serious about finding a bride."

Mama's brows knit together. "Why do you say that, Constantine?"

Con shrugged. "He has rarely attended events in the past, and the marquess spends far more of his time in the card room than dancing when he does come to a ball. Huntsberry may be one of those gentlemen who plans to enjoy bachelorhood for many years to come."

She only hoped that Mama would set her sights on anyone other than the Marquess of Huntsberry.

Her first partner came to claim her, leading Lucy onto the ballroom floor. They had only exchanged brief greetings when groups formed, and the country dance began. Lucy had always enjoyed dancing, and did so even more this evening, knowing she wore a beautiful ballgown and was becoming a part of Polite Society tonight.

Her partner escorted her back to her mother, who told Lucy that her father had already retired to the card room.

The next partner arrived, an earl, and the same pattern repeated. They went to the center of the floor, barely exchanged two sentences, and the dancing commenced again. Lucy decided she would not have time for any conversation this evening and so gave herself over to the music.

After the next set ended, the musicians took a short break, and her partner offered to bring her something to drink. He did so, asking shyly if he might call upon her the next afternoon.

She could not begin to recall his name, but she said, "I would be happy to have you visit us, my lord."

He said, "Then I will see you tomorrow, my lady." Bowing,

he left her with Con.

"Are you enjoying yourself?" her brother asked.

"I am enjoying the dancing immensely, but I can find no time for conversation."

"There never is at a ball," Con agreed. "It will be a little different at a garden party. Even a card party. There is always time to exchange pleasantries as someone is dealing a hand."

"I do not remember a single name of anyone I have met this evening," she admitted. "Is it always like this?"

"You will see these people all Season, Lucy. They will soon become familiar to you. I would not worry about it right now."

She danced a few more sets, and then she stood again with Mama, who crisply said, "This next dance is the supper dance, Lucilla. You will accompany your partner into the supper room and sit with him. Usually, a gentleman who is interested in a particular lady will ask to reserve the supper dance because it allows him to spend more time with her. Who is your upcoming partner?"

Consulting her programme, Lucy said, "A Lord Perth," she told Mama.

Gentlemen began claiming their partners, and she waited for Lord Perth to appear. She thought he was about Con's height, with blond hair, but she could not be certain.

Then her belly tumbled several times as she saw Lord Huntsberry making his way toward her. His determined stride let her know she was his final destination, but she couldn't begin to fathom why.

He bowed. "I am sorry to inform you that Lord Perth had to step out to attend to a pressing matter, my lady. He will be unable to dance the supper dance with you."

Disappointment filled her. She felt all eyes would be upon her because she would have no one to escort her into supper, and she would be forced to find her parents and dine with them.

"I, on the other hand, was not engaged for this dance, Lady Lucy." He paused, their gazes meeting.

She swallowed. "What are you saying, my lord?"

The marquess smiled charmingly at her, taking her breath. "I would be happy to take Lord Perth's place if you are amenable."

Without waiting for her answer, Lord Huntsberry took her hand and placed it on his sleeve, leading her onto the dance floor.

CHAPTER EIGHT

JUDSON HAD DELIBERATELY gone counterclockwise around the ballroom when he had arrived, wanting to avoid Lady Lucy for as long as possible. He feared if he greeted her and her family too early, she would still have empty spaces on her dance card.

And he was *not* going to dance with her.

He arrived long after the crush did and took his time, actually speaking to a few others, stopping to sign the programmes of two young ladies making their come-outs. One was a stunning beauty. The other was plain of face, but her figure—and reportedly large dowry—would ensure that she secured a husband by Season's end. Judson found he wasn't interested in either of them. In fact, no lady seemed to draw his attention, as he'd continued around the ballroom, finally reaching Lord and Lady Marley.

He was relieved when Lady Marley informed him that her daughter had no available dances. It was what he had hoped for Lady Lucy. She was a pretty thing, with a sweet nature and a bosom that would appeal to any man. Judson had bid them good evening and left to claim the beauty for the opening set. As he danced with her, though, she lost her appeal. For a young lady making her come-out, she seemed far from innocent. He yearned for Lady Lucy's chaste sweetness.

Dancing the second set, he kept his eye on Lady Lucy more than his own partner. She danced in a group next to them, and Judson finally chastised himself, directing his focus back to his own dance steps, which he had muddled some. He returned his partner to her mother and left the ballroom to play cards. His idea of finding a bride suddenly didn't appeal to him in the least.

Judson played at one table and then moved to another. As usual, his luck held, and he won more than he lost. He left play for a while, stretching his legs and slipping into the ballroom again for a few minutes. When he located Lady Lucy on the floor, he saw she danced with both grace and exuberance, her cheeks flushed, her smile wide. Something stung inside him, and he forced himself to return to the card room.

Spying an empty seat, he moved toward the table, seeing two of its occupants engaged in conversation. The third accepted a new deck of cards from a footman and was unsealing them.

"Is this seat taken?" he asked, sliding into it.

"It is now," the man with the cards said, shuffling them.

Then he heard Lady Lucy's name come from another gentleman at the table.

"I will be dancing the supper dance with Marley's daughter," the man said. "Lady Lucy. She's quite pretty—and looks as if she has never been kissed."

The other man laughed. "Then she is like most of the young ladies in this come-out class. What of her dowry?"

"I know nothing of it." He paused, a smile growing on his face. "Yet."

Rage filled Judson. He knew how young debutantes were gossiped about. Their looks. Their wardrobes. Their families. Their dowries. But this was Lady Lucy.

He glared at the man who was to dance with her. "Are we going to play cards or not?"

The man, sensing Judson's mood, quickly said, "Of course, my lord."

They played for half an hour, and he took a good amount from the cad, giving him some satisfaction. Then the butler announced that the supper dance would start soon, followed by supper itself. Most of the card room's occupants began wrapping up their games. His table did the same.

As the men at his table stood, Judson said, "Wait a moment, Perth. I wish to speak to you." He had learned the man's name through conversation.

From his tone, the other two card players knew to make themselves scarce and quickly left the area.

"You mentioned you are dancing the supper dance with Lady Lucy Alington if I heard you correctly."

"Yes, I am," Perth said, a bit defiantly.

His defiance began to fade as Judson continued to stare hard at him. "I believe you are going to give that dance to me instead."

"Why would I—" Perth's voice faded as Judson cracked his knuckles. Suddenly, he changed his tune.

"I suppose I can accommodate your request, my lord."

"You must not let Lady Lucy see you. During the supper dance or at supper itself."

Perth started to speak and then closed his mouth. He merely nodded.

"You may appear after supper. After you have taken care of the business which detained you from enjoying the ball for a while. Do you understand?"

"I do, my lord."

Rising, Judson said, "I would not call on Lady Lucy if I were you. Tomorrow—or any other afternoon."

Swallowing, Perth said, "I will not be doing so. There are far too many fish in the sea. I will catch one of them instead, my lord."

He nodded. "A wise decision."

Quitting the card room, Judson returned to the ballroom and located Lady Lucy. He knew he was doing exactly what he had told himself he would not do, but he couldn't leave her in the hands of Lord Perth, who was terrible at cards and most likely, a fortune hunter.

Before he could change his mind, knowing if he did it would leave her stranded and without a companion for supper, Judson headed directly to her and bowed when he reached her.

"I am sorry to inform you that Lord Perth had to step out to attend to a pressing matter, my lady. He will be unable to dance the supper dance with you."

He watched her reaction, feeling the disappointment that washed over her. Not wishing to leave her in limbo, he quickly added, "I, on the other hand, was not engaged for this dance, Lady Lucy."

Their eyes met, and he became lost in her amethyst ones for a moment, as if hypnotized.

"What are you saying, my lord?" she asked.

Knowing he played with fire, Judson smiled at her, a true smile. He could not recall the last time his heart felt so light and he *wanted* to smile, much less at a woman.

"I would be happy to take Lord Perth's place if you are amenable."

Then an irrational fear seized him. What if she turned him down? Made up some excuse not to be seen with him?

Before his worst fears could come to fruition, he took her hand and placed it on his sleeve, guiding her to the dance floor. They arrived and completed a group just as the musicians picked up their instruments and began playing a lively tune. For the first time in his life, Judson enjoyed dancing. Prior to this moment, it had been a social obligation he had fulfilled. But one look at Lady Lucy's face, and all her joy in the act poured into him.

This woman was a balm to his soul.

The dance ended, everyone winded by the strenuous activity. He heard their host announce that supper was now being served, and the mass of people began heading from the ballroom to where the buffet was laid out. Not wanting his partner to become separated from him, he slipped his hand around hers.

A perfect fit . . .

Slowly, Judson guided Lady Lucy to the edge of the crowd, allowing most of those in attendance to pass them. Only as the majority had left did he tuck her hand into the crook of his arm.

Glancing down at her, he saw her face flushed from exertion and realized she wasn't just pretty.

Lucy Alington was beautiful.

"How are you enjoying your first ball, my lady?" he asked, steering her toward the exit.

Her eyes sparkled with excitement. "It has been the best night of my life," she declared.

He liked that about her. Most any other lady in this ballroom would have said it was a lovely time or something else which conveyed nothing. Not Lady Lucy. She was enjoying herself and was not ashamed or embarrassed to let anyone know it.

The din in the corridor leading to the supper room was so loud that he did not attempt any further conversation. He was aware of the warmth of her hand. The heat of her body. The faint smell of lavender coming off her skin.

As they entered the supper room, it was a sea of others, along with long tables laden with appetizing foods.

"Oh! Ariadne is waving to us. Should we go and sit with her and Julian, my lord?"

Judson was faced with a quandary. Already, he knew the gossips would be taking note of who accompanied whom to the supper room. To sit with Lady Lucy was one thing. To sit with her and her family was quite another. It would indicate to others he was truly interested in her. But the tables had filled quickly, and he didn't spy another place for them to sit with anyone he knew.

"The devil take all," he murmured under his breath, and then he added so she might hear, "Yes. We shall go to them."

As they reached the Marquess and Marchioness of Aldridge, he saw a look pass between them. Not certain of what it was, he merely seated Lady Lucy and took the chair beside her.

"I did not know you were dancing with my cousin this evening," Lady Aldridge said.

"Her partner had some brief business to attend to, so I agreed to step in for him. Lady Lucy was gracious enough to accept me as a substitute," he said glibly, which amused him because he had never been glib before.

"We will provide the sustenance for this evening," Aldridge said. "Come along, Huntsberry. We have plates to fill."

Before he left her side, Judson asked, "Is there anything in particular you do not like to eat? Or something you favor?"

She worried her lip a moment, causing a rush of desire to pour through him.

"Anything sweet, Lord Huntsberry. I have always had a sweet tooth."

He nodded and joined the marquess, heading to one of the buffet tables. They chatted a bit about the ball and the food. Judson had the feeling Aldridge wanted to ask him something, but their conversation never veered from being polite.

Returning to the table with a plate for each of them, Judson put one in front of Lady Lucy. Her eyes grew wide.

"Oh, this is so much, my lord. I cannot eat half of what you brought to me."

"Then start with the sweets you love. If you have any room left over, eat something of the rest," he advised.

She giggled, causing his heart to melt. "Mama would be appalled."

He briefly touched her chin, turning her to face him. "Your mama is not here. Do as you please." Smiling, he added, "After all, a perfect night should start with dessert."

She regarded him solemnly a moment—and then burst out laughing.

"This cake has whispered to me that I must take a bite of it," she said facetiously.

Immediately he took a bite of the cake, savoring it. "The cake does not lie," he said straight-faced, causing her to laugh again.

Judson rarely stayed for a midnight buffet, preferring to leave a ball early and go home to his bed, or upon rare occasions, that of his mistress. He found himself enjoying his conversation with Lady Lucy and her relatives. Still, he knew this was all pretend.

He could not afford to pursue her or continue to lead her on. Many years of unresolved anger churned within him. He already knew the kind of husband she sought, and Judson possessed none of those qualities.

Tonight's dance and supper with Lady Lucy had been a fantasy, one which he had indulged in briefly. He sought a marriage of convenience. One where he would give his name to a woman, who would then provide him with an heir. They would live separate lives. He had nothing to give to any wife, much less one such as innocent and playful as Lady Lucy.

The Aldridges excused themselves, saying they were going home for the night.

"You are already leaving the ball?" Lady Lucy asked, appearing baffled by their early departure.

"We must be at Oakbrooke Orphanage tomorrow morning at ten," the marchioness said. "Besides, we have already introduced you to a good number of gentlemen this evening, Lucy. We are ready to go home."

"And do a little more dancing," the marquess said quietly to his wife.

Judson did not think Lady Lucy heard the comment, but he certainly had—and knew exactly what kind of dancing the couple would be doing.

"If Aunt Charlotte will have us, we will come for tea tomorrow," Lady Aldridge said. "That way, we can hear all about your night."

"I will tell Mama you are coming and that I invited you," Lady Lucy told her cousin.

Lady Aldridge kissed her cousin's cheek and then said, "Goodnight, Lord Huntsberry. It was good to see you and Lucy dancing together."

That was exactly the kind of thing he didn't want to hear, much less have Lady Lucy hear. He needed to set things straight between them now.

"I hope you do not mind that I stepped in for Lord Perth," he began after the other couple had left.

"Oh, I did not mind at all," she said, looking at him dreamily.

"My lady, I did it as a favor. What I said before stands. We would not suit. I will not be dancing with you again. I will not be amongst your many suitors. I simply wished to help you this evening so that you would not be left alone during supper."

Tears sprang to her eyes, and Judson hated hurting her.

"I see," she said softly, glancing down at her hands, which were folded in her lap. "I must thank you for being so thoughtful, my lord." Clearing her throat, she said, "If you will excuse me now, I need to go to the retiring room."

He rose quickly and helped her to her feet. Blinking back the tears, she said, "Thank you again for being a part of a wonderful night."

Judson admired her because she didn't rush away. Lady Lucy left the ballroom, her head held high, without a backward glance at him.

"Bloody hell," he said under his breath, repeating it again.

He had been a fool to push Lord Perth aside. Judson should never have asked her to dance, much less shared supper with her. It angered him that he had hurt her and tarnished her evening.

Strengthening his resolve, he left the supper room and the townhouse, striding toward his carriage. He would never attempt to spend any time with Lady Lucy Alington ever again.

CHAPTER NINE

JUDSON ENTERED HIS carriage, sitting back against the cushion and closing his eyes.

Tonight, he would ask to speak to Lady Harriet's father.

After having danced with Lady Lucy and supping with her during the opening night of the Season, he had withdrawn from all social activities for a week. During that time, he had constantly thought about the tawny-haired beauty. She dominated his every waking thought. He had even dreamed of her each night.

That convinced him he needed to get serious and find himself a bride. Returning with new resolve to the social whirl, he had approached this past week with an eye to finding a wife on the Marriage Mart. He had decided upon Lady Harriet, who had been out for three Seasons. She was average-looking and very dull. He knew she would make no demands upon him, which was exactly what he was looking for.

In other words, she would be his ideal wife.

The carriage rolled to a halt, the door opening. Judson descended the stairs and headed across the street toward the townhouse, where tonight's musicale would be held. He spied Lord Eaton and Lord Humley ahead of him. Seeing the pair from his past left him feeling unsettled. They were close to him in age and had been two of the worst bullies whom he had eventually dealt with. Eaton had been the ringleader, with several minions, including Humley.

He forced himself to turn away from thoughts of his past. He had handled these two years ago, and they had never spoken to him again, with Eaton even leaving school. They ran in a fast crowd now, and both had terrible reputations within the *ton*.

Once he entered the townhouse, he found his host and hostess in the ballroom, where the musicale would take place. Chairs had been set on three sides of a raised dais. The invitation he had received mentioned it would be a famed Italian diva who performed for them tonight.

That led him to think about Antonia. Judson had not been to visit his mistress in almost four weeks now. In fact, he had actually forgotten about her. He supposed he would be visiting her with more regularity once he wed. Something told him that his wife would not begin to satisfy him in the bedroom. At least he had Antonia to meet his needs.

He scanned the room quickly, spotting Lady Lucy and her brother engaged in conversation with another couple. Their parents were a short distance away, speaking with an ancient duke and his very young duchess.

He located Lady Harriet, standing with one of her wallflower friends, and went to greet her.

"Good evening, my ladies," he said, gallantly kissing both their hands.

Lady Harriet, as usual, appeared tongue-tied around him, while her friend merely giggled uncontrollably, irritating him to no end. He did his best not to compare his intended to Lady Lucy, but he couldn't help turning his gaze across the room and seeing her animation as she spoke.

Looking back to Lady Harriet, he asked, "If you are not otherwise engaged this evening, my lady, perhaps we might sit together and enjoy the music."

Her eyes grew round in surprise. "Yes, my lord. Thank you, my lord."

The friend, thankfully, drifted away, and Judson tried to have a decent conversation with Lady Harriet. She seemed too in awe of the fact that a handsome marquess paid her attention. Her answers were either yes or no, with *my lord* tacked onto each response. Intellectually, he knew he was making the right decision in offering for this woman. She would cause him no problems throughout their marriage, and he hoped she would produce a suitable number of children, including his heir and a spare.

His heart, however, rebelled at the idea of being shackled to her for the rest of his life. He toyed with the idea, far down the line, of engaging Lady Lucy in an affair once she had wed and provided her own husband with his heir. Though the practice of affairs was common within the *ton*, something told Judson that Lady Lucy would never betray her wedding vows, even if she had a husband who strayed.

He took Lady Harriet's hand and placed it atop his sleeve, escorting them to a seat. As others did the same, he saw Lord Eaton and Lord Humley approach Lady Lucy and her brother, causing his blood to boil. The viscount said something to the two men and abruptly turned, leading his sister to a seat on the end of a row and then taking his place beside her.

Judson would have to keep his eyes on those two. He wanted the duo to have nothing to do with Lady Lucy. While he had every faith that Lord Dyer could keep his sister safe, it wouldn't hurt to have an extra set of eyes watching protectively over her.

Their host gave a flowery introduction as the musicians took the stage. They were joined by the opera singer, whom he had seen perform on a previous occasion.

As she sang, he let his thoughts wander, deciding he would ask Lady Harriet's father for an appointment tomorrow morning. There, he would offer for her, and Judson hoped they might arrange a time for the marriage settlements to be written up. He would be generous in the contracts, wanting both his wife and their children—beyond his heir—to have secure futures once he was gone.

His decision made, he ignored his heavy heart as the songstress ended her performance. He joined in with the applause. Their hostess appeared, saying the diva would rest her voice for the next hour. Guests were encouraged to go into the supper room for light refreshments and socializing until the singer took the stage again.

Dreading spending an entire hour with Lady Harriet at his side, he nevertheless put on a smile. "Would you care for something to eat or drink, my lady?"

"Oh! Yes. Please, my lord."

Judson escorted her to the supper room, where they joined a few others at a table. He was thankful the others kept up the conversation because he could think of absolutely nothing to say to his companion. In a way, that solidified his decision to wed Lady Harriet. He had absolutely no emotional attachment to her. That was the way a marriage should be.

Then his thoughts drifted to Lord and Lady Aldridge. The couple always was affectionate with one another. Sometimes, the glances they shared pierced his heart. He would never have love in his life as they did. Judson must accept that—and move on. Perhaps he might feel some affection for one or more of his children. He simply had no idea what his future held in that regard.

He had loved his father. At least, he thought it had been love. Judson had spent very little time in his parents' company, though. And with his mother having died giving birth to him, he had never known her nurturing hand. He vowed to try his best to always be kind to Lady Harriet and their children. Beyond that, he could make no promises.

Helping her from her chair, he escorted Lady Harriet to her mother. It was time to locate the chit's father and ask to come and see him.

"If you will excuse me, my ladies," he said, leaving the supper room to wander about and find his future father-in-law.

Before he could change his mind.

Lucy had enjoyed the musicale so far. She had sat with Con during the first half, happy that she didn't have to worry about some suitor sitting next to her.

They were two full weeks into the Season, and she had callers every afternoon. Their drawing room filled with flower arrangements each morning, and she knew she would have her pick of suitors. She had even discussed three or four of them she was interested in with Con, and he told her each of the gentlemen had his own merits. Con had emphasized he would not dictate whom she should choose as her husband. He simply was there to rule out the unsuitable ones, such as Lord Eaton and Lord Humley.

The two had approached Con and her earlier in the evening, and she had taken her cue from her brother. He had been polite enough to briefly introduce her to them and then wished them a good evening, leading her away from the pair. Lucy did not even bother asking why he did so. It was obvious that neither would be suitable for her. Even without Con telling her so, she had heard talk of these two in various retiring rooms, ladies issuing warnings to one another about their wicked reputations. Lord Eaton was supposedly the leader of a group of rakehells. Between Con's warnings and that of Lord Huntsberry, along with other ladies, she would steer clear of the pair and their set.

Once the opera singer ended the entertainment, Con led her to the supper room. They joined a table of six others, and Lucy enjoyed herself tremendously. She was beginning to make friends with other girls, even one whom Mama had told her to avoid. Lucy suspected the reason Mama had warned her off the girl was because she was absolutely beautiful and had numerous gentlemen vying for her hand. Still, she thought her new friend kind and had ignored Mama's advice.

They finished dining, and she sipped a glass of ratafia before deciding she would slip out and go to the retiring room. Lucy leaned over to Con to excuse herself, and left the room. Unfortunately, she had to walk by Lord Huntsberry's table, where he sat with Lady Harriet and a few others. Lucy had decided the marquess was courting Lady Harriet. She had seen them dance together a few times this past week, twice in one evening, and everyone knew that if a gentleman danced more than one time with a particular lady in a single night, he was staking his claim on her.

She did not know Lady Harriet, who had been out for a few years and seemed most diffident. Lucy hoped Lord Huntsberry would be happy with his choice and when the betrothal was announced, she would wish the pair every happiness.

Even while her heart broke.

Lucy realized she had not a ghost of a chance with Lord Huntsberry. Because of that, she did her best to ignore him. She truly was enjoying her first Season, meeting new people and having a wonderful time at the various events. Eventually, she would settle on a gentleman and hopefully receive an offer from him. Money and a title didn't mean much to her. She simply wanted to wed a man she liked, one she had things in common with. A man who would make a good husband and father.

That man could never be Lord Huntsberry, and Lucy had accepted this outcome.

She had overheard other girls talk of having their hearts trampled upon, so she assumed it was a common thing within the *ton*. After all, couples did not wed for love. They wed to increase their social standing. Lucy did not love Lord Huntsberry—but she thought given the chance, she could have. That chance would never materialize, though, so she directed her attention to her future.

After her trip to the retiring room, she left to rejoin Con. As she moved along the corridor, Lucy saw Lord Humley rushing toward her. No one was in sight, which caused Lucy's heart to speed up.

He approached her, looking out of breath. "There you are,

my lady. Your brother is looking for you. Your mother has taken ill."

Concern quickly filled her. "Mama is ailing? Has she been taken to our carriage already? I must go to her at once."

"She fainted, my lady, and was carried by footmen to the library. I am certain she would be relieved when she awakens to see you by her side. Naturally, a doctor has been called for. Let me show you where she is."

They went down the hall and turned. Lord Humley paused as they reached a door, which was partially open.

"Lady Marley was taken here, my lady."

Lord Humley pushed the door open wider, and Lucy rushed into the room. Glancing about, she saw it was empty. Confused, she thought Mama must have awakened or been moved while Lord Humley came to look for her.

She turned—only to find Lord Eaton standing before her, his smile like that of a fox who had just slipped inside an unguarded henhouse.

"Excuse me, my lord," she said crisply, with more confidence than she felt.

Lucy started around him, but he grasped her shoulders, his hold strong. Panic filled her. It struck her what was happening.

"My mother is not ill, is she, my lord?"

"No, Lady Lucy. Lady Marley is in excellent health. When I last left the supper room, your mama was holding court, as always."

"Release me, my lord," she said firmly, only to find his fingers dug more deeply into her shoulders. Lucy bruised easily and knew evidence of tonight would be present.

"Your brother was quite abrupt in turning away from us," he told her, a gleam entering his eyes which brought her fear to the surface. "He is quite protective of you, isn't he?"

"Yes, he is. Con will be looking for me. I ask you again, Lord Eaton. Please, let me go. I will speak no further of this incident."

"Incident," he mused. "Yes, I suppose compromising a woman could be classified as an incident."

Panic seared through her, causing her to tremble, but Lucy tried to keep a cool head. "No one has seen us alone together, my lord. Please, leave this library at once," she pleaded. "I will stay a bit and then make my own exit."

"I think not, my lady."

She struggled to get away from him, demanding, "Why are you doing this?"

He shrugged. "In part, because your family has always pretended to be so much better than other ones in the *ton*. And because I have seen Lord Huntsberry looking longingly at you."

Perplexed, Lucy asked, "What does Lord Huntsberry have to do with any of this?"

"I shall merely say that the marquess and I have a past together. A very unpleasant one. Huntsberry did something vile to me, which I can never forget." His tone was wintry now.

"I have no idea what occurred between the two of you, Lord Eaton, but I played no part in it."

"I think the marquess pines for you, my lady. Hurting you?" His smile turned fiendish. "That is merely a way to hurt him."

Then he yanked her roughly to him, his mouth coming down hard on hers, their teeth clashing. Lucy struggled, trying to push him away, but the more she fought, the tighter he held onto her.

He forced her lips open, ramming his tongue inside her mouth, causing her to gag. She wanted to scream but was afraid if she did, it would draw unwanted attention.

And the last thing she wanted was to be chained to this uncouth rake for the rest of her life.

With as much force as she could muster, Lucy thrust her knee upward. Her action did the trick. Lord Eaton released his hold on her, a yowl of pain coming from him. She started to take a step back, but he grabbed her elbow.

"You little bitch," he growled.

Then before she knew what was happening, he slapped her, causing a world of pain and a mass of stars to momentarily blind her. Her hand flew to her cheek, feeling the heat of the slap, and she realized Lord Eaton had released her elbow. Blinking, trying to regain her vision, she heard a loud crack—followed by an even louder thump. Her vision cleared, and she saw her attacker lying on the floor.

And Lord Huntsberry hovered over him.

CHAPTER TEN

JUDSON MOVED ABOUT the townhouse, growing frustrated when he could not locate Lady Harriet's father. He decided the best plan was to return to the ballroom and sit with her again. When the concert ended, he could return her to both her parents and then ask to speak to her father sometime tomorrow.

As he turned a corner, he saw Humley leaning against a door, one ankle over the other, his arms crossed. His gut tightened at seeing the pose. Many a time, a boy had stood in that exact manner, guarding a door as Judson had been carted away by bullies, tormented for hours.

Striding toward one of his former haters, he saw the moment when Humley spotted him. Immediately, the man stood tall, defiance in his eyes.

"What do you want, Huntsberry?"

"I want to see what is behind that door," he stated, knowing he looked intimidating with his size and scowl.

Humley's eyes darted about, as if he looked for help. "There is nothing to see, my lord," he said.

"Then you won't mind if I take a look myself."

"No!"

In a flash, he knew no good occurred behind this closed door. And considering Humley was usually seen in Eaton's company, Judson surmised his old enemy was on the other side, up to no good.

He roughly pushed Humley aside, knocking him off-balance, and opened the door. To his horror, he saw Eaton strike Lady Lucy. Rage filled him, and Judson rushed the short distance, ripping away Eaton's hold on her. Years of honing his boxing skills came into play as Judson threw the hardest punch of his life, knocking Eaton to the ground. Blood spurted from the rakehell's nose, and from how crooked it sat, Judson knew it was broken.

He leaned down—and saw fear in Eaton's eyes.

"Leave town. Now. Take Humley with you. I do not wish to see either of you for a good year. Perhaps even more." Fisting his hands, he held them up. "You know the power of these fists, Eaton. You have suffered from them before. I advise you keep silent and never speak of this night to anyone. Nod if you understand."

Eaton did so, a mixture of fear and anger in his eyes. At some point, Judson supposed Eaton would try to punish him, but he would be ready. He was always ready.

He took a step back as Humley hurried to his friend's side, helping him to stand.

"Get out. Be gone," he told Humley. "Or you will suffer my wrath as never before."

Humley helped Eaton to his feet, but Eaton shrugged off any help. He never looked at Judson as he left the library, Humley trailing after him.

Quickly, he turned, seeing Lady Lucy looked a mess. The mark of Eaton's hand still showed on her face. The slap had caused a few pins to come loose, and part of her hair tumbled down her back. She quivered all over.

Judson moved toward her, wrapping her in his arms. "There, there. Hush, now. You are safe."

She had started to sob quietly and now buried her face against his chest. Her fingers clutched at his coat, tightening and loosening, almost as if she were a kitten kneading her paws. He wouldn't chastise her. Obviously, she had gone through a traumatic experience. It hurt him, though, that she was hurting now, and he had no way to fix things for her.

"Did he force himself on you?" he asked gently, smoothing her hair.

She raised a tear-stained face, their gazes meeting. "They tricked me. Lord Humley said Mama had taken ill. I was coming from the retiring room. He led me here." She swallowed. "But no one was here. Or so I thought."

A fat tear rolled down her cheek, and Judson wiped it away with the pad of his thumb.

"I thought Mama had been moved, but when I turned around, he . . . he . . . was there. Eaton. He would not let me pass." She hiccoughed. "I realized then they had laid a trap for me. He wanted to compromise me." She paused, frowning, gazing up at him. "Because of you."

She began crying softly again, and he brought her head back to his chest. Anger boiled through him. Judson knew Eaton never would have wed Lady Lucy. He deliberately had set out to ruin her. The cad must have caught Judson watching her and surmised he had feelings for her.

Hurt Lady Lucy. Hurt him.

"I will kill Eaton. Humley, too," he said, causing her to jump.

"No." Her gaze met and held his. "You will do no such thing, my lord. You have already ordered them gone from town. I cannot have you committing murder over something so . . . so . . ."

"Eaton nearly ruined you, Lucy," he told her. "And rakehell that he is, he never would have wed you. By God, I would have not allowed you to wed such a despicable, immoral toad."

"But you interrupted him," she said. "You saved me, Huntsberry."

Her eyes swam with tears and her lips still trembled, but she was the loveliest creature he had ever seen.

"Did he hurt you?" he asked, afraid to hear her response.

"I am certain to have bruises where his fingers dug into me, keeping me from fleeing. And he forced a kiss upon me." Disgust showed in her face. "His tongue . . . oh, it was so awful." She shuddered.

Judson did not want her afraid of men. Or of kissing.

"I am sorry he abused you so, Lucy. Not all men are like Eaton and Humley. And kissing with tongues can be quite pleasant."

She frowned up at him. "What? You actually *do* use your tongue to kiss? But . . . you did not do so with me. Your kiss was gentle. Sweet."

"There are many kinds of kisses. They can bring about a plethora of emotions and physical desires."

She trembled in his arms. "I will never allow a man to kiss me that way. Never!"

"But you should," he said softly. "If it is not forced, it can be most delightful."

Doubt filled those enchanting, amethyst eyes.

"Do not be afraid of kissing. It is a way a man brings pleasure to a woman."

She shook her head. "No. I am not sure if I will ever want to kiss a man again."

That was when Judson knew he had to act. To show her not to be afraid.

His mouth moved to hers, slowly kissing her as he had before. She stiffened at his touch, but gradually, she relaxed. He increased the pressure of the kiss, his hand going to her nape, anchoring her. Breaking it, he slowly used the tip of his tongue to sweep back and forth across her full, lower lip. She whimpered, clutching him more tightly.

Judson outlined her entire mouth with his tongue, his touch light as he glided along. Then he swept it along the seam of her mouth, urging her to open to him. She did, without protest, and he knew he had cleared a hurdle with her. He slipped his tongue inside her mouth, beginning a leisurely exploration that caused his own pulse to jump and her breath to hitch. He took his time, not wanting to rush her, needing her to feel comfortable with what he did.

Then he allowed his tongue to glide against hers, causing another whimper. He pinned her tongue lightly with his teeth and then sucked on it, bringing a rush of emotion through him. Desire for her filled him, and Judson knew he needed to back away now. She had been exposed to a different kind of kissing. Playfully, she now answered his kiss, kissing him back. She might have been hurt, but she was far from broken. His job here was done.

Easing from her, he said, "See?"

"That was nothing like Lord Eaton's kiss," she marveled. Then she said the words which undid him. "I want more, Huntsberry. More of it. More of *you*."

Her hands moved up his chest, her fingers plunging into his hair. She grabbed onto it, forcing his mouth to return to hers. They kissed a long moment, Lucy taking the lead. Judson tried to hold back.

And finally gave in.

He deepened the kiss, wanting the taste of her, enjoying the feel of her warm body pressed against his, her lavender scent filling his nostrils. If he died right now, it would be a happy death, for kissing Lucy was the highlight of his life.

"My, my," a voice said. "How interesting."

They sprang apart, dread already filling him, because he recognized who had spoken.

Lady Billingsley stood in the open doorway, a few feet from them. Two years ago, she had wed an earl old enough to be her grandfather. Rumor had it that she had forced the man to her bed for hours each night, wearing him down and finally killing him with her physical demands. Less than a month after they wed, the bride became a widow. She had spent her year in mourning, returning to Polite Society with vast wealth, eager to work her way through the men of the *ton*.

When she had approached Judson, he had brushed her off. Lady Billingsley had demanded to know why he refused to make love to her, saying she was beautiful and available, two things which should appeal to him. He had insulted her, calling her a lightskirt and said he had no interest in coupling with a woman who had bedded half of the men in the ballroom where they stood.

Lady Billingsley had eyed him for a long moment and then told him he would rue the day that he had ever spoken to her in such an ungentlemanly manner. Then she had left and was soon dancing with a slew of other men.

Judson had forgotten the incident, but the memory of their conversation came crashing back to him now. She was going to make him pay.

And Lucy Alington would be the one who suffered the most.

"I see Lord Huntsberry is human, after all," the countess said. "Others have accused you of having no heart." She laughed cruelly. "And I was one of them. But it seems you have quite the *tendre* for Lady Lucy, doesn't it?"

"You misunderstood what you saw, my lady," Lucy said. "I was very upset about something which had just occurred. Lord Huntsberry, who is a friend of my brother, Lord Dyer, heard me crying. He only wished to comfort me."

Lady Billingsley's brows shot up in disbelief. "With his tongue rammed down your throat, my lady? Or was that your tongue down his?" she mused.

Hating to leave Lucy's side, he moved toward the countess. "I beg you, my lady. Please, keep what you have seen to yourself. Lady Lucy is making her come-out this Season. She has many suitors and a bright future ahead. Do not ruin her."

The woman's eyes flicked to Lucy and back to him. "I do believe you were the one doing the ruining, my lord." Her eyes gleamed at him with a viciousness that stole his breath. "I will merely let others know what I stumbled upon. It is up to you whether or not this, what would you call her? *Lightskirt,* perhaps? Whether she is totally compromised or not."

She threw his own word back at him, and Judson knew the

die was cast.

"Lady Lucy is pure," he insisted. "She has done no harm to you, my lady. Punish me. Not her. I will do whatever you ask."

"Will you?" Lady Billingsley challenged. "Somehow, I think not. I cannot envision you kissing me the way you did her. No innocent kisses like that," she said dismissively. "I am off to share what I have witnessed."

Then she was gone.

Turning to Lucy, Judson said, "She is the worst of those who gossip in the *ton*." He paused. "I am sorry. We must announce our betrothal at once, else your reputation will be in tatters by the end of the evening."

"No," she said quietly. "I cannot do that to you, my lord. You made it perfectly clear to me that you had no interest in wedding me. I have seen you with Lady Harriet and assumed you would be offering for her."

He had totally forgotten about his mission to find Lady Harriet's father.

"No," he said firmly, taking her elbow and guiding her from the library. "We are going to wed. It is the only way. I will not allow any argument regarding this."

She halted in the tracks. "So, I have no say in the matter?" she asked angrily.

Knowing he would hurt her pride, he said, "I am afraid not. Come quickly."

"Wait," she begged. "I must return to the library."

Breaking away from him, she entered the room again and fell to her knees. She began picking up hairpins, and he realized they could not appear in front of others with her hair half up and half down, or a scandal even larger than the one Lady Billingsley stirred would occur.

She huffed a moment in frustration and then began removing all her pins. Judson didn't stop her, trusting that she knew what she was doing. With quick efficiency, she twisted her hair several times and began pinning it into a simple style.

Looking up at him, she asked, "Am I presentable?"

He offered his hand, helping her stand. "You are breathtakingly lovely, my lady."

"Then let us go and see my parents."

He tucked her hand close to him, and they moved along the corridor, returning to the ballroom. Guests were taking their seats, and he supposed the diva was about to begin the second half of her performance.

Spying Dyer, he guided Lucy to her brother.

"No time for questions," he said brusquely. "Your sister and I will be wedding by special license as soon as possible."

The viscount looked at him in disbelief. Then anger filled his eyes. "You bastard," he said, his voice low and deadly.

"It is not his fault, Con," Lucy said quickly. "Lord Huntsberry saved me from a dreadful situation. If he had not, the gossips would be talking about Lord Eaton compromising me."

"Eaton?" Dyer hissed.

"Where are your parents?" Judson asked. "Wait. I see them. Come along."

He took Lucy with him, her brother dogging Judson's heels.

"Lord and Lady Marley, we have good news to share with you," he said, giving the countess his most charming smile. "Lady Lucy has agreed to wed me. That is, with your approval, of course."

Lord Marley looked surprised, while his wife looked joyful. "Oh, Huntsberry, you devil," the countess said. "And here I thought you had lost interest in our daughter."

"We are most eager to wed, my lady," Judson continued. "In fact, I will purchase a special license tomorrow morning in Doctors' Commons. Might we hold the ceremony the day after tomorrow? Perhaps at Lord and Lady Aldridge's residence. I believe Lady Aldridge would be happy to host our wedding breakfast."

Lady Marley appeared surprised but said, "Your marquess is certainly a determined man, Lucilla. We do not want to disappoint him, now, do we? Yes, I will speak with Ariadne."

"We thought we could do so ourselves, Mama," Lucy said. "Papa, why don't you ask our host if you might announce our betrothal? Then we will slip out—Con can come with us to chaperone—and we will go to Ariadne and Julian's."

"Splendid idea," the earl said, offering Judson his hand. "You have chosen wisely, Lord Huntsberry. Welcome to the family."

The next few minutes passed in a blur. Lord Marley made the betrothal announcement. Guests surrounded them, offering good wishes. He saw Lady Billingsley standing to the side, looking on in amusement. Something told Judson he had not seen the last of her and her venomous ways.

They went to his carriage, and he told his coachman to take them to Lord Aldridge's townhouse. His future brother-in-law sat opposite Judson, his arm about his sister.

"I want to hear it all," Dyer said. "You may keep the full story from Mama and Papa, but I want to know. Now."

"Could we wait until we reach Ariadne's?" Lucy asked her brother. "We will share it with all of you then."

They arrived and were taken to the drawing room. After several minutes, the Aldridges appeared, the marquess holding Penelope.

"What the devil are you doing here?" Aldridge asked. "We actually had to dress simply to see you. And Penelope is fussy tonight." He rubbed the babe's back, her head on his shoulder.

"We have come to ask if you would host our wedding breakfast," Judson began. "The day after tomorrow. If that is convenient with you."

Lady Aldridge gave a pitying smile to her cousin. "You were caught kissing Lord Huntsberry?"

"It is more complicated than that," Lucy said.

Between the two of them, they explained the situation, taking turns. They left out the part where they were kissing passionately, however. Judson merely said he was comforting Lady Lucy because she was so shaken, and Lady Billingsley had stumbled across them as they embraced.

"Oh, my goodness," the marchioness said. "Lady Billingsley is a horrible woman. One of the worst gossips in Polite Society. She will likely embellish the story and say Lord Huntsberry was ravishing you or some other such nonsense." Sympathy filled her eyes. "I am sorry you are being forced to wed, but it can be a good thing. You already know one another. Have a friendship between you. It will make for a good foundation for your marriage," she assured them.

Judson wondered if Lucy might ever tell the entire truth to her cousin or Lord Aldridge. He knew beyond a doubt she would never speak of what had occurred between them with her parents.

"We are ready to make the best of things," he said lightly.

"We would be happy to host your wedding and the breakfast," Aldridge said. "If you would like, I can accompany you to Doctors' Commons tomorrow to arrange for your special license."

"Thank you, my lord. I would be grateful for your guidance through the process."

"Enough of formality," Lady Aldridge declared. "You are going to be family. We are Ariadne and Julian to you now."

He glanced to Lord Dyer, who still harbored doubt in his eyes. "I am Con," he said sternly.

"And I am Judson," he told them. He slipped his hand around Lucy's, finding it cold. "We should probably get you home. Your mama will most likely keep you busy the entire day tomorrow, preparing for the wedding."

"I suppose she will," his betrothed said quietly.

They went out to his carriage. He handed up Lucy. Her brother glared at him.

"I believe parts of your story—but not all of it. I am angry that my sister's choice was taken from her hands."

With honesty, Judson said, "I will be the best husband I can be to her. That is my promise."

But as his carriage left the square, he wondered just what he had gotten the two of them into.

CHAPTER ELEVEN

JUDSON ARRIVED HOME and went straight to his study. First, he wrote a letter to his solicitor, Mr. Baker, informing him that he would wed later in the week and needed marriage settlements drawn up quickly. He asked that the solicitor be available tomorrow afternoon for this purpose and would send his carriage for Baker and a clerk.

Next, he wrote to Lord Marley, thanking the earl again for granting his permission for Judson to wed Lucy. He mentioned how he wanted the marriage contracts written up before the ceremony and asked Marley if tomorrow afternoon at one o'clock would be convenient. Lucy's father seemed a good sort who would want his daughter properly looked after, so Judson believed they could quickly hammer out the details of the marriage contracts.

After that, he wrote to Lord and Lady Aldridge, thanking them for their kindness in agreeing to host the wedding breakfast. He liked the couple a great deal and was grateful they stepped up in this time of crisis. With the marquess and marchioness hosting the wedding and breakfast, it would signify their approval of the match. Such a gesture would go a long way in restoring Lucy's reputation, especially since Judson had no idea exactly what gossip Lady Billingsley had already spread.

Finally, he wrote a heartfelt letter to Lord Dyer. It was obvious the viscount loved his sister a great deal, and Judson wanted to assure the man that he would look after Lucy and treat her well. In it, he asked for Dyer to be present during the making of the marriage settlements.

He sealed each of the four notes and left them on his desk. He would have Tim deliver them first thing in the morning.

Going up to his bedchamber, he found the valet waiting for him.

Coming to his feet, Tim asked, "How was the musicale, my lord? I know you aren't much for music. Hopefully, it was tolerable."

"I am to be married, Tim," he said abruptly, causing his friend's jaw to drop.

"What?"

"You heard me. It is time I got an heir, so I offered for a woman this evening."

He began unknotting his cravat but made a mess of it. Tim took over.

"I think this is a good thing, my lord," the servant told him, patiently working through the knots Judson had created. "It's time this house was opened up and a little happiness let in."

The valet's remark startled him. Judson had lived simply, but Tim was right. The furniture would need to be uncovered in rooms throughout the townhouse. A lady—his marchioness— would be in residence now. He would need to make certain Lucy understood she could make any changes she believed necessary. She would also want to invite others to tea, meaning the drawing room would need to be made ready, along with the rooms reserved for his marchioness. Restoring those rooms would take top priority.

For a moment, Judson imagined Lucy in his bed, her hair unbound, falling to her waist, the rest of her naked. He swallowed. He wasn't going to ask her to make love with him just yet. He would need to take some time to think about just what he wanted from their hasty marriage. Most likely, he would go to her bed and then return to his own when they coupled. Yet the thought of cradling her in his arms throughout the night and waking to make love to her in the morning sunlight caused a sweet ache within him.

"When will the marriage take place?" Tim asked, startling him from his reverie.

"The day after tomorrow. I will purchase a special license in the morning so that we might wed immediately. I also have several letters which need to be delivered early tomorrow morning. I am entrusting you with this task. You may find them on my desk."

"Of course, my lord. Might I ask who your bride will be?"

"Lady Lucy Alington. She is the daughter of the Earl of Marley. She has a younger sister who is not out yet and an older brother, Viscount Dyer."

His clothes now stripped away, a weariness fell over him. He asked Tim to return and have him dressed by eight o'clock the next morning and then dismissed the valet.

Climbing into bed, Judson lay awake, looking at the ceiling, wondering how his life would change in the next forty-eight hours. Now that Lucy was to be his wife, he wanted the same closeness with her as he saw between Lord and Lady Aldridge. Yet he knew that would be impossible. Long ago, he had closed off his emotions, giving up on people and the world. He could never share with her what his childhood had been like. The best he could do would be to show Lucy respect.

He would also make abundantly clear to her that they would have a marriage of convenience.

After a restless night with little sleep, Judson rose and washed. Tim appeared and helped him to dress.

"I found the letters to be delivered, my lord," his valet said. "I will leave now and see they arrive at their destinations."

"Thank you, Tim. Take Baker's to him first. I want him to know I have immediate need of him today."

Judson left for the breakfast room and before he could be served, he told Clippman, "Gather the staff. I need to address them."

Looking puzzled, nevertheless the butler said, "Yes, my lord."

It didn't take long. For a marquess, he only had a handful of servants. The Clippmans. Cook and a scullery maid. Two footmen and a housemaid. His coachman. He supposed with his marriage, he would need to hire more. Or leave that to Lucy to do. The household would be her domain, and she could run things as she saw fit. That would include hiring the help she wished to have.

"I asked you here today to inform you that I am to be married tomorrow." He paused, seeing the startled looks on the faces of his servants. "Mrs. Clippman, please see that the rooms designated for my marchioness are aired and up to snuff."

"Yes, my lord," the housekeeper said. "Will Lady Huntsberry be bringing her lady's maid with her?"

He hadn't a clue, but since Mrs. Clippman had mentioned it, Judson supposed it was a common practice.

"I would think so. Better have a room readied in the servants' quarters for her, as well."

Cook spoke up. "Does her ladyship have any particular foods she favors, my lord? We want to make her feel welcome."

For the first time since his one careless action resulted in an impromptu marriage proposal, Judson smiled. "Sweets, Cook. My betrothed has a sweet tooth."

Cook grinned. "Ah, that's good to know, my lord."

"That will be all," he said, causing the servants to disperse to their various tasks.

His breakfast was served to him, and as he finished, his butler came forward to clear the dishes himself.

"My lord, on behalf of the entire staff, I want to wish you well in your marriage."

Seeing compassion in the butler's eyes, he replied, "Thank you, Clippman. I believe all the servants will be taken with Lady Huntsberry. She is a very kind and caring person."

He went to his study and paced, having nothing to do until Aldridge's carriage arrived. When it did, Clippman let him know, and Judson went outside, having to use his umbrella because of the downpour. Selfishly, he hoped the rain would stay away tomorrow.

"Good morning, Judson," Aldridge said.

Recalling he had been granted leave to call the marquess by his Christian name, he said, "Good morning to you, Julian."

"Ariadne was up early this morning, meeting with our cook about the wedding breakfast. She told me to ask you whom you wished to invite to the ceremony."

He had no one. No relative. No friend. And then he changed his mind.

"It may seem an odd request, but I would like my valet to be present."

Julian didn't seem bothered in the least, causing Judson to ask, "Aren't you curious about my only guest?"

"Why should I be? If your valet is a loyal servant and you obviously value him a great deal since you wish him to witness your marriage, it is none of my business."

"Tim is a good friend to me." He hesitated. "My mother died giving birth to me. My father was in poor health his entire life and passed when I was ten. Tim was always there, cheering me up, taking care of me from the time I was a boy. Until now."

"He sounds a good sort. And a good friend to you." The marquess' gaze met Judson's. "I had no friends when I came into my title. I was a common laborer on the London docks. I worked long days and then put in a few hours as a clerk in a solicitor's office each evening."

Julian's words shocked Judson. While Aldridge had a look of danger about him, he dressed impeccably and sounded as cultured as anyone Judson had gone to school with. He never would have suspected the man seated across from him had earned his living by doing back-breaking work.

"I won't bore you with my story," the marquess continued. "Suffice it to say that when I became Lord Aldridge, I did not even have a Tim of my own to call friend. My mother had just died. Through an almost unbelievable set of circumstances, I found out I was the heir apparent to a marquessate. The former Aldridge died minutes after I met him, leaving me in a world I did not know or comprehend.

"So, if you need an ear—beyond Tim's—I am here for you, Judson. Val and Con, as well, though I know things are strained between you and Con now. He and Lucy are close. Con is upset with the situation more than he is with you. Try and remember that when dealing with him."

Still reeling from what Julian had disclosed, he said, "I will do my duty. Lucy will lack for nothing."

Julian studied him a moment, looking conflicted. Finally, he said, "I hope the two of you will be even half as happy as Ariadne and I are."

That would never come to pass, but he wasn't going to press the issue.

"Thank you for your offer of friendship. I am sorely in need of a friend."

"We will be family, as well as friends," Julian said. "Our bonds from now on are strong."

They arrived at Doctors' Commons and, thanks to his companion, the way was smoothed. In less than an hour, he held in his hand the special license which would allow him to wed Lucy at the time and place they wished anytime during the next month. Slipping the folded document into his coat's inner pocket, he accompanied Julian back to his carriage.

"What of the marriage settlements?" his friend asked.

"I wrote to both my solicitor and Lord Marley. I would like to see them drawn up this afternoon."

"Good. That will go a long way in appeasing Con."

They returned to his townhouse, and Julian said, "We will see you tomorrow morning. If you have need of anything before then, send word."

Leaning over, he offered his new friend his hand, and Julian took it.

"I am glad things are not awkward between us. I also appreci-ate you revealing a bit of your past to me. Perhaps one day, I can return the favor."

Julian shook his head. "It is not necessary. Share if you wish, but I think we can move forward, all the same."

Judson left the carriage and returned inside his residence. Clippman awaited him.

"You have received replies to your notes, my lord. I have left them on your desk."

"Thank you," he said, heading to his study, hoping the ar-rangements he had proposed had fallen into place.

Reading the first note, his solicitor agreed to be at the ready whenever Judson needed him this afternoon. He set Baker's letter aside and opened the next one. Lord Marley was agreeable to meeting at one o'clock this afternoon and would have his own solicitor on hand.

He opened the final letter. In it, Lord Dyer assured Judson he would be on hand this afternoon as the marriage contracts were drawn up. The note was terse and mentioned nothing else. It was easy to understand how upset the viscount was. His beloved sister's choice in a husband had been stolen from her. Once again, he would do all in his power to see Lucy cared for in these settlements, hoping it would appease both Dyer and Marley, as well as ease his own conscience a bit.

Judson rang for Tim and told the footman to go straight to Baker's office and tell the solicitor the carriage would call for him at a quarter past twelve. He wanted to give plenty of time for them to arrive at the Marley townhouse.

"I'm off then, my lord," Tim said.

"Wait," he said.

The valet turned. "Is there another note you need delivered, my lord?"

"No. I simply wanted to invite you to tomorrow's ceremo-ny."

The servant looked stunned. "Me? Go to your wedding? You

aren't thinking straight, my lord."

Patiently, he said, "Tim, you have always been a shoulder I could lean on, whether I was ten or even now. You stood up for me. Stood by me. Your loyalty and support have not gone unnoticed. Frankly, I have no idea what I would have done if I had not had your ear all these years. I am honored to call you my friend—and I would appreciate your presence."

Tim shook his head in wonder. "I only did what was right, my lord." He grinned. "I'm proud to think of you as my friend. Yes, I am honored to come see you speak your vows with Lady Lucy."

"Thank you. It means a great deal to me to have you there."

Beaming now, the valet said, "I look forward to meeting Lady Lucy. She must be special to convince you it was time to get married."

Lucy was special. He only hated that she would not be wedding her first choice. In the rush of events, he hadn't even asked her if she'd had another gentleman courting her.

Tim left to give notice to Baker, and Judson took out parchment, composing a list of items he believed should be a part of the marriage settlements. A few years ago, he had actually come across a copy of the ones written before his parents' marriage, so he had an idea what could go into them. It saddened him that the provisions for his siblings, including dowries for the sisters he had never had, had never come to pass. Nor had the monies settled upon his mother since she had passed a decade before her husband did.

He told Clippman when he wanted the carriage to be ready and then went upstairs to see where Lucy would settle in. He had never been into the rooms designated for the marchioness, and curiosity brought him here now.

Both his housekeeper and the maid were hard at work. The curtains had been drawn back, and the windows were opened, letting in the cool, fresh air. Dust covers had been removed from the furniture. Rugs were rolled up and standing against the wall, and he supposed they would be taken outside so that the dust might be beaten from them.

"Lord Huntsberry!" Mrs. Clippman said, stopping to come to him. "I was just polishing the furniture. Bed linens have been placed on the bed. The wardrobe has been emptied. When Tim returns, I'll have him take the rugs downstairs. Don't worry, my lord. Everything will be ready for Lady Huntsberry by the time you return tomorrow."

"Flowers," he said. "She should have fresh flowers to greet her."

"Yes, my lord. I will see it," the housekeeper promised. "Do you have any particular blooms in mind?"

He shrugged. "You would know more about something like that than I, Mrs. Clippman. I will ask Lady Lucy this afternoon about her maid joining her, but go ahead and have a room readied for her as we spoke of, just in case."

"Of course, my lord. Leave everything to me."

Judson left, wondering how often Lucy might welcome him into her rooms. He thought of the kisses which had placed them in this situation and knew within her, a passionate woman existed. Whether she let that passion fly free would be another thing. His impression was that ladies of the *ton* remained ladies—even in a bedchamber with their husbands. It was the reason why so many men took on mistresses.

He realized he had lost all appetite for Antonia. He would need to visit her soon and let his mistress know she was free to select another protector. Even if he and Lucy coupled only infrequently, Judson could not see himself breaking his wedding vows to her, with Antonia or any other woman.

When he returned downstairs, Clippman told him the carriage was ready, and he took it to his solicitor's office. His footman summoned Baker, and a clerk accompanied him. The two men climbed into the carriage, and the coachman set off for the Marley townhouse.

Handing over the list he had written out, he said, "These are some of the terms I would like to see when the marriage contracts are written up today."

Baker spent several minutes reading over Judson's list, nodding his head occasionally, and even frowning once.

"These are most generous, Lord Huntsberry. More so than any other marriage settlements I have supervised."

"I wish them to be so," he said firmly. "I want no doubts regarding my marchioness' future. The same with any issue of our marriage."

The solicitor handed the pages to his clerk, who placed them into a portfolio. Then Baker said, "I wish you felicitations, my lord. I hope you and Lady Lucy will be most happy."

Judson wasn't sure what happiness lay in their future. He had never been happy, and with Lucy forced to wed him, he wasn't certain if she ever would be. Still, he thanked Baker, who had been loyal and watched out for Judson ever since he came into his title.

"Before we arrive, my lord, I must speak to you about another urgent matter. It is in regard to Mr. Jarvis."

Bile rose in his throat at the mention of his uncle, and Judson swallowed it. "What of him?"

"He came to see me recently. He . . . wishes for an increase in his quarterly allowance."

Anger sizzled through him. "My uncle knows the terms—and that they are not to be changed."

"I told him that very thing, my lord, but Mr. Jarvis insisted prices have gone up since you negotiated things with him several years ago."

"No," he said flatly. "He can make do with what I give him. Turn him away if he comes to see you again, Baker, and tell him that if he asks you again for an increase, he will lose even what I give him now."

"Yes, my lord," the solicitor said.

They reached Lord Marley's townhouse and were welcomed by the butler, who showed them into the library. Judson did not catch sight of Lucy and decided he would ask to see her once they concluded their business.

Lord Marley welcomed him, while his son's greeting was much cooler. Judson was introduced to the Marley solicitor, and he, in turn, introduced Baker and his clerk.

"Before we start, I would like to share with you what I would like to see present in the documents we draw up," he told the others. "Baker?"

Baker's clerk handed the earl the list which Judson had composed. He watched as Marley read through it, passing the pages to Lord Dyer, who then gave them to their solicitor.

When all three men had read the entire contents, Judson said, "Those points are non-negotiable, gentlemen. I am certain you might also have things to add."

"My lord, these are most liberal," Lord Marley proclaimed. "Why, Lucy will have everything she could ever desire, both now and after your death. You also are handsomely providing for your future children, as well."

"I want to do right by Lady Lucy," he told them, glancing to Dyer.

The viscount said, "You are starting the marriage off right, Lord Huntsberry. I am pleased my sister will be taken care of so well."

"It is the least I could do," he told Dyer, who knew much more about the situation than did his parents. "I told you I would try to be a good husband to your sister."

Lord Dyer inclined his head.

"I cannot see anything our side needs to ask for, Lord Marley," his solicitor told him. "Shall we make things official?"

While the clerk and two solicitors went to work at a table, Judson sat with his future in-laws, discussing nothing of great importance, merely killing time until the documents could be fashioned. Once they were, the three noblemen read through them.

"Everything looks to be in order," he said. "Make a copy for

Lord Marley, his solicitor, and one for Lady Lucy. I would like her to have access to what her future holds."

Baker had him and then Lord Marley sign the original marriage settlements and said, "My clerk will make the copies you have requested, my lord. I can have them delivered tomorrow."

"See that you do," he said. "My carriage will return you to your office now, Baker. For now, I wish to see my betrothed and spend some time with her before tomorrow's ceremony."

"I can take you to the drawing room," Lord Dyer offered.

On their way there, the viscount said, "I am still not pleased with having Lucy's hand forced into this marriage, but I compliment you on having her welfare at heart, Lord Huntsberry." He paused. "Or I suppose I should call you Judson now since Ariadne and Julian are doing so."

"I would be honored if you would," he said honestly.

"Then please call me Con," Dyer said as they reached the drawing room, and he opened the door.

Two things struck Judson. One was the huge number of bouquets which filled the room.

The other was the dozen suitors which lingered in the drawing room, paying court to *his* fiancée.

CHAPTER TWELVE

LUCY STOOD IN a circle of seven gentlemen. All had previously called upon her. Another half-dozen sat on settees and in chairs as her mother chatted and laughed with them. She had a headache from the heavy fragrance of roses in the arrangement behind her.

All she wanted was for all these men to go away.

Mama had gotten her up early, going through Lucy's new wardrobe, deciding what she should wear for her wedding tomorrow morning. Her mother had chosen a gown Lucy liked, but it would not have been her choice to wear for the ceremony. As usual, she decided it would be easier to keep silent and simply wear what Mama told her to. Soon, she would be gone from this house and free to make her own decisions.

Or would she?

She had no idea what her future held. What kind of husband Lord Huntsberry would be. What it would be like living in his London townhouse, especially having heard he did no entertaining and only used a handful of rooms within it. Then there was his country estate, which he never visited. Would he be willing to do so once they wed?

Though Lucy had enjoyed the time she had spent in town for her come-out, she was a country girl at heart. She enjoyed walking and riding, as well as visiting tenants. She even made clothes for the tenants' babes at Marleyfield. Spending all her time in town did not appeal to her at all. Would she have any say regarding where she resided? And if she chose to move to the country when the Season ended, would her husband come with her?

Misery filled her.

It had shocked her when Annie had told her that her mother requested Lucy's presence in the drawing room, and she had found previous suitors present. She had gone straight to Mama and told her that these gentlemen should leave immediately, especially because she was now betrothed and would be a married woman in less than a day. Mama had laughed, telling Lucy to enjoy this afternoon and the many flower arrangements which had arrived, then gone off to speak to an earl and two viscounts.

Not wanting to appear rude, Lucy had joined some of her suitors, who kept up a constant conversation, not even allowing her to insert into the conversation that she had become betrothed at last night's musicale. Apparently, none of the visitors here had been present last night, so not a one knew she was no longer on the Marriage Mart.

Then she spied Con and Lord Huntsberry enter the drawing room. Her betrothed's face darkened in anger as he scanned the room, seeing the many callers she and Mama entertained.

"Out!" he shouted, causing all conversation to cease.

"Beg pardon, my lord?" the earl next to her asked.

"Leave now," Huntsberry demanded, crossing the room until he reached her. Possessively, he slipped an arm about her waist. "My betrothed and I have important matters to discuss."

"Betrothed, you say," said a baron whose name she could never recall. "Why, this is the first I am hearing about it."

Those present murmured as Lord Huntsberry glared at them. Suitors started rising, telling her mother goodbye and then her. One cheeky earl said, "I suppose I won't be asking for a dance at tonight's ball, Lady Lucy."

"Out!" her fiancé repeated, and Lucy could feel the heat of his anger coming off him in waves.

Once the final gentleman exited the drawing room, he turned to her. "Enjoy entertaining your many beaux, my lady?"

His tone was sarcastic, something she had never associated with the marquess. It caused tears to spring to her eyes.

"Let her be, Huntsberry," Mama said. "After all, it was her last afternoon to enjoy being the center of attention."

He turned to Mama. "So, this was your idea to allow my betrothed to entertain a bevy of suitors?"

Her mother shrugged. "I cannot help it if my daughter is popular. And they now know she is no longer eligible to be courted."

"I would speak to my fiancée now. Alone," the marquess said, his arm remaining about her. Lucy couldn't help but be drawn to his warmth and masculine scent.

When Mama started to protest, Con interrupted. "They are engaged to be married tomorrow morning, Mama," he said in a placating tone. "Let them have some time together."

Her brother led Mama from the drawing room. Lord Huntsberry seemed to visibly relax once they were gone.

"Might we sit, my lady?" he asked, leading her to a settee.

"I am sorry you witnessed that. I was trying to announce my new status." She gave him a rueful smile. "But I noticed just how much these other men talked. They did not let me get in a word edgewise. I had thought I had been making conversation each afternoon and learning something about my suitors, when all along, they were learning nothing about me."

His face relaxed some, and relief swept through her. "Was it that bad? I have never called upon a lady during the Season, so I have not a clue what goes on in a drawing room."

"Usually, they only come in small groups of three or four and stay a short while." She paused. "I believe that Mama actually instructed our butler to let them all inside the drawing room at once." Shaking her head, Lucy added lightly, "I think since Mama knew you would be here for the marriage settlements, she wanted you to see the jewel you are getting."

Looking at her solemnly, he took her hand and brought it to his lips, kissing it gently. "You are a jewel. A rare lady full of grace and compassion. I am only sorry your choice in the matter was removed from you."

She sighed. "I was the foolish one, my lord. I believed the lies of a known rakehell. Girls talk in retiring rooms, and I had heard gossip regarding Lord Eaton and Lord Humley. If I had not been so worried about Mama's health, I would have easily discerned it was a trap."

He continued holding her hand, which proved to be pleasant. "You are innocent in all of this, Lucy."

She noticed he called her by her given name and it reminded her that he had done so last night, as well.

"I am only sorry you were dragged into such a horrible scheme. I went to school with Eaton and Humley. They were despicable then and are even worse now."

Though Lucy wanted to ask him about why Lord Eaton would try and exact some kind of revenge upon the marquess years after their schooldays, she was hesitant to ask.

He squeezed her hand. "It is not only that pair who is to blame. I should have left you in that library and gone to fetch your mother so that she could have comforted you. For that, I will never forgive myself. That—and kissing you."

She felt her cheeks heat, thinking about the kind of kissing they had done.

"I doubt I would have let you go, my lord. I was shaking all over. I would have been terrified being left alone."

"Even so, I took advantage of the situation. I never should have kissed you."

Lucy eyed him steadily. "Do you regret having done so?"

His gaze met hers. "Only because it forced your hand." The marquess sighed. "I had some foolish notion that I was helping you."

"By kissing me?" she asked, not following his logic.

"You were terribly upset. I thought you would swear off all men and flee to the country, negating your Season. I worried that you would never let a man kiss you again because you were now afraid of it."

Understanding filled her. "So, you thought if you gave me a true, pleasant kiss, I would calm. That Lord Eaton would not have won."

"Exactly," He released her hand, raking his hair. "Instead, Lady Billingsley saw us."

"You know her, don't you?" she asked softly. "She seemed intent on hurting you."

He shook his head. "Not really." He cleared his throat. "This is an uncomfortable matter to discuss, even with my future wife."

Lucy waited him out, determined to learn of their connection.

Finally, he said, "Lady Billingsley is a widow. Her elderly husband left her a fortune, and she has used her freedom as a widow to . . . make her way through Polite Society."

"You are telling me that she is known for taking lovers."

He winced. "Yes."

"And she asked you to become hers."

"She did. I had no interest in her offer and told her so in no uncertain terms." He shook his head. "I suppose I could have let her down more gently, but I was shocked by how brazen she was."

"And she found a way to retaliate against you last night. You hurt her—and she wished to hurt you."

"I suppose so."

"Well, it isn't all bad. You will not have to peruse the Marriage Mart anymore," she teased. "At least that is over and done. Though I am sorry that the situation caused an end of your association with Lady Harriet."

"Lady Harriet bored the hell out of me."

Lucy didn't know which shocked her more. His profanity—or his admission about Lady Harriet.

"Then why were you paying attention to her?"

He shrugged. "I thought she would make for a good wife."

She unraveled his logic. "Oh. I see. As a lady out for several Seasons, Lady Harriet would be grateful for an offer of marriage. She would allow you to do as you wished."

"Isn't that what marriage is about within the *ton*?"

Hurt filled her. She knew most marriages in Polite Society were arranged ones. Lucy had hoped things would be different for her and her husband, though. It seemed she had been wrong about that.

"What are our plans?" she asked, changing topics. "After we wed."

"Do we need any?" he responded. "Oh, I suppose you are referring to a honeymoon."

"No, I do not need to be taken anywhere. I merely wondered if we would continue to attend events together."

"I don't see why not. You have only been out for two weeks. The Season continues through the end of summer. Perhaps you can still enjoy yourself. Make some new friends. You will always be able to spend time with your cousin."

"Yes, I would like that. Why, I have yet to attend the theater or even the opera."

"I have seats at some of the theaters. We can go anytime you like."

"Truly? I have always wanted to attend a play. Con, Dru, and I used to put on some for our servants. I would love to see a play in person."

"We can look at what is being offered, and you may choose which ones you wish to see."

"Will . . . will you escort me, my lord?"

His gaze pinned hers. "I am your husband. It is my duty to do so. Let me know what play or social event you wish to attend. I will take you to everything you desire."

"I appreciate that, my lord." She lowered her gaze, still unsure about so much with this man. A man she would be spending the rest of her life with. A man she would be intimate with. A man who would be the father of her children.

He took her chin in his hand, raising it until their eyes met. "We are to be husband and wife, Lucy. It is time you call me Judson. At least when we are in private."

Licking her lips, she tried it out. "Judson." She liked how it sounded, so much that she repeated it again. "Judson."

He laughed softly. "Thank you."

Confused, she asked, "For what?"

"You could have railed at me for getting us into such a mess. Instead, you have taken things in stride." He hesitated. "I hope I will not disappoint you."

"I hope not to disappoint you."

He rose abruptly. "I should be going. You must have much to do in order to be ready for tomorrow. Might I ask if you are bringing your lady's maid with you?"

"I am. Annie has always been destined to accompany me to my new household."

"My housekeeper, Mrs. Clippman, inquired if you would. She is preparing a room for Annie, as well as readying the marchioness' rooms for you."

It had yet to strike her, but she *would* be a marchioness, a very high position in Polite Society. Not only that, but her quick marriage would also cause her to be an object of gossip, especially if Lady Billingsley's tongue had wagged too much.

Judson helped Lucy to her feet. He brought her hand to his lips and kissed it tenderly.

"Until tomorrow. If you have need of anything before then, simply send me a note and I will see to it."

"Might I have my things delivered to your townhouse during the wedding breakfast?"

"Of course. Do have you have other things at your parents' home in the country?"

"I do. Some clothes and books. A few sentimental items. But that is in Somerset." She paused. "Perhaps we might go there at some point? I would like you to meet Dru and see where I grew up."

Judson stiffened. "We will see. In the meantime, if you need any of your belongings from there, I can send a servant to Somerset to retrieve them."

He had changed so quickly, from being kind and warm to suddenly distant.

"No, there is nothing I require from Marleyfield that cannot be brought at a later time," she told him.

Leaning down, he pressed a soft kiss against her cheek. Lucy wished for a better kiss, but she kept that to herself. Hopefully, there would be plenty of time for kisses—and more—tomorrow night.

"I will see you at the Aldridge townhouse tomorrow morning," he promised before taking his leave.

Lucy sat again, pondering their conversation. She still had no idea if he would wish to remain in town as he always did or if he might agree to open his country house and come with her. She tried to picture them arriving at events, acting as husband and wife. Also, at some point, she wanted to discover why Lord Eaton despised Judson so much.

And then there was the wedding night itself. Ariadne had sent a note earlier today, saying that she would come for tea this afternoon because she wanted to help Lucy understand a bit about what lay ahead in the marriage bed. Obviously, kissing was involved. If the kisses Judson had given her last night were any indication, she would very much like what was in store in her future.

For now, though, her betrothed remained an enigma to her.

CHAPTER THIRTEEN

L UCY AWOKE, THINKING it was the last time she would do so as an unmarried lady. She lay in bed, thinking how radically her life would change in the next few hours.

She had yet to write her sister this Season. Dru had told her that she knew Lucy would be busy and that writing would be unnecessary unless she did become betrothed. Of course, Lucy had thought her wedding would happen either at the end of the Season or in Somerset itself this coming autumn, and she had anticipated Dru would be present to witness the ceremony. With the speed of the wedding, however, her sister would be left out of the festivities.

She didn't even know what to write. At this point, all she could tell Dru was that her groom was incredibly handsome. That he kissed remarkably well. And that she knew very little about him beyond that. Lucy was still uncomfortable with the fact that Lord Huntsberry never even visited his country estate.

Would they lead separate lives, as so many wedded couples in the *ton* did?

The answer to that question made her fearful.

Instead, she wrote a brief letter to her cousins, informing Lia and Tia of her upcoming nuptials and pointing out the coincidence that Ariadne and Julian's country estate in Surrey abutted that of her new husband's. She omitted the fact that the marquess never went there. Knowing the twins had spent last Christmas with Ariadne and Julian, there was a possibility they might do so again and expect to see a lot of Lucy and Lord Huntsberry.

No, Judson. She needed to honor his request and start thinking about him that way. The name fit him well. It was strong. Commanding. She would say proud, as well, but she knew so little about the man she would wed today that she could not even say that about him.

She rang for Annie, and the maid appeared.

"We'll get you ready in a simple gown, my lady," the servant said cheerfully. "After all, your wedding gown has been sent over to Lady Aldridge's. I think that's right smart for you to get ready there since that's where the wedding will be. I'll wait and dress your hair there, too. No sense in mussing it when you change gowns for the ceremony."

After Lucy was dressed, she gave the letter to Annie to post.

"I'll see it gets taken care of right away, my lady. I'll be back soon with some breakfast for you. Just a little something to tide you over until after the ceremony."

Lucy paced her bedchamber, her nerves increasing as she did so. Relief filled her when Annie returned with tea and toast. A good cup of hot tea would settle her down.

But would it change the misgivings that continued to plague her?

She accompanied Annie downstairs, where Julian's carriage conveyed them to the Aldridge townhouse. Once Annie finished helping Lucy prepare, the maid would return and finish packing Lucy's things, seeing them brought to Judson's townhouse this morning.

After she bathed, Annie dressed Lucy with care, finishing with an elaborate hairstyle which complimented the simplicity and elegance of her wedding gown. At the last moment, she had rebelled against the dress Mama had wished for Lucy to wear and sent this one to her cousin's. She had decided it was her special day, and she should wear the gown of her choice. While Mama would no doubt be upset, she would never interrupt the ceremony and demand that her daughter change. After it ended, Lucy would be a married woman, and Mama would never be able to tell her again what to do or say. That would certainly be an advantage to being married.

Lucy hugged her maid. "Thank you so much, Annie. Not only for preparing me for my wedding today but also accompanying me to a new household. It must be hard for you to leave your friends behind."

"I couldn't let you go off by yourself, my lady. I'll always take care of you. You can count on me."

She cherished those words. She might be going to a strange house, but Lucy would always have Annie by her side, and that was a great comfort.

A light tap sounded at the door, and Ariadne entered. Her cousin's slow smile spread across her face, assuring Lucy that she looked her best.

Coming toward her, Ariadne said, "My, Lucy. You make for a most beautiful bride. I would embrace you, but I do not wish to muss you in any way. Come, let us have a seat and talk a bit."

Annie left the room, and they took the two chairs by the window. Lucy had mixed emotions about the topic they were going to discuss. Her cousin had come for tea yesterday, which was only to be the two of them. Instead, Mama had come in and taken over the conversation, and Ariadne had not had time to share with Lucy about what marriage consisted of.

"Although I do not know Aunt Charlotte well, I doubt she has prepared you for your wedding night," Ariadne began. "Is this true?"

"As I mentioned before, Mama is all about appearance. I have two lovely new night rails to wear. Beyond that, Mama simply said I was to do everything Lord Huntsberry asks of me."

Her cousin was silent a moment and then said, "I know you have kissed Judson because that is what led to you being here today. Did you enjoy his kiss?"

Lucy answered honestly. "Very much so. He is the only man

I have kissed, and I must say, he is most skilled at it. His kisses made my heart flutter wildly in my chest." She hesitated and then added, "I want more of them."

Ariadne nodded. "That is a very good start. Passion in a marriage will strengthen your bonds."

Over the next several minutes, her cousin explained several eye-opening things. Lucy drank them all in, having had no idea about relations between a husband and wife. She had not known she would remove all her clothing to make love and worried what Judson would think of her body. She was still trying to understand the mechanics of everything, but Ariadne assured her instinct would take over.

"Judson will know you come to him as a virgin, and he will be tender toward you. I believe he will take very good care of you, Lucy. Not just tonight—but in all the nights to come."

"Do I . . . go to him? Or does he come to me? How often do we couple?"

"That is something which the two of you will have to decide. Julian and I are different from most couples within the *ton*. They keep to their own rooms. I only use mine as a dressing room because I spend all my nights in my husband's bed."

Hearing that shocked Lucy to her core. She could not imagine her parents ever spending a night together. In fact, it surprised her that they had come together enough to produce their three children.

"If you have any questions in the future, feel free to talk about them with me. Or better yet, talk over any concerns or questions you have with Judson."

She was still getting used to the idea of the two of them shedding their clothes and being together in an intimate fashion for lovemaking. Lucy felt the blood rush to her cheeks in embarrassment, thinking how awkward it would be to ask Judson any question. After all, Ariadne and Julian were a love match. She and her intended were the exact opposite.

Perhaps not total opposites. She did know a little bit about him, whereas many girls who become betrothed knew little to nothing of their husbands-to-be. Arranged marriages were still common amongst the members of Polite Society. At least her parents had not promised her to a stranger. She believed Judson would always be honest with her, which was very important to her. Now, she wondered if he would also be faithful to her. It had not occurred to her to ask if he had a mistress, much less if he would keep a mistress after his marriage. Lucy could not fathom bringing up such a topic with him, wed or not.

She felt a rising panic beginning to grow within her. Her heart started beating madly. Her head swam. Suddenly, she realized she was making a terrible mistake.

"I do not think I can go through with this!" she cried, leaping to her feet.

Ariadne rose and put her arms about Lucy. "You do not need to be nervous. I believe Judson is a good man, and he will take care of you."

"This is wrong," she said, shaking her head. "All wrong. I must speak to him. Now. I cannot wed him."

Her cousin studied her a moment. "All right. I will send him to you."

Once alone, Lucy began pacing the bedchamber, her breathing erratic. Mama would think it the height of impropriety, Lucy being alone with Judson in a bedchamber before they spoke their vows. She did not care.

She could not go through with this marriage.

A knock sounded at the door. Lucy rushed over and opened it.

Judson stood before her, his expression grim. He had never looked more handsome than he did now, and Lucy knew what she would say would upset him.

"Come in," she told him, stepping aside so he could enter. Once he did so, she closed the door, not wanting anyone to overhear their conversation.

Facing him, she found her mouth dry and was unable to

speak. He took her hands in his, and she realized how cold hers were.

"You are having doubts, Lucy?"

She nodded mutely.

"I think it is only natural that we both have some."

"You also have doubts about our union?" she asked.

He said, "Yes. I fear I am ruining your life. Forcing you into a marriage you do not want. But what choice do we have?"

"We can call it off. I know you warned me of how it would damage my reputation and that of my family, but I do not want to hurt you. You told me from the start that you had no interest in me. Now, you are being leg-shackled to me for a lifetime. I simply cannot do that to you, Judson. I won't."

He released her hands, framing her face with his hands, and looked at her almost lovingly.

"Lucy, the reason I did not pursue you was because I wanted to."

Frowning, she told him, "Your words confuse me. Explain yourself, Judson."

Slowly, his thumbs caressed her cheeks, making her dizzy.

"I have always been drawn to you, Lucy. I was attracted to you from the start. But I told you there is a darkness in my soul, and I did not want to dim your bright light."

"You truly like me?" she asked, tears misting her eyes.

Judson smiled. "Quite a bit. I knew you would have a bevy of suitors wooing you. I wanted better for you, Lucy. I am only sorry you are stuck with me and not happy being with one of them."

His words changed everything. He did like her. He was attracted to her. Perhaps he even had feelings for her, which he had yet to admit. She still did not know what created this darkness in him which he spoke of, but she was determined now to wed this man—and make him happy. He seemed so lonely. So hungry for affection.

"I will wed you, Judson. I will be a good wife to you."

"I know you will, little love."

Hearing the endearment caused a warmth to fill her, that warmth pushing aside any doubts she had about this man.

"You should return downstairs," she suggested. "I will come when I am summoned."

He bent and lightly brushed his lips against hers. The gesture held no passion, but it did reassure her.

"I will see you shortly," he told her, exiting the bedchamber.

Calm now, Lucy also became determined to fight Judson's demons alongside him. Ariadne was right. The Marquess of Huntsberry was a good man. He merely needed a little assistance in discovering that for himself.

And she would be the one to make certain that he did.

Ariadne came to her, saying, "It is time." She took Lucy's hands in hers. "Is this what you truly wish for? To go through with the ceremony? If not, Julian can tell the others to leave."

"No," Lucy said, resolve filling her. "I am most eager to wed Lord Huntsberry. I believe that not only is he a gentleman, but he also sincerely cares for me and my well-being." She paused. "And I think that I will be able to bring out the best in him, Ariadne."

Her cousin smiled in relief. "That is good to hear. I have high hopes for this match. Come. The others are waiting. Let us see you wed."

Ariadne walked with her to the drawing room, where Papa stood waiting at the entrance.

Smiling, he said, "You look so very lovely, Lucy. Lord Huntsberry is a fortunate man to be wedding my daughter."

She had always been amused how Papa called her Lucilla whenever he was in Mama's company. If the two of them were alone, however, she was always Lucy to him.

"I believe we are both fortunate, Papa. I am looking forward to marrying the marquess."

Her father led her into the drawing room and across its length. Lucy saw Mama standing with Con, and Ariadne was next to Julian. Besides the vicar, she also noticed another man whom she wasn't familiar with, one who smiled broadly at her. Her gaze, though, quickly turned to her groom, who stood straight and tall. Judson smiled gently at her, and Lucy was at peace with her decision to wed him.

CHAPTER FOURTEEN

J UDSON HELD HIS breath as Lucy and Lord Marley moved toward him. She was a vision of loveliness, absolutely the most beautiful woman he had ever seen.

And she would be his . . .

He had worried that might not come to pass, especially after Ariadne sought him out and explained to him that Lucy was having a bad case of nerves. She had instructed Judson to go to Lucy, who was agitated and restless. After they spoke, though, she calmed down. It had taken him admitting that he was attracted to her before she did so. If Judson hadn't done that, he doubted he would be waiting for her to speak their vows together.

It was terrible that she had lost her choice in this matter, thanks to Eaton. Banishing him to the country, along with his cohort, wasn't good enough. At some point, Judson knew he would have to deal with his enemy in a more permanent fashion. The fact that Eaton had tried to corrupt Lucy and ruin her simply because he despised Judson made him seethe with anger. It would take much thought, but Eaton and his companion would need to pay for destroying Lucy's future.

They reached him now, and the smile she bestowed upon Judson was radiant. Even his cold, hard heart melted a little at it. Lucy was so vibrant. Sweet. Caring. It would be a wonderful thing that she would be the mother of his children. She would teach them well. He would not have to worry about them being unkind or spoiled. Lucy would see to that.

He still planned to keep his distance from her, though. Wanting her wasn't enough. He had already deprived Lucy of wedding a good man, one who might even love her. Since he could never give her the love she deserved, it would best to stay away from her as much as possible. She had a large family who would constantly surround and support her. Judson would do his duty and then give Lucy the space she needed. He could even see her working with Ariadne at the orphanage.

The vicar, reading from *The Book of Common Prayer*, began the ceremony. Judson had never been to a wedding, having no friends and family, and so he was hearing these words for the first time. He understood this ceremony would be not only legally but spiritually binding.

Lord Marley handed his daughter off to Judson, and Lucy now stood beside him, just the two of them. The scent of lavender was present, as usual, and he would never inhale it without thinking of his wife.

His wife . . .

Just thinking of Lucy as his marchioness caused him a moment of panic. He ignored it, knowing he had to be stoic for her. If he crumbled, the entire thing would fall apart, and her reputation would be forever ruined. Instead, he concentrated on the words the vicar spoke. They each repeated certain parts of the ceremony to one another, and Judson knew he would not take these vows lightly. He might not love Lucy—or be the best man for her—but he would never forsake her for another. The Lady Billingsleys of the *ton* could leap off a cliff as far as he was concerned.

The clergyman indicated for Julian to hand Judson Lucy's wedding ring. He had long ago found the ring his father had given to Judson's mother, and this was the ring he had decided his bride should wear to signify their union. It was a plain, gold band. No ornamentation. Something told him Lucy would prefer this type of wedding ring over more ostentatious ones. He only hoped he was right.

Repeating after the vicar, Judson declared to those present and his bride, "With this ring I thee wed, with my body I thee worship, and with all my worldly goods I thee endow. In the Name of the Father, and of the Son, and of the Holy Ghost. Amen." He slipped the ring onto her finger.

He caught the smile on Lucy's face as she gazed down at the ring which now adorned her hand. A warm glow spread through him. Then he cursed himself for not being able to love her. Desire her, yes. He was most eager to get her into his bed. But the thing Lucy deserved the most was the exact thing Judson could never give to her. He would honor her. Respect her. Make certain she had every material possession possible.

But he could never love her. He simply had no love to give.

Suddenly, the clergyman announced they were husband and wife. He lightly brushed his lips against Lucy's and then received congratulations from those around them. The vicar pulled him aside, telling him they would need to sign the wedding registry at some point. Judson had already given the man the special license before the ceremony had begun. He promised they would do so and then rejoined his bride.

Tim stood off to the side, and he led Lucy to his valet.

"Lady Huntsberry, I would like you to meet Tim. He serves as my valet and is the most loyal friend I have."

Without hesitation, his new wife offered her hand to Tim, who looked surprised, but he took it.

"I am delighted to meet you, Tim. My husband is always turned out so well. Now, I know that it is you who keeps him in line and makes certain he can appear in public."

Tim grinned. "Nice to meet you, my lady. I'll keep doing what I can for his lordship, but I think it's your turn to keep him in line."

Lucy laughed, and pride swelled within Judson. He had fully expected her to be a bit cool to Tim, being a servant, but his bride was as welcoming to Tim as she would be the king himself.

"We should go into breakfast," Lucy said. "Ariadne is signaling me."

"I'll take my leave now, my lord, my lady, and let you celebrate with your family," Tim said.

"You are family, too, Tim," Lucy said. "You should join us."

"Thank you for your warm greeting, my lady, but I know my place—and it's not with the others. I will head home now." He looked to Judson. "Thank you, my lord, for inviting me to witness your marriage. You have come a long way from the young boy I knew."

"Thank you for coming, Tim," he said. "We will see you later today."

Ariadne led everyone into the breakfast room, saying, "Since we are such a small group, I thought this would make for a cozier celebration."

A buffet was set out for them, and he led his wife through it, with them being the first to partake. Everything tasted wonderful, and the conversation was lighthearted. He complimented the Aldridges and asked that they pass along his compliments to their cook for such a fine meal.

As they finished eating, a cake was rolled in atop a teacart, and everyone gasped.

"Is it from Gunter's?" Lucy asked, clearly delighted by the three-tiered cake, decorated with yellow flowers and green stems.

"It is," Ariadne confirmed. "Julian knows how you and I favor Gunter's. They bake many of the wedding cakes served in the *ton*. I thought you would be pleased they took on yours."

"Especially on such short notice," Lucy marveled. "Oh, it is a wonderful gift. Thank you, Julian, for thinking of it. And you, Ariadne, for hosting our wedding and breakfast."

"Yes," Judson said, speaking up. "I know we did not give you much time to prepare for it, but everything has been absolutely perfect."

They talked for another hour, lingering over tea and cake,

and then Ariadne said, "We do not wish to keep you, Judson."

He knew that was her polite way of sending them and the other guests along their way.

"Will you be at tonight's ball?" Lady Marley asked.

Lucy frowned. "No, Mama. We will celebrate our wedding day privately. There is no sense in attending a ball when there are still so many of them left in the remainder of the Season."

"I see," Lady Marley said, her disapproval evident.

He was glad his wife had spoken up to her mother. Lady Marley was far too domineering, and he did not want Lucy to ever be under the woman's thumb again.

Everyone went outside, and where his carriage had been, a barouche stood in its place.

Julian came to him. "I sent your carriage home. It is such a beautiful day, I thought you might like to drive in an open carriage through the park."

Lucy clapped her hands. "Oh, what a wonderful idea, Julian. Thank you." She kissed his cheek.

"Have your coachman return it when you are done," Julian continued.

Judson handed up his wife and then climbed beside her, taking the reins. "Good day!" he called, driving the vehicle from the square and in the direction of Hyde Park.

He glanced to his bride, who had her eyes shut and her face turned up to the sun, basking in its warmth. An ache began throbbing inside him. He wanted to do right by her. Make certain that she was happy in their union, despite it being forced upon her.

She opened her eyes. "Everything about today has been perfect," she proclaimed. "I have never attended a wedding ceremony. To think my own wedding was my first!" she said, laughing.

"The same for me," he told her. "We are quite the pair."

"Yes, we are," she said, slipping her hand through his arm.

They drove through the park for an hour. It was clear of

traffic because everyone in the *ton* was calling upon others or at tea. Only in the last few minutes before they departed did they run across others in open carriages. Judson nodded politely to them but did not stop the horses to chat.

Once they arrived home, Clippman greeted them. "Lady Huntsberry, your staff is assembled and waiting for you inside the house."

"Oh, thank you so much. What is your name?"

"Clippman, my lady. Mrs. Clippman is your housekeeper."

Judson leapt from the vehicle and handed Lucy down. "Lord Aldridge's barouche will need to be returned to him, Clippman."

"Yes, my lord. I will have it done as soon as Lady Huntsberry is acquainted with the other servants."

They went inside, and he saw his small staff lined up inside the foyer. Mrs. Clippman greeted her mistress and introduced Lucy to the rest of the servants.

"Annie has already settled into her room," the housekeeper said. "She is in the marchioness' rooms now, seeing to your wardrobe, my lady."

"Thank you, Mrs. Clippman."

"Would it be convenient for you to meet with me tomorrow morning, my lady?" the housekeeper asked. "Much of the house has been closed off until recently. I assume you will want it opened up."

"Yes, I will," Lucy replied. "I believe we will need to hire more servants, though." She looked to Judson.

"Do whatever you need to run this household the way you see fit, my lady. If you wish for furnishings or curtains to be replaced, that is your prerogative. You are now mistress of this house, and I want you to make it comfortable for you so that you view it as your home."

"Thank you, Huntsberry," she said, her eyes sparkling. Glancing back to the housekeeper, she added, "We can tour the house tomorrow at ten o'clock, Mrs. Clippman. I wish to see it from top to bottom. I will also want to meet with Cook and discuss this week's menus with her."

"Yes, my lady," Mrs. Clippman said, clearly understanding now who was in charge.

"For now, I wish to see my rooms. If you would have Cook prepare a small supper for us, we should like to be served in an hour's time. Somewhere other than the dining room. That is too large for the two of us."

"I would suggest the winter parlor, my lady, but it needs a bit of tidying up. Perhaps the breakfast room?"

Lucy nodded firmly. "Yes, that will do nicely. Thank you, Mrs. Clippman."

"Let me take you to your rooms," Judson offered, guiding her up the stairs.

"Was I too firm?" she asked. "I wanted your servants to realize that though I am young, I do know how to run a household. Please, give me your honest opinion."

"You were perfect," he told her. "They will come to adore you."

She giggled. "Mr. Clippman is so very proper. And Mrs. Clippman looked as if she were hiding that her nose was slightly out of joint."

"She has been the housekeeper ever since my father's days. Since my mother died giving birth to me, Mrs. Clippman is really the only feminine hand the house has known for almost thirty years."

Lucy stopped, squeezing his arm in sympathy. "Judson, I am so sorry. I did not know that."

"It's neither here nor there," he said brusquely.

"No, do not brush it off. Or me," she told him. "Not having a mother is very sad. I am sorry you never knew her. Moreover, I am sorry she did not live to see the good man you have become."

He didn't feel especially good. It was what his father had wanted of him, but Judson had failed miserably to live up to that. He had been vengeful. Cold. Dispassionate. He saw nothing good in him.

Yet this woman did. His wife. His throat grew thick with emotion. "Come. I want you to see your rooms."

They arrived, and he led her through the suite, trying to view things through her eyes.

"It is obvious no woman has lived here for a very long time," she finally said. "The wallpaper is faded. The carpeting thin. The rooms are crowded with too much furniture." She smiled brightly. "But all of that is easy to remedy."

"I meant what I said. You can make any changes to this house that will please you. Strip every room. Bring in painters or carpenters or whomever. You can purchase new furniture. Art. Whatever you wish to make this your home."

"I am grateful you trust my judgment, Judson. I will make some changes, but I would like to share those with you before I do so."

He did not want to spend hours with her, looking at samples of wallpaper or carpeting. Judson needed to spend as little time as possible with Lucy because he did not want her to grow too attached to him.

Nor him to her.

"No," he said firmly. "The household is your domain. You are to make all the decisions. You are its mistress. I will be happy with whatever you alter."

Disappointment flashed in her eyes, but she hid it quickly. "Very well."

She moved through the sitting room into the bedchamber, where her lady's maid was still unpacking.

"Finding a place for everything, my lady," the servant said. "Good evening, my lord. I'm Annie."

"It is good to meet you, Annie. I hope Mrs. Clippman and the other servants have made you feel welcome."

"They have, my lord. I look forward to living in your household."

He looked at his bride. "I will come for you in an hour's time. We can dine then."

Judson left her, returning to his own rooms, where he found Tim waiting for him.

"She's a keeper, my lord," Tim praised. "Did you see how kind she was to me? Didn't bat an eye when she heard I was your valet. Was just as nice as she could be."

"Yes, my wife is very kind," he agreed. "She is wanting to make some changes to the house, though. Help her in any way you can."

"I certainly will, my lord."

Judson called for his wife at the appointed time, and he escorted her downstairs to the breakfast room. Cook had prepared a cold supper for them, consisting of chicken, cheese, bread, fruit, and wine. He sent Clippman away after the butler uncorked the wine, not wanting the servant hovering nearby and hearing every word of their conversation.

"Do you often dismiss your servants?" Lucy asked. "I rather like having a bit of privacy."

He poured her a glass of wine. "Not usually. But I saw no need for him to stay and wait on us."

She drank her wine but merely nibbled at the chicken and ate a few grapes. Judson decided that she was growing wary of what lie ahead.

They finished dining, and he took her back up to her rooms. Pausing outside them, he said, "I know you are weary. It has been a long day. A rather long few days, truth be told. I will bid you goodnight."

"You . . . are not joining me? Or will you send for me later this evening?" she asked, concern obvious in her voice.

Facing her, he said, "No. I will have no need of you tonight."

She bit her lip, a habit he'd noticed. "Have I done something wrong, Judson? Angered you in some way?"

He placed his hands on her shoulders. "Not at all. But you must understand, Lucy, that what we have is not the love match of your cousin and her husband. This is a marriage of convenience. In truth, we are practically strangers and know little about one another. Giving yourself to me is an intimate act. One that should not occur until we do know one another better."

"But we are husband and wife," she protested.

"We are. I have a copy of the marriage settlements for you to read. In them, you will see how well I have taken care of you and any children we might have. Your future is secure, even after I am gone, and any daughters we have will receive ample dowries. Any sons beyond the heir apparent will also be financially secure."

Judson paused. "I told your brother I would be a good husband to you, and I do not accept those responsibilities lightly. I want you to know you will have everything you need. You will want for nothing. But we are not and never will be a love match. I will do my duty and come to your bed when the time is right because I know how much you want children.

"For now, though, I think it best to wait until we are more comfortable and know one another a little better."

He kissed her brow. "Sleep well."

Knowing she wanted more from him—and knowing he couldn't give it to her right now—Judson walked away. His desire for her grew stronger each time he was in her presence, but he must temper it. He did not want her to confuse passion and desire for love, and Lucy was innocent enough to make that mistake.

Judson entered his own rooms and stripped off his clothes, not bothering to ring for Tim. He got into bed.

And lay awake for a long time.

CHAPTER FIFTEEN

LUCY ENTERED HER rooms, numbness filling her.
Judson had rejected her.

She moved as if in a dream through her sitting room and entered the large bedchamber designated for the marchioness. Annie sat in a chair and immediately sprang to her feet.

"We need to get you ready for his lordship, my lady."

Glancing to the bed, she saw one of the new, delicate night rails laid out upon it. She wanted to protest and tell Annie there was no need to place it on her tonight.

Because her husband did not want her.

The words wouldn't come, however, and Lucy responded as a doll, allowing Annie to undress her and dress her in the night rail. The maid had her sit at the dressing table as she unpinned the elaborate hairstyle, chattering away. Lucy never said a word.

Annie began brushing Lucy's long tresses, but instead of plaiting her hair, as usual, the servant left it unbound.

With a wink, Annie said, "His lordship will probably favor your hair this way, my lady." Then the servant stopped, misreading Lucy's expression. She placed her hands on her mistress' shoulders as their gazes met in the mirror. "No need to worry, my lady. Lord Huntsberry will take good care of you. I know your mama may not have told you much about what is to come, but it will be fine."

Weakly, she said, "Thank you, Annie. I will see you in the morning."

The lady's maid squeezed Lucy's shoulders in reassurance, and Annie left the bedchamber.

Lucy went to the bed, which Annie had turned back for her. She crawled into it, pulling the bedclothes over her. Then the tears came. She wanted no one to hear her despair and sobbed into the pillow until it was soaked with her tears.

She had never been more dejected in her life.

She lost track of time, lying in the dark, misery filling her. As Lucy stared up at the ceiling, though, anger began to rise within her. Judson had told her she was the marchioness and in charge of this house. She decided it was time to exercise her authority.

Rising from the bed, she washed her face, hoping it would help reduce the swelling about her eyes. She had not bothered to extinguish the candle when she climbed into bed, and so she took it now with her as she entered her dressing room. Beyond it stood a bathing chamber, which she was to share with her new husband. Ariadne had shocked Lucy, telling her there might even be times when she would wish to bathe with Judson. Knowing he was a few doors away, she gathered her courage and opened the door on the far side of the bathing chamber, entering his dressing room.

Immediately, she caught a whiff of his cologne. Lucy froze, doubt filling her.

Was she mad to confront him?

She had already come this far, however. Turning back was not an option. Pushing open the final door, she entered his bedchamber, knowing he was on the other side. The room was flooded with moonlight, and she realized the curtains had not been drawn. She almost stumbled over clothing scattered about the floor, deciding he had not bothered to ring for Tim after they had parted.

Approaching the bed, she saw her groom lying in it. He was bare to the waist, the bedclothes covering the rest of him, and she wondered if he slept in the nude. She moved closer to the bed and couldn't help but admire his broad, muscled chest and arms.

Arms she had thought would be wrapped around her by this point.

His eyes flicked open, meeting hers, surprise in them.

"What are doing in here?" he asked, his tone harsh.

She flinched but gathered her courage and came to the bedside, setting down her candle.

"I am here because we need to consummate our union to be officially wed."

Something flickered in his eyes. Something she didn't quite understand, but it drew her in.

"I thought we were going to wait until we knew one another a little better before doing so."

"There was no *we* in that decision, my lord. *You* decided it for the both of us—and I do not agree with your decision."

His eyes darkened now, and her husband looked at her with hunger. She decided it was desire in his eyes. Playing on that, she told him, "I know you want me. I am here, Judson. I am yours for the taking."

He moved so quickly, it was as if he were a blur. Suddenly, he was out of the bed, standing next to her, those powerful arms encircling her, drawing her close. His kiss was not gentle, but Lucy did not want gentle.

She wanted fire.

Wrapping her arms about him, she felt the immense heat coming off him in waves, easily radiating through her thin night rail.

He kissed her the way he had in the library that night. She had learned enough from him to respond, kissing him back. Judson deepened the kiss, a growl low in his throat, and she knew she had made the right decision to come to him. Lucy realized her husband had no one in his life before her. No friends beyond Tim. No family. No one to love him.

She would change that. Because her heart told her in this moment that she did love this man.

Judson scooped her up and placed her gently on the bed. He

gazed down upon her a moment, and Lucy was able to see all of him. His manhood jutted straight out from a nestle of dark curls, and she swallowed, feeling a bit intimidated by its size. Thank goodness Ariadne had told her some of what to expect in lovemaking.

He slipped into the bed next to her and huskily asked, "Are you certain you wish for us to do this, Lucy?"

"Yes."

He kissed her softly, the heated kisses from moments ago now gone. She didn't understand how his passion could cool so quickly. Why he seemed to pull back. She would have asked him, but his mouth continued a series of soft kisses, placating her momentarily.

From what Ariadne had mentioned, he was supposed to remove her night rail, but he didn't do so. Instead, he took the hem of it and raised it some, his hand beneath it to caress her leg. His fingers danced up her calf and then her thigh. Already, her core pounded unmercifully, begging for his touch. She knew his fingers would reach it soon.

When he slowly raked one along the seam of her sex, Lucy gasped.

Breaking the kiss, Judson said, "I must make certain you are ready before we couple."

She didn't ask how he would do that—because she trusted him.

He pushed a finger inside her, causing her to mewl like a kitten.

"This will help prepare you," he told her, his lips close to her ear.

His finger stroked her, causing tension to coil within her. Another one joined it, and he continued these deep caresses, murmuring into her ear, "You are almost ready. You are wet for me, Lucy. It will make things easier."

Then a pressure built within her. It suddenly erupted, a new sensation which caused her to cry out his name. She bucked against his hand, feeling warmth spread throughout her, culminating in a final peak of pleasure.

"What was that?" she asked, breathless.

He didn't reply. By now, Judson hovered over her, hiking her night rail to her waist. Then she felt the tip of his manhood where his fingers had been. With one, powerful thrust, he entered her. She was startled by the quickness of it, and the momentary flash of pain.

He stilled. "Get used to me."

Lucy looked into his eyes, but he averted his gaze. Then he began moving, slowly at first, and she picked up on his rhythm. Her hips rose and fell in a kind of dance between them. Judson increased the speed of his thrusts, and that wonderful, incredible feeling of a few minutes ago began building inside her again. Anticipation flooded her, and she wrapped her arms about him, holding onto him tightly.

Suddenly, they both cried out in unison, the new sensations flooding her. Her husband collapsed atop her for a moment, and Lucy reveled in the weight of him. The musky scent of him. The feel of them joined together as one.

Quickly, he pulled out of her and left the bed, pouring water into a basin and bringing it and a cloth back to the bed. In an intimate gesture, he washed her.

Judson returned the basin to its stand and came to her again. Taking her hands, he lifted her from the bed and set her on her feet. Kissing her brow, he said, "Go back to your bed, Lucy."

Disappointment flooded her. She didn't know quite what she had expected, but it wasn't this abrupt ending.

Her husband reached for the candle and handed it to her. Numb again, Lucy made her way back to her own bedchamber. This time, she blew out the candle before she climbed into bed. She remained awake for a long time, going over everything that had happened between them, again and again. Instinct told her that Judson had held back. Yes, he had kissed her passionately at first, but she thought it was because he had not been expecting her to appear in his room. Once he gained control of himself and found she wasn't going anywhere, it seemed he had done his duty, keeping himself at a distance.

Yes, he had given her pleasure, as Ariadne had spoken of, but even he had told her it was to make their coupling go more smoothly. To her, it seemed there had been none of the tenderness her cousin had talked about, beyond the way he had cared for her afterward. Her cousin had mentioned that her new husband would explore her body, and she would do the same. That had not occurred. Judson did his marital duty—and no more.

A deep ache filled her now. She had enjoyed their lovemaking, but Lucy believed there was much more to it. Perhaps he had been right in saying they didn't know each other well. Over time, she hoped to explore the hard planes of his body and wished he would do the same with her.

A thought struck her. She was a lady of the *ton*, and perhaps Judson kept her at a distance and didn't ask certain things of her because she was a lady. Would he now go to his mistress, if he had one, to find complete satisfaction? How was she to tell him she was ready to explore this new, sensual world with him, eager to do anything he asked?

Lucy fretted now. Instead of enjoying the feelings of euphoria her husband had brought to her, she was disheartened.

And it was made all the worse because she now knew she loved him.

CHAPTER SIXTEEN

J UDSON AWOKE, IMMEDIATELY angry with himself.

Why had he made love to Lucy last night?

His bride had definitely surprised him, showing up in his bedchamber last night. Especially after he had told her to go to bed. Apparently, Lucy wasn't the well-behaved girl she had told him she was. He liked how she had stood up to him. Asserted herself. For the first few minutes she was with him, Judson had let his desire for her take over. He thought back to those kisses, which caused his body to shudder.

Fortunately, he had come to his senses. He did not want to confuse his young wife. Despite the fact that she never mentioned seeking a love match, she had to have stars in her eyes after witnessing the relationship between her cousin and Aldridge. It would be natural for her to confuse passion with love. He could never have Lucy love him. He was unlovable. Unfeeling. His past had impacted his present—and the future.

He had done as she asked and made love to her in the most dull, unremarkable way possible. The wild kisses had turned sweet. Judson had kept his lips on her mouth and not anywhere on her body, which he yearned to taste. He had brought her to orgasm, though, before he entered her. He owed her a bit of pleasure and had known it would smooth the way for her when he took her virginity. For a bit, though, he had lost his head once again, being inside her, feeling the exquisite tightness of her, knowing he was the only one who had ever breached that wall.

She was his—but he didn't want her.

No, that was a lie. He did want her. Desperately. But he could not become emotionally involved with her. He must keep his distance. Judson would do his husbandly duty. Perhaps last night they had created their first child together. But he could never give her anything of himself. He only hoped she hadn't realized how he had held back. Lucy was smart, though. He wouldn't put it past her to speak to Ariadne of last night's experience. If the two women compared experiences, Lucy would know her husband had not fully given everything to her.

He threw back the bedclothes. It was a waste of time to worry about such matters. Judson had done his duty. He would continue to couple with her until she was with child. Then he would leave her be. A part of him hoped she would ask to go to the country. It would be easier on him if she did. He could remain in town and then go to see their babe once it had been born. Of course, that would mean a great deal of time would need to be spent in getting Huntsworth up to snuff. The house hadn't been inhabited in years. Though he had a caretaker looking after it, it would need a thorough cleaning from top to bottom. The house's interior would certainly need painting. Even new furniture might be required.

That thought eased his mind. If he could send Lucy to the country, she would be busy with refurbishing Huntsworth and seeing it brought back to its former glory. And hopefully, not miss him.

He rang for Tim and quickly picked up his clothes from where they lay on the ground, setting them in a chair.

Tim appeared, his mood jovial as usual. He shaved Judson and then helped him to dress. Not having a clue if Lucy had arisen, he made his way to the breakfast room.

She was already there.

"Good morning, Huntsberry," she said brightly, buttering a toast point.

"Good morning, my lady," he replied, taking the seat to her right. "I hope you slept well."

"Yes. It is always difficult getting used to a new mattress, but I was quite comfortable. Thank you for asking."

A footman poured coffee for him. Another one brought his breakfast, placing the plate on the table before him and lifting the cover. He glanced over and saw Lucy had poached eggs and bacon before her.

"What do you have planned today?" he asked.

"I will tour the house with Mrs. Clippman. Once I have seen every room and made notes of what I wish to be done, I would like to go over those with you."

"I have told you to do as you wish," he said lightly, not wanting to encourage her spending time with him.

Not backing down, his wife said, "And I have expressed how I wish you to discuss the changes with me."

Judson saw a footman bite back a smile at their exchange.

"Yes. Whenever you would like, I am happy to discuss the matter with you."

"I would like to go the garden party being hosted this afternoon."

This came out of the blue. They had not talked about when they would begin attending events together.

"I am happy to escort you," he said genially. "When does it start?"

"Two o'clock. We would need to leave here by a quarter past one."

"Then I will make certain I have returned by then."

Her brow furrowed. "Where are you going?"

He wasn't used to having to explain his actions. He supposed this was as part of marriage, but he didn't want to make a habit of it. Judson wanted to go his way and allow Lucy to go hers.

"I box several mornings a week."

Her eyes lit up. "Oh. So that is where all those muscles come from," she quipped.

This time, both footmen reacted. One coughed to cover his laugh, while the other turned his head to avoid being caught smiling by his employer.

He had no response to her comment and continued to eat his breakfast. When a footman tried to refill his cup with more coffee, Judson waved him away.

"Where do you box?" Lucy asked.

"A place called Gentleman Jack's. It is next to a fencing academy. I participate in both sports."

"I thought boxing was illegal."

"Boxing matches are. This is merely a place owned and run by a former successful boxer where gentlemen might take some exercise." He took a sip of his coffee.

"I think I would like to see you box, Huntsberry."

Judson almost spewed what was in his mouth across the table. Recovering—and swallowing—he told her, "It is not a place for ladies."

A smile played about her lips. "Then perhaps you might show me when we are in private."

Tossing his napkin onto the table, he tried to ignore the servants. "That is enough," he declared, standing and leaving the breakfast room. He had thought his new wife would be unassuming. She had always been polite and discreet. Their breakfast exchange, though, showed an entirely new side of her. One he was not going to tolerate.

Clippman followed him from the breakfast room. "Might I have your carriage readied, my lord?"

"Yes," he barked, storming off and into his study. He sat, doing nothing, until the butler let him know the carriage awaited him outside.

The coachman drove him to Bond Street, and Judson hurried from the vehicle and inside, in such a hurry that he crashed into none other than the famous Gentleman Jack himself.

"My, you're in a hurry, Huntsberry. Eager to spar today?"

He had already sparred verbally with his pretty new wife.

Judson was now ready to take out his anger on someone else since he couldn't on Lucy.

"I need a sparring partner at once, John."

"Is your marriage not to your liking, my lord? I saw the notice in the newspaper."

Being in town year-round, Judson frequently saw the former boxer. They had become friendly, and Judson even referred to him by his given name of John and not his nickname. He did not want to bite off the man's head, much less reveal the state of his marriage, and merely said, "The marriage is fine. Lady Huntsberry is beautiful and cultured."

"But you feel the need to soundly thrash someone this morning."

"That is correct."

"I'll send Jones over after you change and warm up."

He went to a room where gentlemen shed their cravats and coats. Judson stripped bare to the waist and returned to the main room. There, he attacked a heavy bag, punching it for several minutes until Jones came to him.

"Best try some of those punches on me, my lord."

They moved into one of the makeshift rings. A few other gentlemen already present set aside their own training and came to watch them spar.

Judson reined in his anger. Anger was not a boxer's friend. Boxing required a cool head and thinking several steps ahead in order to best an opponent.

Jones took several hard shots to his torso from Judson, as well as a sound punch to the nose. Despite the fact the other man was from the lower class, he did not hold back, giving as good as he got. Judson knew he would be sore tomorrow and have a few bruises to show for today's efforts.

Gentleman Jack called a halt to their sparring just as Jones threw a final punch. Judson had already lowered his wrapped fists and realized too late he could not ward off the hit. Jones' fist connected with Judson's left eye, and he stumbled back.

"Bloody hell, Jones!" the owner shouted, cursing at his worker.

"No," he said, stepping between the two men. "The shot was fair. I hold no ill will."

"I am sorry, my lord," his sparring partner said apologetically. "You're going to have a shiner."

"Get Lord Huntsberry some ice," barked Gentleman Jack. He looked around. "Nothing to see here, gentlemen. Go back to what you were doing."

The others began to move away. Judson raised a hand to his eye, touching it, finding the area tender.

"Guess you won't be going to any fancy balls with that new wife for a few days."

"I promised to take her to a garden party this afternoon."

John grinned. "Perhaps she'll change her mind when she sees you. Or leave your sorry arse at home."

The thought of Lucy going to the party without him, flirting with other men, left a sour taste in Judson's mouth.

"My apologies to Jones. I was rough on him."

John snorted. "He's a boxer. He can take whatever punishment you give." Pausing, John added, "Perhaps you should stay away from boxing for a week or so, Huntsberry. Let your wife fuss over you a bit."

That was the last thing he wished for. Still, he would respect the owner's wishes. "I will see you once the bruises have faded, John."

Returning to the dressing room, he put on the rest of his clothes. Jones showed up with some ice wrapped in a cloth, and Judson accepted it, apologizing to the boxer for the intensity of today's punches.

"I didn't mind at all, my lord. You always offer a challenge. Keep the ice on for another five minutes," Jones advised as he left the room.

Judson sat for a few more minutes and then returned to his carriage, asking to be taken home. Once he arrived, he was glad to avoid seeing Lucy. He ordered a bath be brought up and retreated to the bathing chamber. Tim appeared, with the hot water following soon after, and Judson stripped and sank into the bathing tub, soaking his already sore muscles.

"Lady Huntsberry will be concerned about your eye, my lord," Tim observed.

He shrugged. "It is a hazard of boxing."

But he knew Lucy would want to fuss over him, which was why he was relieved he hadn't run into her when he arrived home.

"Everyone likes her," Tim told him.

"That is good to hear," he said, impatience in his voice.

After that, Tim sat quietly, waiting until Judson nodded, and then the valet helped scrub away the sweat. He allowed Tim to dry and dress him and then went to his study. He wouldn't say he was hiding from Lucy. He was merely enjoying time alone.

Without warning, the door flew open. Lucy rushed in and stopped in front of the desk, her expression pained.

"Oh, it looks bad, Judson," she said, coming around the desk and bringing her fingers to his face. Tenderly, she touched the sore area. "It will bruise. Soon, you will be all shades of the rainbow." Then she did the unthinkable.

She plopped into his lap.

Before he could protest, she took his face in her hands. Her gentle touch almost undid him. Moving toward him, Lucy gently kissed below his tender eye. The corner of it. His brow.

Her actions moved him, and Judson found himself taking her nape, pulling her mouth to his.

The kiss started gentle, but he increased the pressure. Suddenly, he wanted to kiss her the way she was meant to be kissed.

So, he did.

CHAPTER SEVENTEEN

THIS WAS THE kind of kiss Lucy had been expecting from her husband. Judson kissed her as if he truly meant it. He was invested in this kiss—and she hoped he also was invested in their relationship, both now and in the future.

She kissed him back with everything she had, all of the longing she had felt for him. Their tongues collided, warring with one another, sending frissons of desire through her. Lucy looped her arms about his neck, pressing closely to him, yearning for him to be inside her again.

It was hard to tell when one kiss ended and the next began because her head spun from the sensations filling her. She only knew that she loved him deeply, and her love would only continue to grow.

Judson broke the kiss, and they both gazed at one another, each a little dazed.

Finally, he spoke. "Will you accompany me upstairs, Lucy?" he asked, his voice low and rough.

If he meant what she thought he did, she was a bit shocked by the impropriety of making love during the day. Yet she was not going to pass up this opportunity by being a proper lady.

"Yes," she told him, resolve in her tone.

He came to his feet, setting her down on hers, his fingers threading through hers. Their bodies may have come together last night, but for the first time since they had spoken their vows,

Lucy felt truly joined with him.

Judson led them from his study, where they came across Clippman.

"We are not to be disturbed," her husband said crisply as they passed the butler.

She felt the blush spill across her cheeks, knowing the servant would know what they were up to.

He pulled her up the stairs, practically running now, asking, "Your rooms—or mine?"

"Mine are closer," she managed to say, trying to keep up with him.

They reached her rooms, and Judson threw open the door and swept her off her feet and into his arms, using his foot to close the door behind them. Her heart was aflutter with such a romantic gesture. Judson strode through her sitting room and entered the bedchamber, where Annie sat in a chair by the window, a gown of Lucy's in her lap and needle and thread in her hand. Annie looked startled by their appearance, and then she broke out in a smile.

Coming to her feet, she said not a word, merely passing by them and exiting the bedchamber, sewing in hand.

Judson set Lucy on her feet. Immediately, his mouth returned to hers, greedily kissing her senseless. He broke the kiss and left her side, turning back the bedclothes. Returning to her, he took her hands in his and smiled wryly.

"I am afraid we will miss the garden party."

"What garden party?" Lucy asked innocently, and they both began laughing.

During the next few minutes, her new husband lovingly removed every layer of clothing she wore, kissing her in between placing each piece on the seat where Annie had previously sat. It surprised her that when she stood before him without a stitch on, she felt not the slightest bit of embarrassment.

Cupping his face with her hands, she pulled him down to her for a long, delicious kiss before ending it and asking, "May I return the favor now, my lord?"

Slowly, Lucy unknotted the cravat at his neck, pulling it from him and tossing it to the ground. Before she could continue, he sprang into action, tearing off his coat and waistcoat, dumping them on the floor next to the cravat. His fingers fumbled at his shirt, and she pushed his hands aside.

"Let me."

Undoing the three buttons for him, Judson took over, pulling the shirt over his head and letting it float to the ground. He stood beside her, looking as if he had been sculpted from stone by a master of old. She placed both palms flat against his chest and began gliding over the sleek muscles, seeing them bunch at her touch.

"I wanted to do this last night," she said softly. "Touch you. I wanted you to touch me, too."

He jerked her to him, his hands roaming her bare back as he kissed her hungrily. They moved lower, capturing her buttocks and kneading them, sending delicious tingles through her. She brought her arms around him, and as she moved her hands up and down his back, dismay filled her.

He was scarred.

Perhaps this was why he had behaved as he had last night, not letting her touch him. But something had changed between them, and Lucy was not going to stop and ask him anything at this point.

Judson released her and took her hand, leading her to the bed. He sat upon it and gazed up at her. "I will need help removing my boots."

"At your service, Lord Huntsberry," Lucy said saucily, causing him to laugh.

He raised his right leg, and she took hold of the heel in one hand and the tip of his toes with the other hand. She yanked hard. It took several tries for the boot to come off, but she flushed with success when it did. The second proved to be easier to remove since she now knew what she was doing.

He stood, their bodies close together now, guiding her hands to the buttons of his breeches. Lucy made fast work of unfastening them, and he peeled them down his muscular legs, discarding them and his stockings. He stood before her now, his manhood once again at full attention. This time, she wanted to satisfy her curiosity, and so she clasped it in one of her hands.

Judson sucked in a quick breath, and she squeezed it lightly before stroking it lovingly. It was hard to the touch and yet his skin was so soft, almost like steel encased in velvet. She brushed the pad of her thumb over its head, and he gasped.

Taking her wrist, he gently removed her fingers from his rod, saying, "Not yet. Your touch makes me want to come—and we have much more to do before that occurs."

He pulled her toward the bed, and Lucy climbed upon the mattress, Judson following her. They exchanged long, drugging kisses, both their hands roaming the other's body as they did so.

His lips left hers, trailing kisses along her jaw and then nuzzling her throat. He found her pulse point, his tongue encircling it, and then he nipped at it, sending a thrill through her. His tongue went even lower, finding the curve of her breast and outlining the tops of each one. Lucy now trembled, wanting him as she had never wanted anything in her life.

As one of his hands kneaded her breast, his tongue and teeth focused on the other one, feasting upon it. The new sensations running through her made her catch fire, and her core beat as her heart did. He sucked and laved the nipple, grazing his teeth across it, causing it to stand erect, begging for more of his touch.

Judson turned his attention to her other breast, murmuring that he was not going to ignore it, causing her to giggle.

His tongue found the valley between her breasts and then moved lower, sliding down to her belly, causing it to quiver. He kept going, though, and she realized what his final destination would be. The thought was scandalous, and yet she wanted him to taste her there.

He reached for her ankles and locked onto them, dragging

her feet so they were flat on the bed, her knees bent. Pushing her thighs open, his tongue settled between her legs, entering her, sending jolts of hot desire through her. Her husband took his time, licking, sucking, using fingers and mouth and tongue to bring her to a height previously unknown. She shattered, calling his name, her entire body shuddering with pure pleasure.

His mouth worked its way back up her body until he was kissing her again. She tasted herself on his tongue, and the erotic moment made her feel like a wanton.

She would remain a wanton—only for her husband.

Judson moved, now hovering over her, his gaze pinning hers as he pushed inside her with one swift motion. It surprised her when she felt no discomfort and then remembered it was only supposed to hurt the first time. Knowing more what making love was about, this time Lucy enthusiastically joined Judson in their dance. Her hands were constantly moving over him, loving the feel of his hard body and musky scent of this man she had committed herself to. Then her release came. She felt him climax at the same time she did, his hot seed shooting into her. She pulled him to her, their mouths fusing as their bodies did.

Spent, he collapsed atop her a moment and then rolled to his side so that they faced one another. He smoothed her hair, tenderness filling his eyes.

She smiled. "That is what was expecting from you last night, Judson."

He winced. "I apologize if I did not make you happy then, Lucy."

"No, you did," she insisted. "What we shared last night—our first time making love—will always be special to me."

She hesitated and then decided she must always be honest with him if they were to have a true marriage.

"But I sensed you holding back last night. It was as if you were doing your husbandly duty with minimal effort and no emotional involvement. Yes, the release I experienced was incredible. I did not know my body could undergo such a thing.

And when we joined, you took wonderful care of me. You saw to my needs, but not your own. You would not let me participate— and I want that, Judson. Desperately. I want to be a good wife to you. I want you to feel all the fantastic things I have."

Lucy placed her palm against his cheek, caressing it with her thumb. "Can you tell me why you kept me at a distance?"

He remained silent, and she decided this was the moment to press him.

"Is it because . . . of the scars on your back?"

"In part," he said hoarsely. "But the larger portion was that I did not want to destroy that light within you."

"I do not understand why you believe you have this darkness inside you, Judson. I know you to be a good man. If I can see it, why can't you?"

She snuggled closer to him, draping an arm and leg across him, resting her cheek against his chest.

"Tell me. I am your wife. I will stand against the world with you if need be."

Silence filled the room for several minutes. Lucy had almost given up hope that Judson would open up to her.

Then he said, "All right. But I warn you now—you may not like the man you have wed once you hear who I really am."

CHAPTER EIGHTEEN

I F HE TOLD Lucy the truth about his background, Judson was afraid of losing her.

When he had just found her.

Lucy was the best person he had ever known. She had such faith in him, even if it was misplaced. She had been honest with him, and he owed her the same courtesy. In fact, it might be a blessing in disguise. When he told her the kind of man he truly was, she would most likely have little to do with him. It would become the true marriage of convenience he had thought to have with her all along. As it was, he prayed that was what it would become.

Because Judson was fast losing his heart to this wonderful woman.

She lay cuddled against him, their limbs entwined, and he knew he might never experience this closeness with her again once he had spoken his truth. He would relish these minutes together and remember to hold her blameless when she heard what a monster he had become.

"I have previously told you I had no mother," he began, his hand absently rubbing her arm. "My father was ill much of his life. I saw him more in his bed than out of it."

"That must have been hard."

"He did the best he could. I cannot blame him for his health being frail." Judson paused, closing his eyes. "I was a small child. Thin. Boney. Underweight. By the time I went away to school, I had yet to learn the things other boys' fathers taught them. How to ride or swim or hunt."

Judson spoke dispassionately now, not infusing any emotion into his voice. "Because of my size, I was picked upon. Bullied by the other boys."

He launched into things which had been done to him, things he had never told a soul. Things he wished he could forget—but couldn't. As he spoke, he felt the tension fill Lucy's body.

"No one would befriend me because they were afraid to be caught up in the campaign of intimidation against me."

He felt her tears against his chest. "Could you not speak to one of your tutors? Or the headmaster?"

"They shut down any talk of such matters. What they do not see or know about simply does not exist."

Lucy raised her head. "But you were a boy!" she exclaimed. "One who was suffering greatly. Oh, Judson, I cannot imagine the fear you lived in. The physical pain you endured."

He pressed her head down, not being able to see the look in her eyes.

"And yet I loved learning," he told her. "In the classroom, I was in my element. I shone in every subject. Of course, I suffered mightily from being recognized—even praised—by the staff. Many of those who bullied me struggled in their studies."

"They were still terribly wrong to hurt you as they did." She sighed. "I am sorry your papa was so ill and could not go to the authorities and make things right for you. As it is, those in charge should have been held just as accountable as those boys who hurt and intimidated you."

He sensed her hesitation and knew what she would ask. Judson decided to beat her to it.

"It got much worse once Papa passed. Huntsworth had always been my refuge from school. I eagerly looked forward to returning home to Surrey between terms. I became the new marquess at ten years of age. Because of my youth, my uncle, Papa's brother, became my guardian. He, in effect, had already run Huntsworth for many years, due to my father's ill health. Uncle Jeremiah despised my father and the fact that he held the title and wealth."

"And then a mere boy became the new marquess," she said quietly. "What did he do to you, Judson?"

His new wife was intuitive.

"His excuse was that he wanted to toughen me up. Constantly, he berated me verbally, but the physical punishments were even worse."

Her head popped up again, her gaze meeting his. "He is the one who gave you your scars."

"He did."

Lucy's pained expression almost undid him. She seemed to recognize this and placed her head again on his chest. Her hand found his, threading her fingers through his, giving him strength to continue.

"Uncle Jeremiah beat me unmercifully for the slightest supposed infraction. He also drove me to my physical limits and beyond. It is hard to say this, but I suppose I have him to thank. He pushed me to the brink of my physical limits. Running. Dragging heavy objects. Lifting weights to help me gain strength. At school, other boys often stole my food. I think half my problem in being so small was the hunger I suffered. At least at Huntsworth, I was able to eat. Most of the time."

She squeezed his fingers. "Go on."

"I began to grow in spurts. At first, it was in height, but due to the intense physical activities my uncle put me through, I also started growing in strength. The time came when my tormentors did not come for me during the night.

"I came for them."

He let those words hang in the air, wishing he could stop there, but knowing he must finish his tale of woe.

"First, I made it evidently clear to the boys in my own class how I would no longer tolerate their abuse. I am not proud of this, Lucy. I used fists. Feet. Even teeth to teach them the lesson.

My father had begged me on his deathbed to become a good man, but I became the opposite of that. I bullied my bullies, taking them to task. Hurting them as they had hurt me. Until they feared me—and hurt me no more."

He found himself holding her hand tightly and released his grip on it.

"Then I went for the older boys. The ones who had taken advantage of someone younger than they, a boy who was thin and undernourished and lonely. I taught them the same lessons and forced them to agree to never bully another boy at school again. I was deadly serious when I told each and every one of them that I would kill them if I came across them torturing any child."

"That was very brave of you, Judson," his wife told him. "To stand up to so many who had tormented you. Did they . . ." Her voice trailed off. "Oh! I understand now. Lords Eaton and Humley were two of your bullies."

"Yes," he said quietly. "Two of the very worst. Eaton, in particular. He was vicious and enjoyed hurting me. And others. Humley was mean, but he took all his cues from Eaton. I did catch the pair bullying a younger boy once, two years after I had issued my edict. I beat Humley badly. He was terrified of me after that."

When he paused, Lucy asked, "What did you do to Eaton? I already know how much he despises you because of the way he spoke of you when he hurt me."

"I dealt with Eaton. He was injured so badly that he left school."

"I am surprised you were not expelled, Judson."

"No one spoke against me. Not a single boy—and yet the entire school knew it had been me who damaged each of them."

He stroked her hair, loving the feel of the silky tresses. "So you see, dear Lucy, I am not a good man. I have bullied and beaten others. I caused an entire school to be terrified of me. Before, no boy befriended me because they were afraid of being sucked into the web of torment I suffered. After, every boy feared me so that no one would look at me, much less speak to me. That evil has remained in me, Lucy. It has festered over the years. Because of it, I have kept myself apart from others. You know Tim is my only friend. Julian has tried to befriend me, but he knows nothing of my past. Even your own brother knows of my reputation. He can verify if you have any doubt."

Judson lifted Lucy, placing her in his lap, needing to see her eyes.

"The darkness will never leave me. I will have no friends. I hated that we were forced to wed and that I sucked you into the blackness of my world and soul."

A fierceness filled her eyes. "You are wrong about everything, Judson. You took the bullying for years and became stronger for it. You grew into a size where you could threaten those who had done you harm. You *protected* other boys by unleashing your wrath upon those who had hurt you so deeply. Think how many other boys would have suffered if you had not intervened."

She cupped his cheeks. "And you came to my rescue. You have given me the protection of your name. You sent Eaton and Humley away. We are man and wife now. We are free to build the future the two of us want. The *two* of us, Judson. Together. You are an honorable man. You may think your soul black, but all I see is a hero who helped so many. And me."

Lucy kissed him softly. "You will not dim any light within me. From now on, you will let your own light shine. Your own goodness and kindness and thoughtfulness. Leave the past in the past, Judson. Stand side by side with me in the present, and help me as we look to our future."

She kissed him again. "You are a good husband. You will be the best of fathers."

"I know nothing about either," he protested, his resolve to isolate from her weakening.

"We will learn these things together" she said, quiet determination in her voice. "Thank you for opening up to me. For telling me all that has happened to you. I think you will be wonderful as a husband and father because of the suffering you have under-gone. You are everything I have ever desired in a husband. You will spend time with our children, teaching them with patience and love."

Lucy grinned. "Why, you might even become more besotted with your daughter than Julian is with his."

Her words—and laughter—caused a lightness to fill him. Judson realized for the first time in his life, he had hope. Hope for what his future would hold. Hope for the good things in life to come his way.

And in that moment, he realized that he loved Lucy. With every fiber of his being.

Before he could tell her, though, she was kissing him again. Passionately. Judson had thought only a mistress could exhibit this level of arousal, but Lucy, though a daughter of the *ton*, was definitely a woman who would always satisfy him.

She broke the kiss. Grabbing a pillow, she walloped him with it—and burst out laughing. Scrambling off the bed, he gave chase, catching her, kissing her, picking her up and taking her back to bed. They wrestled. Kissed. Laughed. And made love to one another, a coupling Judson would never forget for as long as he lived.

He had found a partner. An equal. Someone to share his life with. A person whom he would always put first.

They stayed in bed for hours, kissing and talking. His wife told him of things she wanted to do inside the townhouse. She valued family greatly, and he caught her enthusiasm, ready to open the house once it was ready and entertain her many relatives.

He agreed to take her to Huntsworth. The ghosts of the past had evaporated, and he began to recall the things he had loved about the estate.

"I enjoy the country," she said. "I hope you will allow us to restore Huntsworth and live there at least part of the year."

"I will go where you go," he said solemnly. "I do not want to leave your side, Lucy. You have opened my eyes to an entire new way of thinking."

"You don't mind if we go to the country?" she asked, biting her lip. "Because I want to be with you, Judson. Wherever you are."

He took her into his arms. "I want to have a normal life with you, Wife. We shall open the country house again and live there most of the year until we come to town for the Season. I hope we will fill it with children, many children, and that we will enjoy spending time with them. Yes, they will need nursemaids and nannies and tutors and governesses, but I want a true family. One I see frequently and let them know how much I love them."

Her luminous smile dazzled him. "And can we bring our children to town with us each year? Ariadne has already started this new tradition. Val and Con agreed they would do the same. We want to come to know all our cousins, and for our children to grow up with one another."

"I think that sounds like the best plan of all," Judson declared. "The smartest thing I have done in my life has been to wed you, Lucy Jarvis." He paused, his heart ready to burst from his chest. "I love you."

He kissed her deeply, making love to his wife, thoroughly pleasuring her.

When they both lay exhausted, wrapped in each other's arms, Lucy said, "I love you, too. Judson. I realized I did but was afraid to tell you."

He kissed her. "You need never fear that again, love. We were meant to be together and love one another."

"Will we always be this happy?" she asked.

He thought a moment. "No. I think our happiness will grow, day by day, Lucy. As will our love."

CHAPTER NINETEEN

JUDSON SAT AT White's, Julian and Con his companions. So much had changed in the last two weeks since his marriage to Lucy. While Julian had always been open and offered friendship to him, Con had finally come around and was treating him decently, seeing his sister was happy in the marriage she had made.

He and Lucy had attended a few events of the Season, but they had also enjoyed time alone. They had taken walks about town, visiting bookshops and Gunter's. Gone for drives in Hyde Park. He was even teaching her how to play chess, which she was picking up with an alarming speed. His Lucy was not only sweet-natured, but she had a bit of a competitive streak when it came to games.

Judson only had one thing left to do—and that was tell Antonia Amato goodbye.

He had sent his mistress a note yesterday, saying that he would call upon her today to discuss an important matter. He supposed Antonia would know what was going to happen. Judson would not leave her destitute. He would make certain she was taken care of until she found another protector.

"How are the changes to your townhouse coming?" Julian asked, taking a sip of his tea.

"Rather well," he replied. "Lucy and I have been from top to bottom of the place, opening rooms and having dust covers removed from furniture so we can see what's actually there. Actually, I believe she is issuing an invitation to tea to family for tomorrow afternoon." He paused. "It will be the first time I have ever entertained—and that we have entertained together."

These two men had known him slightly at school, so they understood what a loner he was. Still, Lucy was bringing him out from his shell. It was almost as if he were a caterpillar, transforming into a butterfly, spreading his wings. He liked having friends. He liked having family.

And he especially liked having a wife.

Lucy had proven to be adventurous in the bedroom. She was open to any suggestion, and their lovemaking was something he looked forward to daily.

"I have a few errands to run," he said, excusing himself. "I will see you at tonight's ball."

His friends bid him farewell, and Judson left White's, focused on the task at hand. He didn't think Antonia would mind that he was ending their arrangement. They saw one another infrequently, and she might enjoy being with a man who spent more time with her than Judson ever had.

Since it was a nice day, he decided to walk the few blocks to the house he rented for his mistress. On his way, he concentrated on what to say to Antonia.

When he arrived, he was admitted by Mrs. Worth, the housekeeper. Judson paid for a housekeeper, cook, and maid, as well as taking care of the rent and other household expenses. He had also given Antonia a few baubles, which he hoped she would know she was free to sell. In fact, he should bring that up to her during their discussion now.

"How are you today, Mrs. Worth?" he asked the housekeeper.

"Very well, Lord Huntsberry," the woman replied. "Miss Antonia is waiting for you in the parlor. Will you be wanting tea?"

"No, thank you, Mrs. Worth. I will not be staying long."

Her brow creased in concern. "Are you ending things, my lord? I am only asking because it means I'll need to look for a new position."

Her words gave him pause. He planned to take Lucy to Huntsworth in a few days so that she might see the estate and view the house. He would be in need of many servants to run the place when they opened it up.

"If Miss Antonia does not need your services anymore, perhaps I will be able to assist you in finding employment."

"My lord?"

Although he knew it was Lucy's domain to hire servants, Mrs. Worth and Cook were excellent at their jobs, and Antonia had always mentioned how pleased she had been with both women.

"I will be opening my country house soon," he explained. "An entire staff will be needed. I would be happy, if you are open to the idea, for my wife to interview you. Cook, as well."

He had eaten many a meal Cook had prepared, and he thought her even more talented than his other cook. Still, he wanted to leave the final decision in Lucy's hands. Judson decided when he returned this afternoon, he would discuss the matter with his wife. It might be a delicate conversation, since he would have to admit to having once kept a mistress, but he hated to lose good servants.

"I know my way, Mrs. Worth. No need to escort me. Think on what I have said, and let me know if you are interested when I depart."

"Of course, my lord," she responded.

Going to the door of the parlor, he knocked upon it and entered, finding Antonia seated on the settee, sewing in her lap. She placed what she was working on in the basket at her feet and rose to greet him. Offering Judson her hands, he took them and kissed both her cheeks.

"Have a seat, Huntsberry," she said, setting herself again on the settee as he sat beside her.

Before he could speak, Antonia said, "I read about your marriage in the newspapers. I hope that it will be a happy one, since you have always been such an unhappy man, my lord."

He placed a hand over hers. "It was nothing you ever did, Antonia. Know that you gave me some of the few happy times in my life. I am sorry if I have been neglectful of you. As for my marriage, I am very satisfied in my choice of wife."

She smiled warmly at him. "I am delighted to hear that. And I expect you are here to end things between us. You have been most generous in our relationship. You demanded very little of me or my time, and you gave me everything I could possibly want." She paused. "Other than a babe."

Judson had always told his mistress he did not want to get a child off her and had used French letters when they coupled.

"I want to thank you for the time we had together," he said sincerely. "I know you will be looking for a new protector now, and I want you to feel free to remain here as long as you wish. There is no need to hurry into a new arrangement. Take your time and choose wisely."

Surprisingly, Antonia burst into tears, something he had never seen before. He had overheard other men discuss how their mistresses used tears as a weapon to wheedle things out of them, but that had never been the case with Antonia.

Placing his hand on her back and rubbing it, he asked, "What is wrong? Do you not wish to form another liaison with a titled gentleman?"

"I want to go home to Tuscany," she told him, removing a handkerchief from her bosom and mopping away her tears.

Gazing at him solemnly, Antonia said, "I have always been faithful to you, Huntsberry. In fact, I have never had relations with any other man in England." She smiled ruefully. "But my heart has always belonged to Luigi."

This was the first time his mistress had ever spoken of home, much less another man.

"Who is this Luigi to you?" he asked gently.

"My first love," she admitted. "We both knew I had a gift in my voice, and Luigi urged me to stretch my wings. He told me he would always love me and that he did not want to limit me. I left him when we were but sixteen years of age in order to pursue opportunities to sing."

Judson had met Antonia two years ago. Although he was not terribly fond of music, he did go to the opera upon occasion and had heard her sing. The diva's voice was high and clear, moving him.

Shortly after he'd first heard her perform, something had ruptured in her throat, leaving her unable to sing at the professional level. At first, the doctors said if she merely rested her voice, she would recover. That had not come to pass—and that was when he had stepped in, offering to make her his mistress.

"While I have enjoyed our arrangement, Huntsberry, I am tired of the gloomy weather here in London. On a whim, I wrote to Luigi a year ago, and he replied. He has never wed. He misses me."

Antonia stood, brushing away her tears, and moved to the window, looking out.

"I told him that my days of performing had come to an end. I even wrote to him of how I was managing to get along now." she turned her gaze to him. "He did not care. He wants me back. He has offered marriage."

"Do you want to return to him?"

She nodded. "I have longed for Luigi—and his babes—for many years. While I do not regret pursuing music and singing to crowds who cheered for me, at heart I am a simple girl who only wants to go home to my true love."

Judson went and joined her. Taking her hands in his, he raised them to his lips, kissing them tenderly. "I will see that happen. What does Luigi do for a living?"

"He is a shopkeeper in Sienna. His father passed away three years ago, and Luigi stepped into his shoes."

"I will make the necessary arrangements for you to travel to Italy."

She frowned. "It will be expensive, my lord."

"Do not worry about the cost. I owe you that much."

Antonia smiled at him. "You are a good and generous man. I cannot thank you enough for taking care of me when I was at my lowest."

Normally, Judson would brush off such a compliment, not believing it to be sincere. Since Lucy had come into his life, however, he wanted to be the best man he could be. For her.

Graciously, he said, "Thank you for the compliment, Antonia. And thank you for being here for me."

She studied him a moment. "I am glad this new wife of yours makes you happy, my lord. Most men in your position would have kept their mistress. It says a lot in regard to your character that you came here to end our relationship to remain faithful to her, much less that you will help me to return home to Tuscany."

Antonia walked him to the door. Judson stepped outside and turned to face her.

"I hope you and Luigi have a good life together. We will not see one another again, but I will wish you the best."

She leaned up on tiptoe and kissed him briefly. "Lady Huntsberry is a very fortunate woman. Goodbye, my lord."

He watched her close the door and then he started down the street, looking for a hansom cab to take him home.

To Lucy.

To love.

LUCY FINISHED HER errands and found herself eager to see Judson. To say that her husband was consuming her every waking thought would not be an exaggeration. As she had finalized her order for new draperies just now, her mind had wandered three different times to Judson. She thought him the most handsome man in all of London and the most caring, as well.

And he was hers. Truly hers.

She looked forward to the time they would spend together in the country. Already, she imagined the children they would have and how they would enjoy playing with them. Already, her marriage was turning into one which was very satisfying, with love blooming in her heart.

Perhaps she should surprise him. Judson had mentioned going to White's as she had left their townhouse this morning.

As she exited the shop, she looked up to her driver. "Head to White's. We shall wait a bit to see if Lord Huntsberry comes out. It would be good to offer him a ride home in his own carriage."

"Yes, my lady," the coachman said, biting back a smile.

A footman assisted her into the carriage, and Lucy settled back against the plush cushions. Wicked thoughts danced through her head. If she were lucky enough to actually see her husband exiting White's, perhaps they could draw the curtains and tell their driver to take his time heading home.

Giving them time to do all kinds of wonderful things to each other.

Oh, Judson had been a bad influence on her. Lucy smiled. Or perhaps the best influence.

The coach came to stand across the street from White's. She would wait half an hour before asking the coachman to head home. She only wished she could step inside the hallowed halls of the gentlemen's club in order to see whether or not Judson was still there, but that simply wasn't the done thing.

Then Lucy spied him coming through the door, her heart speeding up, and she wondered if it might ever grow old, catching sight of him.

Before she could call out to Judson, he strode down the street with purpose. The footman appeared at the window.

"Shall we catch up to his lordship, my lady?" the servant asked. "The coachman wishes for your instructions."

"Yes, please," she replied.

With the heavy stream of traffic, it was impossible to turn the carriage around, and so the driver took them down the block before turning on a side street. He turned twice more, eventually taking them in front of White's again, this time headed in the opposite direction. Lucy hoped they hadn't lost Judson and leaned out the window, finally spying him far ahead. She relaxed against the cushions, knowing they would soon catch up to him.

After a few minutes, the coach came to a halt. She peered outside, seeing her husband entering a townhouse more than a block ahead.

"Why have we stopped?" she called out.

The footman appeared next to the carriage. "It seems a costermonger's cart of vegetables was struck by another carriage, my lady. The cart has toppled over, and vegetables are strewn everywhere." He glanced ahead. "I think the carriage which struck the cart is having a problem with its wheel. It's caused a bit of a mess."

"See me out," she instructed, and the footman opened the door. Looking up to the coachman, Lucy said, "I will go ahead and meet Lord Huntsberry. Pull over next to the pavement here. I will return shortly."

"Yes, my lady," the driver replied.

Lucy moved along the pavement, taking a moment to view the accident that had clogged the road. She proceeded past it and stopped at the next block, not quite certain which townhouse Judson had entered.

And curious now as to who he was visiting.

Not wanting to knock upon the doors of a few strangers, she waited a few minutes, hoping Judson would come out soon. Deciding her idea had been foolish, she started to return to the carriage when the front door to a townhouse three down from her opened.

Lucy stood and watched as the dark-haired beauty kissed Judson. Her belly clenched, tears springing to her eyes.

Her husband had a mistress.

She should not be surprised by this information. It was common knowledge that many men of the *ton* did have one, both before and after their marriages. She had thought things would be different between her and Judson.

The past two weeks now seemed like a lie.

Quickly, she turned to hurry away, only to see that the marquess' vehicle had made it through the traffic and now pulled up beside her.

Lucy glanced up at the coachman, refusing to meet the driver's eyes, knowing he had witnessed what she had. Wordlessly, she allowed the footman to hand her up. As she sat in the vehicle, no tears came. She thought they would at some point, but she was too numb now to even think.

She arrived home, handing her reticule and bonnet to Annie, who greeted her.

Turning to Clippman, who stood nearby, she told him, "I have a headache. I do not feel like tea or dinner. Please inform his lordship of that if you would."

Annie had remained in the foyer and went up the stairs with Lucy.

"You look white as a ghost, my lady. Is it just a headache?" Annie smiled slightly. "Or could it be more?"

"I do not know what you mean, Annie," she said flatly.

"Well, I suppose it is a little too soon. I was just thinking that you might be with child and nauseous from the babe growing inside you."

Tears sprang to Lucy's eyes. She had thought each time she and Judson had made love that there was the possibility a babe had been created. Now, she did not want one growing inside her. She felt incredibly betrayed by her husband.

She supposed they would go back to having a marriage of convenience. The closeness which they had shared the past two weeks would be no more. Lucy knew she would mourn that loss. She still believed Judson had good in him, but she felt so betrayed by him keeping silent—and keeping a mistress.

In her bedchamber, Lucy allowed Annie to undress her and help her into a night rail before she climbed into bed.

"Is there anything I can bring you, my lady? Rub your temples? Fetch you some tea?"

"No, Annie. I merely wish to be alone. Hopefully, I can get some sleep. Do not disturb me. I will ring for you tomorrow morning."

"Very well," the maid said, leaving the room.

Once Annie had left, Lucy rose from the bed. She went to the door to her sitting room and locked it. Then she locked the one that connected her bedchamber to her dressing room. She did not want to see her husband tonight. She did not want to deal with anything.

Lucy merely wished to be left alone to wallow in her sorrow and mourn the future she had dreamt of, one which would never come to pass.

CHAPTER TWENTY

JUDSON HEADED STRAIGHT for his solicitor's office, wanting to get everything squared away regarding Antonia. He had no secretary, and so over the years, details such as this had fallen to Baker to attend to. Once he arrived, he was shown in to see Baker, despite the fact he had no appointment. He supposed that was the beauty of being a marquess.

"Good day, my lord," Baker greeted him. "It looks as if marriage is agreeing with you."

"Yes, I made the right choice in wedding Lady Huntsberry."

The solicitor smiled shamelessly. "Oh, I knew she was the one for you, my lord. The fact you are a love match was obvious to me. Gentlemen rarely take such extraordinarily good care of a lady in the marriage contracts."

In part, he had felt guilty in Lucy being forced into marriage with him, which was why he had wanted the contracts to favor her, but the largest part was wanting to do right by his new wife. He wanted her to be cared for if anything should happen to him, and he had wanted any future children looked after, too. For a moment, Judson wondered if he might have loved Lucy all along and hadn't admitted it to himself.

"I do thank you for your help in drawing up the marriage settlements. I am here on another matter, however."

"What can I attend to, my lord?"

"It is Antonia Amato."

"Ah. The mistress." Baker shook his head. "Is she asking for more, now that you are wed? A larger allowance or even larger house?"

"Quite the opposite."

Judson explained how he had gone to break things off with Antonia, only to learn she was homesick and wished to return to Italy.

"She is from a town in the Tuscan region. Sienna. I told her I would make the arrangements for her to return home."

Baker chuckled. "You mean I would make them for you?"

"Yes. I have no wish to see Antonia again. She was always kind to me, and I want to return the favor. Could you see to arranging her transportation, as well as ending the lease on the house she occupies? Also, she will need funds to use as she travels home."

"I can handle these arrangements, my lord. What of the staff? Do you wish a small amount of money settled upon them before they are dismissed?"

"I may have need of them. Lady Huntsberry and I have decided to open my house in Surrey. She enjoys country living. Her cousin has wed the Marquess of Aldridge, and they happen to be our neighbors. We will see much of them while we are in the country."

His solicitor now beamed at him. "I am very happy for you, Lord Huntsberry. I know you have avoided Huntsworth for the past decade."

"We hope for a large family. Raising them in the country will be important." He rose. "If you will handle the details regarding Miss Amato, I would be grateful, Mr. Baker."

"Consider it done. And congratulations again on your marriage, my lord."

"Thank you."

Judson left the solicitor's office and hailed another hansom cab to convey him home. He hoped Lucy would be there by now. She had gone to meet with someone regarding new fabrics for the curtains in several of the rooms and also to discuss paint colors. He liked that they had opened many of the rooms in his London townhouse. Hopefully, the nursery might even be occupied when they came to town for the Season next year.

The driver dropped him at home, and he entered the townhouse. Clippman greeted him, saying, "Would you care for tea in your study, my lord? Lady Huntsberry has a headache and will not be coming down."

"Is she all right?" he asked quickly.

"She seemed a bit pale and asked to be left alone. Annie told me that her ladyship wished to sleep."

"Thank you, Clippman. No tea is necessary. I will go upstairs and check on my wife."

He took the stairs two at a time, worried about Lucy. She always seemed the picture of health and had never mentioned headaches to him.

When he reached her rooms, he pushed open the door and softly closed it behind him. Crossing the sitting room, he tried to open the door leading to her bedchamber—and found it locked. Not wanting to knock and disturb her if she were sleeping, he retraced his steps and went to his own rooms, From them, he went through the bathing chamber and her dressing room.

And found the door to her bedchamber locked.

Concern filled him. Yet he did not want to overreact and have Lucy upset about him fussing over her.

He returned downstairs and asked Clippman, "When did Lady Huntsberry return from her appointment?"

"Less than two hours ago, my lord."

"Send for Annie if you would. I will be in my study."

The maid arrived several minutes later, and Judson asked, "Does Lady Huntsberry suffer from headaches often?"

"No, my lord," the servant replied. "I can only recall one other occasion when Lady Lucy—Lady Huntsberry, that is—had a headache. It was a fierce one, though, and she slept most of the day and all the night. When she awoke the next morning, it was gone. She hasn't had one since. That was three, maybe four years ago."

"Thank you, Annie."

The servant left, and Judson found himself unable to concentrate. He was worried about Lucy, and it consumed him. He forced himself to remain downstairs, though, knowing she needed her rest.

He ate dinner by himself, something he had done most of his life. After only two weeks of having Lucy as his dinner companion, though, he felt very lonely. He wondered how he had existed before Lucy had come into his life.

After dinner, he went upstairs and waited a few minutes before he couldn't stand to wait any longer. He went to her bedchamber door and knocked softly, pausing to listen. When she didn't respond, he knocked again.

"Lucy, love, are you all right? Is there something I can do for you?"

After a long pause, he heard, "No. Just leave me alone."

Then silence.

Slowly, Judson made his way back to his own bedchamber. He told himself not to fret. That Lucy didn't feel well. She needed her rest. Yet once he had summoned Tim and undressed for bed, he missed his wife. The large bed felt empty without her in it. He needed her warmth nestled against him. The sweet scent of lavender wafting off her skin. Judson lay awake for a long time, not knowing how to fall sleep without his wife in his arms.

He rose the next morning, ringing for Tim. The valet shaved and dressed him, and Judson headed downstairs to the breakfast room. Relief swept through him when he saw Lucy present at the table.

Going to her, he bent and kissed her cheek. For a second, he almost thought she cringed, which was ridiculous.

"How is your headache?" he asked, taking a seat to her right.

"Better," she replied, focusing on buttering her toast points.

He was used to Lucy being cheerful and talkative. This morning, she was neither.

"Should I summon the doctor? You do not quite seem to be yourself."

"No. That will not be necessary."

She avoided meeting his gaze.

Something was wrong.

"Do you have plans today?" he asked, cutting a bite of the ham from the plate a footman had brought to him.

"Yes."

Another succinct response. This was not the Lucy he knew. Judson wanted to ask her more, but he was keenly aware of the presence of the footmen and Clippman. Whatever needed to be said between them was a private matter.

After that, he gave up on conversation, and they finished their breakfasts in silence. When Judson saw she was about to rise, he asked, "Are you feeling well enough for our visitors at tea this afternoon? Or should we postpone?"

Her eyes widened, and he guessed she had forgotten she had issued the invitation. She said something under her breath, but he couldn't make out what.

"I will be ready for them," she promised, no warmth in her voice.

Before a footman could come to assist her, Judson stood and pulled out her chair from the table, even taking her hand and helping her to rise. Once on her feet, she pulled away from him.

He followed her from the room and kept his distance as she hurried up the stairs. Then he raced up them, wanting to speak to her before she locked herself inside her bedchamber again.

"Lucy," he called, but she continued moving down the corridor, ignoring him.

Running now, he caught up to her, clasping her elbow before she could enter her rooms. She glared at him, shrugging him off.

"What have I done?" he asked, his eyes pleading with her. "Why are you suddenly so cold to me?"

She hesitated and for a moment, Judson thought she would

reveal why her behavior had changed so radically. Then it was as if a curtain descended, hiding the truth.

"I must ready myself. Please ask Clippman to have the carriage readied."

Then she stepped inside—and locked the door.

Defeated, he slowly walked down the hall, returning to the ground floor, instructing the butler to have the carriage prepared. Not wanting the servants' pity, he retreated to his study, where several minutes later, he saw his wife step from the house. She spoke to the coachman for almost a minute, and then a footman handed her up into the carriage. Judson had no idea where she went.

Nor why he was being punished.

LUCY SAT IN the carriage, cold determination filling her. Breakfast had been absolutely awful. Even if Judson was treating her disrespectfully, it was hard to stay mad at him. He had looked at her with such anguish as she had spoken coolly to him, and she had almost opened up and told him what she had accidentally seen yesterday, him kissing his mistress.

She had spent much of last night awake, reliving memories from the past two weeks, which had been the best days of her life. Lucy wanted more of those days in the future.

But first, she would need to deal with this mistress.

Determination filled her. She was not going to be the good girl she had always been, the child who never caused her parents a moment's worry. Today, she was going to stand up for herself—and her marriage.

She had instructed the coachman to take her back to where they had been yesterday. He had reluctantly agreed to do so after she reminded him that he worked for her and her husband and if he wished to retain his position, he would drive her where she requested. Lucy had never abused her authority, but she realized the driver had probably driven Judson to the address many times and knew she planned to confront the mistress.

On the way there, she debated what to say. Her thoughts were so scrambled that she finally decided she would have to speak spontaneously. She only hoped her mission would be successful.

The carriage slowed, and a footman opened the door. Normally jovial, he merely handed her down, averting his eyes. Lucy ignored her racing heart and dry mouth and marched to the door, rapping upon it, wanting to retch. She swallowed, trying to calm herself.

The door was opened by a servant. "Yes?"

"I am Lady Huntsberry. I wish to speak to your employer at once."

The servant's eyes widened. "Lady Huntsberry? Oh, my." She looked over her shoulder and then back at Lucy. "Would . . . would you please come in, my lady?"

"Thank you," she said crisply.

Lucy swept by the woman, whom she guessed to be the housekeeper from her dress and manner. Several boxes sat on the floor next to the staircase, along with a trunk.

"The parlor is this way, my lady."

She followed the servant into a cozy parlor and took a seat, afraid if she didn't, her knees would give out and she'd tumble to the floor. Still, she kept her posture erect and held her head high.

"I will let Miss Amato know you are here, my lady." The housekeeper fled the room, closing the door behind her.

"You are here for a good reason," she told herself quietly. "You are here to try and save your marriage."

She repeated this silently several times until the door opened again. The dark-haired woman from yesterday came into the room and looked intently at Lucy for a moment. Then she glanced over her shoulder. "Thank you, Mrs. Worth. You may continue supervising the packing."

The woman the servant had called Miss Amato approached her, and Lucy was taken with her beauty. Flawless skin. Deep brown eyes. Luscious lips. A figure that would appeal to any man.

"Good morning, Lady Huntsberry. I am Antonia Amato." She took a seat. "How may I help you?"

"By keeping your hands off my husband," Lucy said brusquely. "And getting out of our lives."

CHAPTER TWENTY-ONE

MISS AMATO LOOKED taken aback by Lucy's declaration. She remained silent for a good minute, Lucy staring at her through narrowed eyes, ready to do whatever it took to defend her rights to her husband.

Then the woman said, "Oh, Lady Huntsberry. You are going to be *so* good for the marquess."

The words were spoken with compassion. For a moment, Lucy couldn't help but wonder not just what had passed physically between the pair, but the emotional bond they shared. Perhaps this was someone Judson needed in his life.

Rising, she said, "I have made a mistake in coming here today, Miss Amato. If you will excuse—"

Judson's mistress came to her feet. "No. Please stay."

Something was in her eyes. Something that made Lucy sit in her chair once again. She didn't know what this woman wanted from her, and so she waited expectantly.

Miss Amato also took her seat again. "Lord Huntsberry has been a very unhappy man. I can assure you that there is no love between us, my lady. The marquess helped me at a time when I was at my lowest." She swallowed. "I was an opera singer. I came from Italy."

That explained her accent. Though the woman spoke excellent English, it was obvious she was not a native speaker.

"I come from a humble background, but I had a talent for

singing. I have sung to audiences in Berlin. Paris. Rome. And of course, here in London."

The woman's gaze met hers. "I suffered a vocal injury. Damage to my vocal cords. At first, the physicians were optimistic and told me to rest my voice. It soon became apparent to me, however, that I would never sing again at the level I previously had. And that is where Lord Huntsberry came in."

Tears formed in Miss Amato's eyes. "The marquess does not even enjoy opera. Still, he had heard me perform and somehow learned of the dilemma I faced. Yes, I know it is common for women in the opera and theater to become the mistress of titled gentlemen. I did not know what I was going to do, and so I accepted his offer of protection."

Miss Amato looked about the room. "Huntsberry provides this house and servants for me. He gives me an allowance so that I feel a small bit of independence. I can assure you that it has not been some avventura amorosa. In fact, I see him only a couple of times each month. I had not seen him since the beginning of March until yesterday. I knew something must be afoot. Then I read of your marriage in the newspapers."

Lucy looked at the former opera singer with more sympathy, putting herself in her place. She was in a foreign country and had lost all visible means of supporting herself. Even she herself might have turned to a similar arrangement in order to survive.

"Yesterday, Huntsberry came to see me. He had written for an appointment, and I knew what was coming." She smiled at Lucy. "He came to end his association with me, my lady. I can tell you that your husband is one of those rare men in Polite Society who takes his marriage vows seriously. He offered to continue supporting me until I found a new protector."

Tears now spilled down Miss Amato's cheeks, and Lucy quickly handed her a handkerchief.

"Thank you, my lady," she said, dabbing her eyes. "You may have seen evidence of me leaving London when you arrived."

She recalled the boxes and trunk in the foyer and nodded.

"I was in love when I was young. I have been writing to Luigi for over a year now after being out of contact for many years. He has taken over his father's shop and has begged me to come home to him." Miss Amato's gaze met hers. "Lord Huntsberry is seeing to those arrangements now so that I might return to Sienna and marry my childhood sweetheart."

Lucy sat, stunned, realizing now that Judson had come to say goodbye to Miss Amato yesterday. That their kiss had been initiated by a grateful woman, thankful Judson had taken care of her so well.

"I must apologize. I barged in and said terrible things to you."

Miss Amato smiled gently. "You are passionate about your husband and your marriage, Lady Huntsberry. You are protective of him and what the two of you have together. Know that I would never come between you. I will soon be gone. The marquess even told me yesterday that we would never see one another again."

Lucy realized how wrong she had been. To come here. To think so little of Judson. She should have trusted her new husband and not behaved irrationally.

"Lord Huntsberry is a good man," Miss Amato continued. "He has been nothing but kind to me, and I believe he will make for an excellent husband. I can see now why he cares so much for you."

They both rose, and Lucy impulsively embraced the other woman.

"Thank you for sharing all this with me, Miss Amato. I hope that you and your Luigi have a wonderful life together."

"And I, too, hope that you and Lord Huntsberry will have a long, happy, satisfying marriage," she replied.

Lucy asked, "Would you write to me? Let me know that you have arrived in Italy and are settled?"

A genuine smile touched Miss Amato's lips. "You are as kind as your husband. Yes, my lady. I will write and tell you when I arrive."

The woman reached for Lucy's hands and squeezed them. "Love him well. He never told me anything of himself. I know he has suffered greatly, but he never spoke of it to me."

She thought of the scars on Judson's back—and soul—and nodded. "I will take care of him," she promised. "I will love him the best I can—and trust him more than I did today."

Miss Amato smiled. "A little jealousy never hurts. In fact, it might even create a new spark within your marriage bed."

Lucy thought the other woman frank, but she liked her very much.

"I will take my leave now, Miss Amato, and let you return to your packing. Have a safe journey to Sienna."

The woman walked Lucy to the door, kissing her on both cheeks. "I think you already know Huntsberry better than anyone ever will. If anyone can heal the scars he bears, it will be you, my lady."

She took her leave and told the coachman to drive her home. On the ride, she reflected on how coldly she had treated Judson when he had only done the right thing. She was ashamed of her behavior and owed him an apology. It would be painful because she would confess all to him, but Lucy now believed their love strong enough to survive any crisis.

The carriage began to slow, and her heart beat faster, anticipating seeing her husband again. it came to a halt, and the footman opened the door, handing her down the stairs.

"Lady Huntsberry!"

Lucy turned, seeing an older gentleman looking to be in his early fifties, hurrying along the pavement toward her.

He approached and said, "You are the only one who can help me, my lady. You must talk some sense into my nephew."

JUDSON HAD SAT by the window, awaiting Lucy's return. He had been miserable the entire time and was determined to clear up whatever misunderstanding had arisen. He would insist that Lucy tell him what was wrong because he wanted to remedy the rift between them before it grew wider.

He saw the carriage pull up in front of the townhouse and sprang to his feet. Hurrying from his study, he went to the foyer and out the front door, only to see his wife engaged in conversation with someone. His gut lurched as he recognized Jeremiah Judson.

Quickly, he rushed toward them, slipping a possessive arm around Lucy, wanting to protect her from his uncle.

"You are a monster!" Lucy spat out, glaring at his uncle. "You treated your nephew abominably. Why would I plead with my husband to increase the allowance he so generously gives you? If you lay dying in the gutter, I would not lift a hand to assist you."

The vehemence of her words startled Judson. Apparently, his uncle had approached Lucy to ask for more money on his behalf.

An old, familiar look settled in his uncle's eyes as he turned his gaze upon Judson. "You are as weak as your father and mother were." Hate dripped in his words. "You have to have your wife champion you."

"I will take Lady Huntsberry as my champion any day. I appreciate her standing with me against you," he said, his tone biting. "You may be my family by blood, but my wife is the family of my heart. I learned early on that you despised me because my father held the title you coveted, and I would do so after him. When Papa died, your mistreatment of me was abominable. I believe you did everything in your power to try and kill me by putting me through such strenuous, physical labors."

Judson couldn't help but smile. "It backfired. What I suffered through only made me stronger. Not only physically but mentally. You lit a burning determination in my soul to outlast you. So no, I will not be increasing your quarterly allowance, Uncle. You should be grateful I even provide one to you. You have been told never to come here. Because you did, you will not receive your next payment."

His uncle gasped. "You cannot do that!"

"Oh, but I can. Because *I*—not you—am the Marquess of Huntsberry." He paused, looking at this man in disgust. "And if you approach either my wife or me ever again, I will cut off all funds. Permanently."

He thought rage might seethe within his uncle and bubble out. Instead, Judson saw defeat in Jeremiah Jarvis' eyes.

"Leave," he and Lucy said in unison, and his heart filled with love for the woman standing beside him.

Dejectedly, his uncle walked away—and out of their lives.

Turning to Lucy, he wrapped his arms about her, kissing her despite the fact they were in public. She answered his kiss, and he could tell all was right again between them.

He ended the kiss. "Thank you for defending me."

"He is a beast," she said, contempt in her voice. "To think of the way he treated you, and then he comes here and expects you to give him more money? You are far too generous as it is, Judson. If I were you, I do not think I could hand over a single farthing to him."

"Come upstairs with me," he said huskily, watching the blush spill across her cheeks.

"It is not even noon," she protested. "Besides, my relatives are coming for tea today. I should meet with Cook."

Judson smiled slowly. "Haven't you already met with Cook regarding our visitors?"

"Yes," she admitted.

"Haven't you already discussed the menu to be served this afternoon?"

"Yes."

"Do you trust Cook to prepare a wonderful tea for the first visitors we will entertain together?"

The corners of her mouth turned up, even as her blush deepened. "I do."

"Then I think we should leave to Cook what is hers to do. That means if you are not otherwise engaged, Lady Huntsberry, I would appreciate your company. In our bed."

Her radiant smile felt like sunbeams warming him, and Judson kissed his wife again. Then he swept her off her feet, moving past two footmen and Clippman as he carried Lucy up the stairs to bed and made slow, deliberate love to her.

After they lay together, their limbs entangled, he kissed the top of her head.

"Judson? I must tell you something important." She paused. "I hope you will not be angry with me, but I went to see Miss Amato this morning."

"You saw Antonia?" He wondered how she had known about his former mistress, much less where to find her.

"Actually, I went to White's yesterday after I finished my errands, hoping to see you come out. You did not see the carriage, and I had the driver follow you." Lucy hesitated. "It was wrong of me to follow you to Miss Amato's. And when I saw the two of you kiss, I will admit that I saw red."

He couldn't believe his wife had witnessed that kiss and realized how deeply she had been hurt by it. Suddenly, everything made perfect sense. Her headache. The sudden, unexplained distance between them.

"I am sorry you saw us saying farewell. I did not kiss her, Lucy. She kissed me."

"I understand that now. And I think she's lovely." Lucy stroked his forearm. "I am glad you had her company. I hope she brought you some comfort during your time together."

"It is done between us," he assured her, his arms tightening about her. "In fact, I had not even seen Antonia after I met you. Until yesterday."

"She told me how kind you were to her. How you are helping her return to Luigi in Italy."

He marveled at what the two women had spoken about. "I hope you do not mind me engaging in this final task. Helping her return to Sienna."

"I think it is wonderful you are doing so." Lucy chuckled. "I even apologized for confronting her."

Curiosity filled him. "Why *did* you go to see her?"

Lucy lifted her head, their gazes meeting. "Because I love you so much. And I was jealous." She bit her lip. "I told her to keep her hands off you."

He grinned. "You did?"

Her palm cradled his cheek. "I most certainly did. Because you are mine. *My* husband. And I refuse to share you. Ever."

"Then it is a good thing that we agree on the matter. I do love you, Lucy. So much it almost hurts. I would do anything for you."

"I understand that now." Her eyes misted with tears. "And I am sorry I did not trust you. I promise I will do so from this day forward."

Judson kissed her tenderly. "We are in this marriage together. Forever. Just the two of us. And we will take the vows we spoke to one another to heart." He smiled. "You are the only woman for me, Lucy. I have bared my soul to you. I want to share everything with you."

Her love for him was obvious, for she was one of those people whose face reflected her every thought.

"I love you so much, Judson. I will always love you." Then she gave him a wicked grin. "I will love you even more after you put a babe in my belly. Perhaps we should work on that again. After all, my family will not be here for a few more hours."

He beamed at her. "I cannot think of a better way to pass the time, Wife."

CHAPTER TWENTY-TWO

LUCY PAUSED IN front of the doors leading into the drawing room, hearing laughter within. She smoothed her gown and took a deep breath before entering the room. It was her first time to entertain guests as a married lady.

And she was late to tea.

She wondered what excuse Judson had given to her parents, Con, and Ariadne and Julian. They had both summoned help to dress when they realized how late it was getting and that their visitors would arrive at any moment. Where Judson only had to run his fingers through his hair a few times to look presentable, Lucy had to have Annie redo her hair completely. After their first bout of lovemaking, several pins had fallen from her hair. Her husband had collected them from the bed and then removed the rest from her hair. He liked her hair when it was down, enjoying running his fingers through it.

Annie had brushed it out and placed it in a simple chignon due to lack of time. Lucy would have to have her maid redress it again for the theater tonight. They were to attend a performance with Ariadne and Julian, the couple sitting in Judson's box.

Taking one final, deep breath, she breezed into the room and headed toward her family.

"I am so sorry I am late to tea," she apologized.

"That is perfectly all right, Lucilla," Mama said. "Huntsberry told us you were finishing up interviewing candidates for when you open Huntsworth again. You can never be too careful when hiring your staff. You want to assess servants carefully and then check out the letters of reference they present. It is always best to speak to their former employers directly or at least write to them for a proper evaluation of a candidate's qualities and skills."

So, that was the white lie her husband had given. After Lucy had admitted going to see Antonia Amato, Judson had told her he wished for her to interview the servants which would be left behind, telling her that Cook was a real treasure and that Mrs. Worth, the housekeeper, and the other servants seemed to also do a good job. She had agreed to interview them all for consideration at Huntsworth, but Judson was to arrange those interviews to begin tomorrow morning. He said that he would send a note to Mrs. Worth once tea had concluded today, and she could inform the staff.

Others might have thought it odd that she would even contemplate hiring staff which had served her husband's former mistress, but Lucy didn't think those servants should suffer because her husband had ended his arrangement with his former mistress. It wasn't as if Miss Amato would be taking any of the servants back to Italy with her. Liking Miss Amato as she did after only their brief acquaintance, Lucy knew the woman wouldn't have tolerated mediocre help. The least she could do would be to interview the handful who would soon be out of a job. If she liked them well enough, she saw no problem in sending them to the country to help with the opening of the Surrey house. If Judson and Miss Amato had been pleased with their performance, she most likely would be, as well. And if she weren't, she could dismiss them after a trial period.

"Yes, Mama. Opening Huntsworth will require hiring a bevy of servants to staff it." Lucy took her seat, avoiding Judson's eyes because she was afraid she might burst into giggles. "We will need a butler and housekeeper. Numerous maids and kitchen help, as well as footmen. And we have yet to discuss the stables."

Her brother's interest was sparked. "Do you have any horses

in Surrey, Judson?"

"Not a one," he admitted. "I do enjoy riding, however, and I know Lucy does, as well." He looked at her with affection. "Darling, please add to your list a head groom and other grooms. I suppose we'll also need to investigate getting a few cats to act as mousers in the stables."

"If you need any help picking out horseflesh, I am at your service," Con said. "Perhaps Julian and I could accompany you to Tattersall's. You and Lucy will each need mounts to ride in the country, and you'll probably want one or two others, as well."

Two maids rolled in the teacart, and Lucy began pouring out for their company. She passed the first cup and saucer to Judson, who made sure Mama received it. She still hadn't been able to look at her husband. Telling a small fib about Lucy interviewing potential servants was a far better choice than confessing they had made love twice in broad daylight and had had to scramble to dress in time for tea.

Somehow, though, she had a feeling that Ariadne knew exactly what they had been up to. Her cousin had flashed a knowing smile at Lucy as she had taken a seat.

After everyone had their cups of tea and plates of cakes, she asked, "How is little Penelope doing?" She knew that would be a safe topic of conversation.

"She becomes more brilliant every day," declared Julian, elaborating on his daughter's latest milestones. "Penelope is eating better and sleeping more restfully. While she still needs a little help with supporting her neck, I can feel it growing stronger every day. Soon, she will be like a turtle, holding it up and moving it about as she explores the world."

"Penelope recognizes our voices," Ariadne said proudly. "While I love to sing to her, Julian enjoys reading to her."

"Isn't she a bit young to be read to?" Con asked, baffled.

"While she does not understand the words, I can tell reading soothes her," the proud papa said. "Besides, the more language she hears, the more quickly she will pick it up, in my opinion."

Talk turned to their evening plans, and Papa asked, "What play will you see performed this evening?"

"It is Shakespeare tonight," Judson replied. *"Henry IV, Part I.* Falstaff is to be played by a relative newcomer. I look forward to his performance."

"I always enjoy a good play," Ariadne said. "At least it will be over before the usual ball."

Con laughed. "You and Julian have slipped out early from many a ball this Season." He glanced to Lucy. "You and Judson, as well."

"It is what newlyweds do," she retorted. "Perhaps one day you shall be a newlywed yourself and better understand."

"Not for a long while," her brother said. "I may be sprouting gray at my temples before I decide to wed."

Mama glared at Con. "It is one thing to sow your wild oats, Constantine, and another bragging about them. You will wed. I need grandchildren from you."

Her brother pointed to Lucy. "Look no further, Mama. I will wager that by this time next year, my little sister will have a babe growing in her belly."

Mama sniffed. "That is all well and good, Constantine, but *you* are the heir to the earldom. That means you need sons, preferably more than one of them."

"All in good time, Mama," Con said placatingly.

"Would you like to show us more of the house?" Ariadne asking, obviously trying to smooth any ruffled feathers.

"I would love to give you a tour," she told her cousin, trying to ignore how Mama would view her brother's children as more important than Lucy's own. "We can leave the men at tea. I doubt they care about talk of bed furnishings and carpets and new paint." Lucy rose. "Mama, would you like to join us?"

"No. You two go ahead. I will make certain the gentlemen have all they need. Someone should remain to entertain them."

She couldn't help but feel that last bit was judgmental. Mama had always been hard on Dru and her, with Con easily being her favorite.

"We will be back in about half an hour," she said, motioning for Ariadne to come with her.

Once they were in the corridor, her cousin said, "Is Aunt Charlotte always so . . . so . . ."

"Overcritical?" Lucy ventured.

"Yes. She did not overtly criticize you, but I felt she judged you all the same. Yes, it would be different if we were not family, but I see nothing wrong with leaving the men to chat while you show off your new home. We leave them to their port and cigars after dinner, and they do just fine without our presence for half an hour."

"I think Mama wishes she had been born a man—and the heir to the dukedom. She always has held strong opinions and is never shy about expressing them. I do think she would have made for a good duke. She has a keen mind and is not afraid to use her authority. She also had little interest in her children growing up. Only Con has any favor with her at all, and it is because he is a male and the heir apparent. I believe Mama is happy to have me off her hands. I do dread things next year when Dru is to make her come-out."

"Will she and Aunt Charlotte clash?"

Lucy chuckled. "Terribly. Dru has expressed no interest in making her come-out. She would be happy to stay at Marleyfield the rest of her life. Marriage and babes are of no interest to her. Where I have tried to play the peacemaker and been the good child who always obeys Mama without question, Dru has forever fought tooth and nail with her. Things have never been rosy between them. Whether Mama realizes it or not, Dru is just like her. Stubborn. Opinionated. Never one to back down."

"Oh, Aunt Charlotte will have her hands full with Dru," predicted Ariadne. "It might come down to Dru deciding to stay with you and Judson if they quarrel so much."

"That is *if* Mama can even get Dru to come to town. I cannot imagine my sister spending hours at the modiste's, deciding on fabrics and styles of gowns. Why, she even goes about the estate in breeches the moment Mama and Papa's carriage is out of sight, and she remains in them for the most part until the Season ends and our parents come home. Except for church," she added.

"I am liking Dru the more I hear about her. Perhaps I should invite her to Aldridge Manor before next spring. Get to know her some. Tell her about the Season. Have her play some with Penelope." Her cousin smiled. "Being around Penelope might even change her mind about babes."

"That would be lovely, Ariadne. She and Mama argue frequently, so keeping them apart is an excellent idea. Why, I could also ask her to come and stay with us at Huntsworth. I know Judson would not mind. That way, we both could see her. Oh, you would also need to ask Toby to come."

"Toby?"

"He is Dru's constant companion. A gray tabby that is two years of age. Toby does not like anyone but Dru. He will tolerate me, but he hisses at anyone else."

"Oh, dear," fretted Ariadne. "That would not be good if he acts that way around Penelope. Julian would toss the cat out the door."

"And Dru would toss Julian out after him."

Both cousins erupted in peals of laughter.

"Come, let us go look at my new home," Lucy urged. "We can start at the top of the house. The nursery is bare except for a couple of cribs, but I would like you to see it anyway."

Ariadne slipped her arm through Lucy's as they climbed the stairs. "I do hope by next Season or the one after that you will have a babe to occupy it. You and Judson will be good parents, Lucy. I can feel it in my bones."

They toured the entire house, with Lucy telling Ariadne about some of the changes she was making to various rooms.

As they made their way back to the drawing room, her cousin said, "It is a fine house. You have done well for yourself, Lucy. I know you were rushed into this marriage with Judson in order to save your reputation, but the two of you seem to be getting along well."

"I visited his mistress yesterday. Told her to keep her hands off my husband," she said proudly.

"What?" Ariadne cried. "You did not."

"I most certainly did. Of course, I learned from Miss Amato that Judson had broken things off with her earlier. That she had not even seen him since he had met me. She is returning to Italy in the next few days."

"Amato, you say?"

"Yes. She was an opera diva who wound up having to leave the stage due to problems with her vocal cords. Miss Amato has a man waiting for her in Tuscany. Her childhood sweetheart. I actually liked her quite a bit."

Ariadne laughed. "Leave it to sweet Lucy to like her husband's mistress."

"*Former* mistress," she corrected. Then she grew serious and had them stop before they reentered the drawing room. "We love one another, Ariadne. Just as you and Julian do."

"Have you said those words to one another?"

She nodded. "And we both meant them. I trust Judson with all my heart."

Her cousin gave her a sly smile. "Were you *trusting* him before we arrived for tea? Is that why you were late?"

Her face grew hot. "Yes. I am interviewing servants tomorrow morning. We lost track of time, and I had to have Annie help me into my gown and repair my hair."

"Oh, Lucy. I am so glad to hear this." Ariadne hugged her. "This is wonderful news. Now, two of the cousins have made a love match."

"Only eight more of us to go," she said happily, and they returned to the drawing room.

Lucy knew how content she was and figured Ariadne was equally happy with her husband. She thought it would be interesting if all of their cousins were fortunate enough to make love matches. It would be up to Ariadne and her to lead the way—and possibly do a bit of matchmaking in the process.

CHAPTER TWENTY-THREE

As THEY REACHED the city limits of London, Judson asked Lucy, "Are you certain you do not mind missing some of the Season?"

She laced her fingers through his. "The Season, for some, is strictly about the social events they attend. Ariadne has a different view, which she has shared with me. She said the Season is time for family to come together. While she and Julian attend some of the events, she told me as their family grows, they will begin to choose only a handful of social affairs to go to."

Lucy squeezed his fingers. "You may not realize this, but bringing Penelope with them to town is quite unusual for parents to do. It is almost unheard of to bring children to town while the Season is in full swing. That is why Ariadne, her brother Val, Con, and I have all made a pact."

His wife smiled at him. "I told you a little about it before, but we were also engaged in other things."

"I do recall you mentioning it." He grinned. "But I am hazy on the details because my mind was on you."

"Then I will simply remind you. We agreed to bring our own children to town each time the Season begins. We ten cousins only met one another one time, and we are of a mind to raise our children together so they will know one another."

"I am all for that, love. Since I do not have a family, I have made yours mine. It would be delightful to have our children play with their cousins while we adults get to spend time together."

"I am glad we are of like minds," Lucy told him, resting her head upon his shoulder. "I also am so grateful that you have agreed to spend part of the year at Huntsworth. I believe raising children in the country is what is best for them. They need a place to roam and enjoy being children. They need to learn to appreciate the estate their family owns and learn about it. I am looking forward to seeing Huntsworth."

He remained silent, fear gnawing at him. Judson had not seen his country seat since he left for university. Mr. Baker had given him a generous quarterly allowance, which allowed him to maintain rooms year-round during his studies. Other young men had gone home at intervals. Not Judson. He had no desire to return to a place where he had been terrorized, to an uncle whom he feared might poison him to gain the title. He had made a deliberate decision to stay away from Huntsworth even after graduating. It was only because he loved his wife so much and wanted to please her that he was willing to go back now and live there most of the year.

"It amazes me that we will be at the house in Surrey in such a short time. I know because of the orphanage, Ariadne and Julian are able to travel to town for a couple of days each week when the Season is not going on. Somerset is far from London. It took us several days to journey from Marleyfield to town, staying at inns along the way."

"Is that the reason you did not see your cousins but the one time? The distance was so great?"

"I assume that to be the case. Uncle Charles and Aunt Alice, Ariadne's parents, live in Kent. My family was all the way on the western coast, while Uncle George and Aunt Agnes live in the north of England, in the Lake District. At least Aunt Agnes and the children do. Uncle George died several years ago. My cousin Hadrian is now the Earl of Traywick."

She sighed. "As an adult, I understand how travel is not easy, especially over great distances. That is why, not knowing where all we cousins will land after our marriages, Ariadne suggested we bring our children to town each spring. Eventually, our sons will be off at school during that time, but they can always join us in town once their spring term ends. The girls will have governesses, so they can continue their education."

She lifted her head, their gazes meeting. "Thank you for agreeing to bring our family to town. It means a great deal to me, Judson. Con, Dru, and I always felt abandoned when our parents left for a good portion of the year." She smiled ruefully. "Not that they paid much attention to us in the country, especially Dru and me."

He pressed his lips to her brow. "We will be different parents to our children than yours were to you and your siblings, love. We will form close bonds with them. After all, we only have to look to Julian's and Ariadne's example."

She chuckled. "Ariadne is a good mother, but I am most impressed at Julian as a father. I wish every titled gentleman in England could witness how batty he is over his daughter and be likewise."

He raised their joined hands and kissed her fingers again. "I hope I will have daughters to spoil in the same manner. Sons, too. Being an only child was lonely. If you are willing, I hope to fill Huntsworth with many children."

"Well, it will not be from lack of trying," she teased.

They switched horses at the halfway point of their journey, and by noon, they pulled into Alderton, the nearest village to his estate. Judson had written to Mr. and Mrs. Paul, his caretakers, as well as Wayling, his steward, so they would be expected.

Their carriage pulled up at the local inn, and he handed down Lucy. They went inside, where he found the Pauls waiting for them. He introduced Lucy to them, and Mr. Paul handed over the keys to the house.

"Everything is in good shape, my lord," the gray-haired man told him. "I walk the outside of the house once a week, while Mrs. Paul checks the inside for things such as leaks. And Mr.

Wayling, of course, handles everything else on the estate."

"Thank you for taking care of the property for me, Mr. Paul," Judson said. "Lady Huntsberry and I will be living at Huntsworth for a good portion of the year in the future. We will open the house back up, so I want to thank you both for your service to me."

"It's been a pleasure, my lord," Mrs. Paul said, beaming at them. "And it's so good to hear you'll be back in residence with her ladyship."

"We will be sending servants down soon," he shared with the couple. "We have hired a butler and housekeeper, as well as a cook, but we'll need several maids and footmen."

Lucy spoke up. "If you know of anyone in the village who might be looking for employment, please let us know. I would like to interview them while we are here over the next few days."

The Pauls left, and the innkeeper came to greet them, telling them their room was ready and their things had been brought up. He also assured them that Annie and Tim had been given small rooms of their own.

"Might I offer you some refreshment?" the innkeeper asked.

He looked to his wife, who nodded. "We would appreciate that."

After a light repast, Judson asked, "Are you willing to stretch your legs a bit? The house is about a mile and half from the village."

"That sounds heavenly," Lucy replied. "I get stiff riding in a carriage after a few hours."

The May day was mild, and he pointed out several shops in the village as they walked through it. When they passed the graveyard next to the church, he paused for a moment.

Lucy, ever attuned to his mood, asked, "Would you like to go and see your parents' graves?"

They entered the graveyard, and he went straight to the section reserved for the Jarvis family. He stopped before his parents' graves, looking at their names carved into the stone and the dates of their existence. A lump grew in his throat, and his fingers found Lucy's, glad she was by his side for support.

"I wish I had known her," he said softly. "Mama. Papa always said she was a gentle soul and that I favored her in looks and manners."

Judson turned his gaze to his father's grave, hurt welling within him. "Papa was never well. I almost feel guilty having robust health."

She squeezed his fingers. "You should never think that, Judson. Think of how proud your parents would be of you. Of what you have accomplished."

"They would have liked you," he said softly. "You are good and kind and have such strength of character." Emotion swelled within him. "I cannot tell you what it meant to me to hear you defend me to Uncle Jeremiah."

"I love you," she said simply. "I would walk to the ends of the earth for you. Do not say his name ever again, Judson. He is no family to you. He is evil incarnate. Banish all thoughts of him."

"I will," he responded, though how he would be able to do so while they were at Huntsworth would prove to be impossible. Every room—every inch of the property—would most likely remind him of the abuse he'd suffered under his uncle's hand.

They reached the estate, and Lucy began speaking animatedly, praising the beauty of the land.

When they reached the house itself, he heard her audible gasp. "Oh, Judson! Your house is beautiful."

He framed her face with his hands. "*Our* house, love. The house where we will raise our children. The house where we become a family."

They approached the front door, and he removed the keys from his pocket and unlocked it. The foyer was dim, so he left the door open.

Lucy said, "We shall open the curtains in every room so we might see things better."

They went up the stairs, starting in the drawing room. He

helped Lucy fling back the curtains, allowing light to enter the large room. She insisted upon pulling covers from some of the furniture, wanting to see what was beneath it.

"Oh, these are some lovely pieces, Judson. Yes, there will be things to do. Rooms to be aired. Carpets to have dust beaten from them. Furniture to be polished and painting to be done."

She twirled impulsively, her arms wide, and he caught her joy.

Lucy flung her arms about him. "We are going to be so happy here, Judson. I promise."

They investigated other rooms. He swallowed the emotions which continued to rise within him, especially when he showed her his childhood bedchamber. He explained how his father had spent most of this time in the room across the hall. Confused, she asked why the marquess had not occupied the rooms set aside for him.

Not bothering to hide his bitterness, he told her, "My uncle took those rooms for himself."

She caught the lapels of his coat and pulled him down to her, kissing him softly.

"Lead on," she told him, and they continued their tour.

Lucy was pleased with how large the nursery was, saying it was one of the first places she wanted to be refreshed. He knew how much she yearned for babes, and he found himself feeling the same.

They returned to the ground floor, looking at the kitchens and a few other smaller rooms. Then they reached the study, where Judson froze in his tracks.

"What is behind this door, Judson?"

"A world of misery," he said dully. "Memories I wish I could forget."

"Then we are here to conquer them," she said firmly, pushing the door open.

She marched to the curtains and threw them open. He stood in the doorway, afraid to step inside what had been his uncle's domain. Lucy came to him, taking his hand, pulling him into the room.

His eyes swept the length of the study. Fear seized him. He had been terrorized in this room more than any other. Beaten. Berated. Made to feel as if he were less than nothing.

A strangled cry escaped from his lips. Judson found himself sobbing uncontrollably.

His wife's arms went about him. "Let it out, my love. All that you have kept bottled up inside you. Allow it to escape—and be gone."

He could not remember the last time he had cried, but a river of tears came now. He should be ashamed of behaving in such a manner, but Judson realized how well Lucy understood him. He let his tears fall, the heaving sobs erupting again and again. Throughout it all, Lucy held fast to him, letting him know he was not alone. That he would never be alone again.

Once the tears ended, he understood how right she had been. They had acted as a catharsis, cleansing his soul. Judson gazed down at her, gratitude now filling him instead of fear and panic.

"You have dispelled the demons from your past, my darling," his wife told him. "You and I will create new memories from this moment forward. This is *our* home. We are going to fill it with love and laughter and many good times. We will have children, and they will be the center of our lives, as well as the love we have for one another. We will have our family visit us here at Huntsworth. From this day forward, this place is one you will always look upon fondly. Happiness will abound at Huntsworth."

Judson knew Lucy was right. It was as if the chains which had bound him, chains of the past, now fell away. He was unshackled. Free to do as he wished. Live as he wanted, no ghosts of the past haunting him.

He gazed down at the woman who had changed his life in such a short amount of time.

"Have I told you today how much I love you?"

"Twice, I believe," she said saucily.

"Then perhaps I should say it thrice—and show you, as well. Christen our new home."

Mischief lit her eyes. "Are you thinking of making love to me here, Lord Huntsberry?"

He yanked her to him. "That is exactly what I had in mind, Lady Huntsberry."

His mouth seized hers, hard and demanding. She yielded immediately. It was hard to explain how hungry he was for her. It was something Judson had never felt for any other woman, but Lucy set him afire.

They kissed for a long time, his mouth finally leaving hers, nuzzling her throat, moving lower, his tongue licking the rounded curves of her breasts peeking out from her neckline. She gripped his cock through his breeches, her hand massaging, teasing, stroking until he was mad for her.

Judson released her, striding to where the desk sat. Ripping off the cloth that covered it, he saw nothing upon it. Just a flat surface that would be absolutely perfect for what he had in mind.

Returning to Lucy, he captured her wrist, pulling her to the desk. His hands spanned her waist, lifting her to sit upon the edge, her feet dangling.

"My goodness, my lord," she purred. "I think I know what you have in mind."

He grinned wickedly. "I don't think you have a clue, my darling."

Easing her to her back, her legs still dangling off the desk, he bunched up her gown, raising it to above her waist. His lips and tongue moved across her belly, and Judson saw her shudder at the touch. He grabbed her ankles, placing her feet flat upon the desk, and parted her legs. Softly, he blew against the seam of her sex, sending another shudder through her.

"I cannot wait to taste you," he growled, licking the seam and then parting her with his fingers.

His tongue plunged inside her, causing Lucy to gasp. "Judson!"

He glanced up, seeing her head raised, and pulled back a moment. "Back down, love," he ordered, and she obeyed him immediately.

Using his fingers, his teeth, and his tongue, Judson made love to his wife, delighting in each moan. Each whimper. Each tremble. Her fingers pushed into his hair, clutching it tightly, as she panted. She tasted sweeter than any treat from Gunter's, and he reveled in the fact that she was his. He was the only man who had touched her thus.

Lucy began to moan loudly now, releasing his hair, her head moving back and forth even as her body began gyrating. He sensed her release and then heard her shout his name. Her body shook as her hips rose, her breathing rapid and shallow. The orgasm went on for a long time, and then she stilled.

Judson stood, leaning over her, pressing his body to hers. "How was that?"

Her dazed expression told him all he needed to know.

"I . . . I had no idea we could make love away from our bed." She smiled up at him. "If I weren't so bloody limp, I would sit up and embrace you, but I cannot seem to even move."

"Then I will move you. Give me a moment."

Quickly, he unbuttoned his breeches, pushing them down his thighs to his knees. Joining his wife on the desk, he lay with his back flat against it before rolling her on top of him.

Lucy's eyes lit up. "Oh, my favorite," she proclaimed. "You know how fond I am of riding. A horse—and you."

She quickly sat up, pushing her gown and undergarments up. "My, Lord Huntsberry. Your manhood already stands tall and proud for me."

He groaned as she hovered over him, taking him into her, seating herself atop him. Ever so slowly, she began to move, the undulating motion teasing him. Tantalizing him. Torturing him. He reached out his arms, and their fingers joined. His wife pressed hard against his arms as she began to ride him, the tempo increasing, his groans growing louder, laughter spilling from her as the wild ride took them to heights they had never known.

They climaxed at the same time, their cries in unison as she fell to his chest, still straddling him. They lay together, their breathing finally slowing. Judson stroked her hair.

Finally, he said, "If I had known how the country air would affect the both of us, I would have abandoned town long ago."

Peals of laughter came from her, and he joined in, hugging her tightly to him.

"No wonder men want such large desks," she mused. "I do believe the study might become my favorite room at Huntsworth."

"I think we should christen every room in the house in this manner," he told her. "And there are a lot of rooms."

"Don't forget the stables," she added. "And if there is a summer house or gazebo, we must not neglect it."

He lifted Lucy slightly so he could kiss her. "And here I thought I was going to be the bad influence on you. Who knew you were the more wicked of the two of us?"

"I like it best when we are wicked together," she declared, kissing him again.

Judson had never been happier than in this moment. He had found love with a wonderful woman, and he knew they had a bright future ahead of them.

CHAPTER TWENTY-FOUR

EVEN THOUGH THEY were living in an inn, the past week had been the happiest of Lucy's life. She had grown even closer to her husband, and she believed that she helped him dispel the demons from his past.

She smiled at him across the table as they finished their breakfast in the common room of the inn.

"So, you will be with Mr. Wayling for a good part of the day?"

He reached for her hand. "Yes. Wayling and I will go over the estate's ledgers for the last decade."

"You will enjoy doing so, Judson. You have expressed your interest in numbers to me. It will be good for you to look at the various trends over the last several years. See which crops had the best yield and which livestock was most profitable."

He rubbed his thumb in a slow circle along her palm, sending frissons of desire running through her.

Quietly, Lucy said, "You have already made love to me once this morning, Judson. I would not wish for you to be late for your appointment with Mr. Wayling."

"Will I see you at the house?"

"I will be there for a short while, and then Mrs. Amesbury has asked me to come and talk with her and some of the other tenants' wives over tea."

Two days ago, the new servants they had hired in town had

arrived, including a butler and Mrs. Worth, who had been Miss Amato's housekeeper. Lucy had found the woman to be a mixture of no-nonsense when it came to tasks at hand and compassionate, a unique blend which she thought would make for a very good housekeeper for Huntsworth.

Lucy had a hired a few local girls from the village to serve as maids, and Mrs. Worth had taken them under her wing as dustcloths were stripped away from furniture and a deep cleaning of the house had begun. By the time the Season ended, and they returned to Surrey, everything would be in good order. She had even hired the local carpenter and his son. Both men were hard at work, making small repairs to the house and painting several of the rooms.

"Will you walk me to the hostler's?" Judson asked.

"I would be happy to."

They left the inn and traveled down the main thoroughfare of the village, greeting Mr. Abel, who had rented horses for them to ride while they were staying in Alderton. Her husband had taken her riding across the entire estate, and she wanted to pinch herself, finding her new home lovely. The only thing that would take a good deal of time and effort to restore were the gardens, which had gone wild during Judson's absence.

"Shall we ride to Huntsworth together?" Judson asked.

"No, you go ahead of me. I intend to write a letter to Dru before I go up to the house."

She had put off writing to her sister when she and Judson first wed, not certain what she wanted to say about her marriage. Now that she felt she was on firm ground with it, she wanted to share her good news with Dru. Lucy doubted Mama would have written to Dru about the wedding because Mama had never written a single letter to any of them while she was away at the Season.

"I will stop by Mr. Wayling's office, however," she told Judson.

The estate's steward had worked all these years from the

cottage that came with his position. Since they were permanently opening the house, Wayling had expressed the desire to use the office within it marked for the steward's use. The room contained all the records of the estate, so it was more convenient for him to work from there. The room had already been given a fresh coat of paint, and the furniture had been polished until it gleamed.

Her husband leaned over and gave her a soft kiss. "Then I will see you later, love."

She liked how he used the endearment with her. It made her glow each time it came from his sensual lips.

Lucy waved as he rode off and told Mr. Abel that she would be back in an hour to claim her own mount. He told her he would have the horse saddled and ready. She returned to the inn and asked the innkeeper to bring her parchment and ink. She chose to remain at a table in the common room since it would be the best place to compose her letter to Dru.

Dru—

I am writing to you about an event which has changed my life. I am a married lady!

The wedding took place almost a month ago. My only regret is that you were not present to see it. My husband is Judson Jarvis, the Marquess of Huntsberry. His country estate is located in Surrey. In a wonderful coincidence, I will be neighbors with Cousin Ariadne and her husband Julian, the Marquess of Aldridge. Julian's country seat is adjacent to my new husband's estate.

Dru, I was reluctant to write to you at first because of the mixed emotions I had regarding my marriage. I will tell you more about what led to our deciding to wed when I see you. I must admit I was not happy at the beginning to have to wed so quickly. I was caught in a compromising position with Judson by one of the ton's most notorious gossips. If we had not wed immediately, my own reputation would have been in tatters. You and Con would also have been affected by that, as well.

The thing is, I already had feelings for Judson before this incident occurred. I was worried going into a marriage where his hand—and mine—had been forced, but I have found my husband to be the kindest, most generous man of my acquaintance.

Dru—I love him. I would sing that to the heavens. I never expected to make a love match. In fact, I had never even considered the possibility until I witnessed the love between Ariadne and Julian and wondered if I might find it for myself. They are meant for one another, just as Judson and I are meant to be man and wife. I love my husband more each day, and he feels the same way about me. He not only loves me, Dru, he values my opinions and treats me with respect. I could not ask for more, and I am the happiest I have ever been.

We have come to Huntsworth, his country seat, to open the house up again. Judson has not been here in over a decade. His family history is a sad one, with him losing his mother during childbirth and his father when Judson was but ten years of age. The house had many sad memories for him, and after university, he chose to remain in town year-round.

We are opening the house again now, however. My husband understands how much I enjoy the country and how I want to raise our children here. He is more than amenable to that.

That means, even though Huntsworth has had a caretaker, there is much to be done at the house to make it livable again. While Judson gets to know his tenants and the property better and is working with his steward, I am supervising our new servants in helping prepare the house for us to live here once the Season ends.

I would like you to come and stay with us, Dru. Please say you will. It would be wonderful to see you again, and Judson is so looking forward to meeting a new sister. He is an only child, and he and Con have become friends. I hope they will grow to feel as though they are brothers. You could also reacquaint yourself with Ariadne and meet Julian since they are nearby. Please consider this. It would also give you time away from Mama. That alone should have you racing to Surrey!

*We will return to town soon and finish out the Season be-
fore coming back to Huntsworth in August. I hope at that time
that you would come to us. Judson has said you may stay as
long as you wish, even up to next spring when you go to town
for your own come-out. Oh, I can hear you now, protesting
about that, but I do believe there is a man out there for you, my
dearest sister. One who will let you be the person you are and
not try to change you in any way.*

*I hope my letter finds you well. Know how much I miss you
and love you. I cannot wait to hear from you. Please write soon,
Dru.*

All my love,
Lucy

At the end of the letter, she added a postscript, indicating her
new address in town, as well as where to write her in Surrey. She
did want to see Dru desperately. They were only a year apart in
age and had always been the closest of friends. Lucy thought it
would be good for Dru to get away from Marleyfield and from
under Mama's thumb.

She addressed the letter to her sister in Somerset and asked
the innkeeper for sealing wax. He told her he would post it today,
and she thanked him.

Returning to Mr. Abel's stables, Lucy claimed her horse and
rode the short distance to Huntsworth. She led the horse into the
stables, empty save for the horse Judson had ridden there. She
and Judson had talked about buying several horses for them to
ride. Their carriage horses would also be kept in the stables, but
they had yet to hire any grooms, so the team currently resided
with other horses at Mr. Abel's.

She left the horse saddled and led it into a stall because she
would only be at the house for a short while. Stroking its neck,
Lucy said, "I will be back soon, pretty one."

Leaving the stables, she went to the house, cutting through
the kitchens to find Mrs. Worth. Together, they walked through

the house so she could see the progress being made.

"How much longer will you be in Alderton, my lady?" the housekeeper asked.

"Now that you are here and things are in capable hands, I believe we will depart either tomorrow or the following day. We will return sometime in August once the Season has concluded. I will be certain to write to you so that you know when to expect us."

"I wanted to tell you how pleased I am with the girls you hired from the village. They are hard workers. All you will need to employ now are footmen and stable help."

"I know one of the maids has a brother who might come to work for us in the stables. Otherwise, I will hire the footmen and others once we return to town. I will send them to Surrey as soon as I can."

"I cannot thank you and his lordship enough, Lady Huntsberry, for offering me the position of housekeeper at Huntsworth. The same goes for Cook and the other maids who served Miss Amato. Forgive my frankness, but not everyone would have been as generous as you in hiring us on."

"I do not look at you as reminder of the time my husband had a mistress," she assured Mrs. Worth. "You are quite skilled at what you do. Besides, Miss Amato was present before I entered my husband's life. She has now returned home to find her own happiness, just as Lord Huntsberry and I have found ours."

The housekeeper beamed at her. "It is not often you see a love match within Polite Society, my lady. I am very happy for you and his lordship."

"Thank you, Mrs. Worth. I am off to see my husband and Mr. Wayling, and then I am going to meet with Mrs. Amesbury and have tea with her and few of the other tenants' wives. If I do not speak to you before we leave, I wish to thank you for all your efforts in opening the house again so that we might live here in comfort."

Lucy went to the steward's office, where she found Wayling

and her husband bent over a ledger. Other ledgers were opened, scattered about the desk. She couldn't help but think what she and Judson had done on the desk in his study and decided a repeat performance might be in order.

"Good morning, Lady Huntsberry," Mr. Wayling greeted.

"Are you finding your office to your liking?" she asked the steward.

He smiled and enthusiastically said, "I am indeed, my lady. It is much easier to work from this office, which is set up properly, than from my cottage."

Judson came to her, taking her hand in his. "Have you concluded your business with Mrs. Worth?"

"Yes. She has everything in hand. I told her we would most likely leave tomorrow or the next day, as soon as you and Mr. Wayling have concluded your own business."

"Wayling and I will finish up today, so we can return to town tomorrow if that suits you."

"Then I shall have Annie and Tim pack for us. I am off to tea now with Mrs. Amesbury and the others."

He brushed his lips against her cheek. "Have a wonderful time, love."

Lucy left the house and returned to the stables. She led the horse out to the mounting block and used it to push herself into the saddle. She and Judson had already visited the area where the tenants had their cottages, which was about two miles away, so she knew her way there.

She spent a good two hours with Mrs. Amesbury and five other farmers' wives. They told her of their lives at Huntsworth and shared stories of their children and some about others in the village. Lucy had regularly visited her own family's tenants, bringing baskets of food and other needed items, celebrating the births of their babes, and letting those tenants know how valued they were. She planned to continue doing the same here at Huntsworth.

"I need to leave," she finally told the group. "Lord Huntsberry and I will be returning to town tomorrow, and so we need to pack our things."

Mrs. Amesbury smiled broadly. "We're delighted to hear of your marriage, my lady, and the fact that you and his lordship will be in residence now most of the year. It is how things should be."

"I could not agree more, Mrs. Amesbury. Thank you for your hospitality." She gazed about the group. "I look forward to seeing all of you again, come August."

Lucy left the cottage and undid the reins tied to a hitching post. One of the younger wives accompanied her, giving her a boost into the saddle. She waved goodbye to the woman and decided to return to the house and see if Judson might be ready to accompany her back to Alderton.

She dismounted and led her horse into the same stall as before, telling it, "I will be back shortly."

Others might think her mad for talking to an animal, but she had picked up the habit from Dru, who loved animals probably as much as she did people, especially Toby.

Lucy closed the door to the stall and suddenly sensed another presence. She glanced to her left, freezing in place. The Earl of Eaton stood mere steps from her. He held a pistol in his hand.

Aimed at her.

CHAPTER TWENTY-FIVE

THOUGH FEAR WASHED through her, Lucy wasn't ready to die yet. She had so much more living to do. She wanted to spend decades with Judson, loving and being loved by him. She looked forward to raising their children and then living to see their grandchildren. She wanted to get to know all of her cousins. Determination filled her.

Calmly, she asked, "What are you doing here, my lord?"

He looked taken aback at her question—and her composure. He licked his lips nervously.

"You should not be here. You should be at your own estate," she continued, locking her fingers together so he wouldn't see her hands trembling. She noticed his nose sat slightly askew from Judson's blow to it on the night Eaton and Humley had tried to ruin her.

He recovered and said harshly, "I am here to do what I started before. Hurt you—to hurt Huntsberry."

She stared hard at him, recalling what Judson had confided to her. "Why do you wish to harm my husband, Lord Eaton?"

"Because he ruined my life," the earl hissed.

"He told me about it. How you and Humley bullied him for years when you were boys. How he finally grew larger and stronger and told you never to bully another boy again, else there would be consequences."

Anger sizzled in Eaton's eyes. "Who was Huntsberry to go

about issuing edicts? Yes, Humley and a few others and I had teased him some, but—"

"You did *not* tease him, my lord," Lucy said, her own anger rising now within her. "You abused him. Tormented him. Beat him. Starved him. Even locked him outside with snow on the ground, his hair and clothes sopping wet. It could have killed him."

Wariness filled the earl's eyes. "He told you that?" Before she could reply, Eaton said, "He is lying. We only had a little fun."

She glared at him. "It was not fun. He was undersized, and you and your cadre of bullies took advantage of him. You hurt him. Embarrassed him. Tortured him. All to make yourselves feel superior. And when Judson finally grew and stood up to you, he was protecting all those other innocent boys from suffering at your hands." Lucy paused. "You deserved everything he did to you—and more."

A growl came from his throat, sounding like a wounded animal. "Huntsberry hurt me physically. Badly. Enough where I left school. And then I had to face my father's wrath."

Lucy kept silent, subtly glancing about the stables, seeing if there was anything she might use as a weapon against him. She decided to try and keep him talking, hoping to buy herself time to get out of this impossible situation.

"What happened with your father, my lord?"

Eaton's gaze pinned hers. "He hurt me worse than Huntsberry," he said, his voice hoarse. "Told me what a coward I had been. He was ashamed that I had let another boy physically harm me and chase me from school." His tone grew deadly. "Father never forgot—and he never forgave me for allowing Huntsberry to get the best of me."

A part of her sympathized with the boy this man had been because of what his own father had done to him. Still, Eaton had bullied and hurt so many others. Lucy wanted to point out to his that his actions had held consequences, but she knew her words would merely enrage him. He had turned his entire focus upon

Judson. Eaton believed everything he had suffered had been her husband's fault and would never accept he was, in large part, to blame.

"Even when he lay dying," Eaton continued, "he berated me from his sickbed. Told me that I was a waste of humanity and would never be a tenth of the man he was. I swore to him as he took his last breath that I would avenge myself. And make Huntsberry pay."

She swallowed hard, forcing down all emotion as Lord Eaton looked away, his memories taking him back to a painful time. He was distracted. Absorbed for a moment in the past. This was her chance.

Lucy made her move.

JUDSON LISTENED TO Wayling, his attention finally beginning to wander.

Back to his wife . . .

He would readily admit he was obsessed with Lucy. She had become his wife, lover, and best friend in a short time. Deciding these ledgers could wait—and his wife could not—he interrupted his steward.

"I think that will be enough for now, Wayling. You have done a remarkable job these past ten years in keeping Huntsworth profitable. Actually, the three years before that, as well."

The steward smiled. "It was a happy day when Mr. Jarvis hired me for the position, my lord."

The thought of his uncle soured his belly.

"I have a good grasp of the state of affairs at this point. We will meet again at length when Lady Huntsberry and I return in a few months."

"It was a pleasure meeting Lady Huntsberry, my lord. All the tenants are most impressed with her. And they are very happy that you have chosen to come back to Huntsworth and stay for part of the year."

"I am sorry if they think I neglected them. I did," he admitted. "But my marriage has changed my view on many things. Huntsworth is now my priority." He grinned. "Next to Lady Huntsberry, that is."

"Have a safe trip back to London, my lord," the steward said. "You will be here in time for the fall harvest. I think you and Lady Huntsberry will help to revive some of the old traditions regarding the harvest with your presence."

Judson knew the harvest involved music and dancing. If dancing in the moonlight hadn't previously been a tradition at Huntsworth, he would make certain it was from this point onward. Having Lucy in his arms and dancing under a full moon seemed the best idea he'd had in a quite a while.

He bid farewell to Wayling and also his new butler and housekeeper before making his way to the stables. He was eager to return to the inn and get his beautiful wife in bed again.

The door to the stables was open, which gave him pause. Lucy would have closed it behind her when she left to go to the tenants' cottages. Concerned, he picked up his pace and moved closer, stepping into a nightmare.

As he entered the stables, he saw Lucy with her back to him. Lord Eaton stood a few feet in front of her, a pistol in his hand. Shock paralyzed Judson for a moment, and then he raced toward his wife, hoping to draw Eaton's attention away from her.

But Lucy, too, began moving, hurling herself at the earl. His arm swung up, and he fired the pistol just as Lucy crashed into him, knocking them both to the ground. A whizz of hot air shot by his right ear, and Judson realized how close he had come to being shot.

He reached Lucy and Eaton, his hands clasping her waist just as she threw a hard punch into Eaton's face. The earl groaned, blood spurting from his nose. Judson lifted his wife from atop Eaton, swinging her away, and then placing her on her feet.

"Judson!" she exclaimed, wrapping her arms about him tightly, burying her face in his chest. He could feel the tremors which rocked her body.

"Are you all right, love?" he asked, dreading her answer.

She sniffed, looking up at him. "I am. He did not hurt me. He was distracted, and I knew I had to act."

"Stay," he commanded, pushing her aside because he saw Eaton staggering to his feet.

"I have failed again. Miserably," the earl said, dejection in his voice. His gaze met Judson's. "I tried to exact revenge upon you by compromising Lady Lucy because I thought you cared for her. Now, my second attempt has gone even worse." He glared at Judson. "I wanted to hurt her so you would suffer as I have."

Judson didn't know if this man had thought to kidnap Lucy. Rape her. Or even murder her. The problem was, even if he tried to bring charges with the local constable's help, Eaton was a peer. And peers were never punished for their crimes.

The only way to hurt Eaton was financially. Or socially.

"Get off my property," he said, his tone wintry. "And know that I will do everything in my power to see you brought to your knees. If you have investments, I will see that you lose money. If you have gambling debts, I will make certain they are all called in at once."

That struck a note with Eaton, who visibly winced.

"You are a plague which must be washed away, Eaton," he continued. "You tried to cause me pain by harming my wife. She is the most precious thing in the world to me, and I would protect her with my life. If you set foot on my property again—if you dare to even address Lady Huntsberry—I will kill you on the spot."

A defeated-looking Eaton reclaimed his pistol. "I will save you the effort, Huntsberry." He brushed past Judson and left the stables without a backward glance.

Lucy ran to him, hugging him tightly, covering his face in kisses. He let her do so, enjoying the feel of her against him.

She finally stopped. "What will you do to him, Judson?"

"You heard what I said."

"Would you truly kill him?" she asked.

He framed her face in his hands. "I will if he threatens you. I love you, Lucy, my darling. I will do whatever it takes to keep you safe."

Judson kissed her, a long, hard kiss that claimed her as his for all time. He thought to hire a Bow Street runner once they returned to town, someone who would keep him abreast of every move Eaton made.

For now, though, all he wanted to do was kiss his wife.

"You know what a treasure you are to me," he murmured against her lips.

"I know my life is richer and fuller and always will be, because I have your love," she responded, grasping his nape and pressing his lips back to hers.

He ended the kiss. "If there were hay in one of these stalls, I would bed you here," he said roughly. "Since there isn't, we should go back to the inn. Do you feel up to riding?"

Lucy's luminous smile dazzled him. "I will race you back to Alderton," she said, breaking away from him and heading to the stall where her horse stood, fully saddled.

She took its reins and hurried past him, and Judson knew she headed for the mounting block.

"You have the advantage," he called after her, rushing to the stall where his own horse stood. "I must saddle my mount."

Lucy appeared atop her horse in the open doorway. "Then that will give me time to be naked and in bed waiting for you, Lord Huntsberry."

Laughing, she nudged her horse's flanks and took off.

Judson had never saddled a horse so fast.

EPILOGUE

August—Final night of the Season

J UDSON PATIENTLY WAITED as Tim tied his cravat. They would be attending the last event of the Season this evening. Tomorrow, he and Lucy would return to Surrey until next spring. He was looking forward to their new life together in the country.

The valet stepped back, eyeing his work, and then smiled. "You're ready, my lord. And everything is packed for the journey, save for the clothes I have laid out for you in your dressing room for you to wear tomorrow."

"I have not asked you, Tim, which is remiss of me, but are you happy to be returning to Huntsworth?"

"I remember those days at Huntsworth, my lord. I know they were difficult for you after your father passed. You have Lady Huntsberry now, though, and she brings light and joy everywhere she goes."

A wonderful warmth filled him. "She does, doesn't she?"

His world was one he shared with Lucy now. His wife had given him a second start at life. He looked forward to their time in the country, where her sister Dru would come to visit them soon. Judson also knew next Season would be a different one because he would have family from the start of it. Family to lean upon. He had already grown closer with Con these past few months, as well as Julian and Ariadne. He had even taken to holding Penelope upon occasion when he could wrestle her away from her father.

Dismissing Tim, he went to box which sat upon a table. He

was gifting Lucy with a necklace this evening.

He only wondered if she might tell him of the child she carried.

Judson had begun to notice Lucy's breasts seemed a bit larger. There was also a slight curve to her belly which had not been there before. It struck him that his wife might not yet realize she was with child. She had been quite innocent when they wed although she was now a woman who enjoyed pleasing him in bed and being pleased herself.

Of course, most girls making their come-outs had little to no knowledge of what took place in the bedroom, and Lucy might not understand she was with child because she had exhibited no signs of the awful retching each morning that many women did once they were increasing. It was early, though, so that might come to pass in the near future.

Still, her courses had ceased, so Judson knew she did carry his child.

No, *their* child. They were partners in every endeavor, and that included the babe which they had made together.

He opened the jeweler's box and removed the diamond necklace from it, slipping it into his pocket, and making his way to his wife's bedchamber. Judson lightly tapped on the door and then entered the room, seeing Lucy seated at her dressing table as Annie put the finishing touches on her hair.

"Hello, my darling," his wife said, their eyes meeting in the mirror.

"Hold still, my lady," Annie lightly chided. "I'm almost done. Another pin or two should do it."

Lucy's tawny hair was piled high atop her head, and all he wanted to do was remove every pin and let it spill to her waist, his fingers running through the long, silky tresses. That would have to wait until later tonight.

"Oh, Annie, it is your best effort yet," Lucy declared.

"Will there be anything else, my lady?" the maid asked.

"No. You may go."

Judson took Annie's place, standing behind his wife, resting his hands on her shoulders. "You are a vision of loveliness, Lady Huntsberry. I think you are lacking one thing, however."

"What?" she asked, clearly puzzled by his remark.

"Close your eyes. I have a gift for you; I wish for you to wear it this evening."

The corners of her mouth turned up. "Oh, a surprise! I do not believe I have ever been surprised with a gift."

"Close your eyes," he repeated, and she did so.

Removing the necklace from his pocket, his fingers found both ends of it, and Judson lifted it over Lucy's head, resting the necklace against her satin skin as he fastened the clasp. He took a moment to admire her image in the mirror a moment before saying, "You may open your eyes, love."

She did, her eyes filled with wonder as her fingertips touched the necklace. "Diamonds? You bought me diamonds? Oh, Judson, they are so expensive. I do not deserve something such as—"

"You deserve everything, Lucy Jarvis. The sun. The moon. The stars. I would give them all to you if I could. I know we wed in haste, and I was remiss not to think to give you a wedding present before now. I thought the last night of the Season would be an appropriate time to do so."

"But I never gave you any gift," she protested.

He helped her to her feet, his arms encircling her. "You have given me numerous gifts, love. The gift of yourself. The gift of helping me quell my demons. The gift of your family, which is fast becoming my own." He paused. "And most importantly, the gift of your love."

Judson kissed her softly, treasuring each moment he had with this remarkable woman.

"Come. We should go downstairs. Julian's carriage will be here at any moment."

He escorted his wife to the foyer, and Clippman told them Lord Aldridge's carriage had just arrived. They were accompanying Julian and Ariadne to this last ball.

"Con!" Lucy cried, seeing her brother had joined their party as she entered the carriage. "How lovely to see you."

"Is that a new necklace?" Ariadne asked. "It is incredible. And diamonds."

Lucy fingered it as Judson took a seat beside her. "Judson gave it to me tonight. It is a belated wedding gift."

"Or it may be a new tradition," he ventured. "I can see giving my beautiful wife a piece of jewelry at the end of each Season to commemorate another year having passed."

"You would have to say that aloud," Julian grumbled good-naturedly. "Now, I will be obligated to do the same with my wife."

Ariadne rested her head on her husband's shoulder. "You are gift enough to me, Julian. You give of yourself to me every single day."

Con chuckled. "Love is oozing from this carriage. Perhaps I should get out and walk so as not to be touched by it."

"I hope you will be struck by Cupid's arrow, Con," Lucy told her brother. "Being in love is absolutely the most wonderful feeling in the world." She slipped her hand around Judson's, lacing their fingers together.

They arrived at the ball, and Julian climbed from the carriage, handing down Ariadne and then Lucy.

As Lucy exited the carriage, Con quietly said, "The coroner's inquest has concluded. Death by misadventure." His brother-in-law bounded from the carriage.

Con referred to Lord Eaton. Not long after Judson and Lucy had returned to town after their encounter with the earl, news arrived that Eaton was dead. Gossip abounded, claiming everything from murder to suicide. Other stories challenged those, saying that Eaton had merely been cleaning his pistol when it misfired, striking him in the head, killing him instantly.

The verdict did not matter one whit to Judson. Eaton was dead and would never trouble them again.

He collected his wife, and the five of them joined the receiving line inside their destination. They greeted their hosts and then entered the ballroom. He thought how different tonight was, compared to the opening night of this Season. He had entered it without friends, hoping to make a marriage of convenience.

Instead, he had found everlasting love.

THE NEXT MORNING, Judson breakfasted with Lucy while their carriages were readied. They would travel in the much grander one, meant to convey him and his marchioness back to Huntsworth. The second, plainer one contained their trunks, along with Tim and Annie. Clippman would supervise the remaining servants in the London townhouse and see to its upkeep, making certain it was already ready anytime they came to town.

He had purchased a few horses at Tattersall's for them to ride and had hired grooms, sending both to Huntsworth last week. It would be good to have his own horse in the stalls and not have to rely on ones from Mr. Abel's stables.

He slipped his arm about Lucy, and she snuggled against him, falling fast asleep the entire way to Surrey. He decided she would need extra rest because of the child which grew within her and he determined to pamper her however he could.

She awoke a few minutes before they reached Alderton, and minutes later, they arrived at Huntsworth. He handed her down, greeting the servants who had all gathered outside to welcome their master and mistress home. It was a good feeling, knowing he owned this house and all its surrounding land and that he had a staff which would make certain that he and his wife spent happy times while they were in the country.

"See that the luggage is brought in," he told their new butler. To Mrs. Worth, he added, "Have Cook send tea and bit of refreshment to Lady Huntsberry's parlor. No, make it the terrace, instead. It is far too lovely a day to remain inside."

They entered the house, and Lucy said, "I am famished. I am glad you asked for tea. Let me go freshen up, and then I will join you outside."

Having tea served on the terrace turned out to be a good idea, and they both decided they would do this several times a week as long as the weather was nice. Judson thought the raisin scones the best scones he had ever eaten. He was glad Lucy had agreed to hiring both the cook and housekeeper who had worked for Antonia. Surprisingly, his former mistress had written to them, and Lucy had explained that she had asked for Antonia to do so. Antonia had been welcomed with open arms by Luigi, and the couple would be wed by the time her letter arrived in London. Judson doubted Antonia would write again, but it was satisfying to know she had found a home and love.

"Would you like to take a stroll?" Lucy asked after they finished.

"I would be delighted to do so."

They went down the stairs of the terrace and walked, hand-in-hand, along the path to the gardens. Both were pleased to see weeds had been cleared and the gardens were starting to take shape. He knew nothing about gardening, but Lucy told him it would take a few years to restore the Huntsworth gardens to their former glory. He hoped by that time they would have at least two children.

Once they reached the gazebo, at the heart of the gardens, he led her up the steps and to its center, happy to be at Huntsworth once again. Although Judson knew he could never erase his past, having Lucy by his side helped conquer the bitter memories, and he knew they would recede over time, replaced by more pleasant ones.

They came to a large oak, and Lucy leaned against it, pulling him close to her. His body brushed against hers, and he gave her a thorough kiss.

"I needed that," she said, once he ended the kiss. Her eyes sparkled. "I have something to tell you, Judson. Something absolutely wonderful."

Knowing what was coming, he kissed her again. "*You* are wonderful, love."

"I am not exhibiting the signs Ariadne told me about. She was terribly sick each morning for a few months, but I do believe I am with child. Our first child." Her smile was blinding.

"That is the best news I have ever been given," he told her, awash with love for her and the child that grew within her.

He kissed his wife, the kiss full of promises he would keep to her throughout the years.

About the Author

USA Today and Amazon Top 10 bestselling author Alexa Aston lives with her husband in a Dallas suburb, where she eats her fair share of dark chocolate and plots while she walks every morning. She enjoys travel and sports—and can't get enough of *Survivor* or *The Crown*.

Her Regency and Medieval historical romances bring to life loveable rogues and dashing knights. Her series include: *The Strongs of Shadowcrest, Suddenly a Duke, Second Sons of London, Dukes Done Wrong, Dukes of Distinction, Soldiers and Soulmates, The St. Clairs, The de Wolfes of Esterley Castle, The King's Cousins, Medieval Runaway Wives,* and *The Knights of Honor.*